D1599441

end over end

end over end

a novel

Kate Kennedy

A small portion of Chapters 38, 1 and 3 and of 8 through 12 appeared in substantially different form as "In Harm's Way" in *The Dissident*, Summer, 1997 and "Self-of-Steam" in *The Dissident*, Summer, 1996.

Copyright © 2001 by Kate Kennedy
All rights reserved.

Published by

Soho Press, Inc.
853 Broadway
New York, N.Y. 10003

Library of Congress Cataloging-in-Publication Data

Kennedy, Kate, 1948–
    End over end / Kate Kennedy.
      p. cm.
    ISBN 1-56947-235-1 (alk. paper)
    1. Trials (Murder)—Fiction.   2. Teenagers—Fiction.
I. Title.
PS3561.E42657 E53 2002
813'.6—dc21   00-05030

10 9 8 7 6 5 4 3 2 1

For Nate

Author's Note

This is a work of fiction. All of the characters, their personalities, mannerisms, thoughts, and words are the product of my imagination. No actual people have been depicted within these pages.

But the landscape is lying on its side, so you
lie down on your side to see, your assumptions
rolling from your pockets into the black acres past the beach.

Jonathon Aaron

part one

◇

one

Blake loves me, Ivory repeats to herself to push away the other words: *He's in love with somebody else.* He said he had to help his uncle skid logs out of the woods before the ground thaws, but outside the narrow bathroom window, stapled over with plastic, she sees mud, her father's footprints, soggy as waffles and leading to the shed.

Maybe Blake doesn't notice the mud, maybe he sees only Charity, the girl from parties at the gravel pit, who flashes her boobs in the school library. They're going to the movies, Ivory imagines, maybe a *Conan* movie.

It's time to shave her legs. She pulls up her pajamas, soaps her calves, her knees, up her thighs. She uses the safety razor her mom gave her last birthday, which she keeps clean and polished, changing the blade before it rusts.

Pamper yourself, she read in a magazine. *Take extra time in the bathroom. Love yourself. Pretend you're somebody else, who loves you and says, You're beautiful, smooth skin or stubble-y . . .*

She's sitting cramped on the counter, one leg in the sink. Outside, her dad's boots suck mud as he passes the window. She nicks her knee. *Hurry.* She shaves the other leg, not the way somebody who loves her would but rush-rush, an everyday job with someone impatient on the other side of the door. She dries her calves. It's spring-time, and Blake's with Charity at *Conan the Destroyer.*

"Ivory!" Her dad's low voice. His cough rattles, stones striking glass in his chest.

She grabs her towel and razor, then opens the door: shame at him catching her shaving, at him catching her. Both legs sting. Her face and hair flame up. He pushes past her, shaking his head.

Blake loved me first, Ivory says on the closed side of her bedroom door. *He'll love me again.* . . . Feet wide apart, she sits down on her bed, slowly, gingerly, needing to protect some organ of memory that's painful to touch. A joint would help, make her drifty so she'd float out the window, over the deep tromp of feet in April ground.

She twists the handle of her razor, removes the blade and rubs it on a corner of her flannel pajama top until it shines. She pulls down her pajama bottom and runs her palm down one smooth leg. *Pamper yourself. Pretend you're somebody else, who loves you.*

She holds the razor the way she holds a pencil to draw with. Skin is paper, blood is lead, pain the bright smell of marigolds. She draws two squares, one stacked on the other, the letter B. And then all the letters lace together into a necklace of red beads.

BLAKE, her leg says. It's so beautiful it's all she can swallow, this beautiful word carved into her skin. The word glows. She imagines cutting it out and wearing it on a gold chain . . . But right now, just for a second, she's outside of wanting anything. Sharp joy is all she feels. *I love you* weighs as much as a heart cut out and saved in a jewelry box, and that's next-to-nothing.

two

"Ivory, c-come here, b-ba-by," Blake says.

He can start to talk her down with that, but when he lies on his bed and pats his bare stomach, he's so beautiful she just caves in. His skin's the smoothest thing she's ever touched, his belly's got no hair. Something like church, the feeling she gets when he pats himself. The sound feels holy. She'd like to drink from this small, perfect bowl.

She remembers a buck she saw once in the woods—the buck saw her too—two Novembers ago. She'd scooped a hole in a pile of leaves and crouched down, breathing their dusty crackle. The sun melted behind the hackmatacks while rusty needles shined yellow, then blue. She wasn't hungry or thirsty. She closed her eyes and held her breath, living on sunlight and leaf dust—light-as-air. Then, the sound of a boy patting his belly, so proud of muscles and tight skin— that's what it seemed like—the drum of his belly beating danger and secrets, but when she opened her eyes, there stood a buck, beating his hooves on the dry ground.

She let out her breath, he didn't move. She opened her heavy wool coat, lifted the sweater Gram Towle knit, the top of her brother's hand-me-down long underwear, opened the button on her pants. She tapped her belly, cupping the buck's rhythm in her palms.

5

"C-come here, b-baby," Blake says again.

He's lying on his back in the dark hole of his room, hands under his head, black hair midnight blue, T-shirt off, smiling at her like somebody's sweet boy, somebody's naughty boy. He blows her kisses. She hates him for something, he did something—Charity again. She cried a whole day and night, home sick from school. He did something, said something.

"I-I d-didn't mean it," he says.

He looks like he might cry. He's her baby, come on, baby. He pats his belly. It's the loneliest drumming she's ever heard, a sound from the distant place where girls go when they run away. But if she ran, who'd coax her back? Who'd hold her, rock her, rub soft lips in the hollow of her throat? Who'd say, *Come on, baby, come on, Ivory, I love you, baby, come.*

The buck watched her, she watched him. His eyelashes were longer than Blake's. She saw his heart beat in his neck, a thrill of drumming just under the skin. He's curious, she's curious back. She rises slowly, leaf fragments tumble from her hair.

"Come here, baby," she says to the buck. He doesn't blink. She's thirsty, parched from breathing November leaves. She drinks his eyes, touches him where his heart's beating just under the skin.

It was hunting season then, now it's May and black flies have stapled her ears.

Blake pats the drum of his belly. "C-c-come here, baby." She kneels on the edge of the mattress, leans over to breathe his breath. He smells like beer and dope, pizza, danger, speed, some other girl he's loved. She forgets why she hates him. She still hates him. She's parched from breathing November leaves. Tomorrow she'll run away, she'll remember why she hates him, she'll remember the taste of where he's been and all the hurtful things he's done.

He pats his belly. He's her beautiful boy.

three

"They're like polliwogs, but with very long tails." Mrs. Cadenza is reviewing.

Geena perks up from a slouch. "Polliwogs?"

"Tadpoles—they turn into frogs," Mrs. Cadenza explains. She dresses like a gypsy with print scarves wrapping her head. She's dying of cancer, somebody says, but somebody else says they saw her hair at Piece of Pizza and it's bright red.

"So," Mrs. Cadenza continues, "these tadpoles are swimming their hearts out up your vagina through your cervix and on to that egg." Her matter-of-factness makes Geena giggle. She likes Mrs. Cadenza, they all do. She's a little weird but kind. Hearing medical sex words in school, right after Practical Math and before lunch, the whole thing feels strange; still, it's a ticket out of English for a few days.

Sex Ed happens every year at the end of May when love heats up the schoolyard. Kids can't keep their hands off each other. Geena's seeing Ricky, Nicki's with Howie, sort of. Ivory's back with Blake, who's off Charity, the slut. This time they mean it.

A honeybee, big as a blimp, has flown in through an open window. Nicki squeals once, but minus the boys, why bother reacting?

The bee is so heavy it barely stays aloft, always on the edge of free-fall. Twice it bumps a closed window.

Geena raises her hand. She's wide awake now, her eyes the blue of electric shock. "How many—polliwogs—go up you in one squirt?"

"In one ejaculation?—which of course we know is really a series of pulses—"

"Yeah, one ejaculation."

"Millions."

"Wow," Nicki says, pushing long rusty bangs off her forehead. A few girls whistle. It's nothing new. It's an impressive statistic, nevertheless, no matter how many times you've heard it. Geena nods, the soul of scientific inquiry, then to Ivory she whispers, "Happy Pastures."

Ivory smiles. Her nose turns red and sweaty, one more cute thing about her. During a grammar-school field trip to Happy Pastures Farm, they witnessed something sensational: a draft horse stuck out his penis, in their faces, and that neon baseball bat—not the ice cream cones they ate or the calves they petted—is all anybody remembers. Even now, four years later, whenever Ivory says she's going out with Blake, Geena does Groucho eyebrows and wishes her *Happy Pastures*.

That's the closest they come to talking about sex. Oh, they joke around, and they're always guessing who'll get pregnant first, but confiding they aren't. Until today, Geena's never wondered how many of Ricky's sperms shoot up her when they—*make love*. That's better than Mrs. Cadenza's *engage in intercourse* or Ricky's *fuck*. Except right at the moment the whole subject makes Geena edgy. Not just for herself, but for Ivory. Ivory's in the middle of a scare—she's two weeks late. Scares happen to everybody. When you're in one yourself, though, you can't think about much else.

"I know this is too early for most of you—" Mrs. Cadenza is saying. Her eyes scan them to detect the sexually actives, but in a nonjudgmental way. Just to be safe, they pull down their masks. *At fourteen we shouldn't even have to hear this junk . . .*

"What is the only one-hundred-percent-effective form of preg-
nancy prevention?" Mrs. Cadenza asks. The bell is about to ring.

Nicki's hand flies up, and her braces gleam. "Suicide?"

Mrs. Cadenza laughs. It's not funny. "Abstinence," she says. She
scans the room again. Half of the girls look bored, the cultivated
boredom of about-to-light-a-cigarette, the others look mortified and
no older than ten or eleven. *Ask the quiet one,* she says to herself.

"Do you have any questions—Ivory, is it?" She recognizes
Ivory—dark hair, carefully pouffed, small features, big eyes ringed
with black liner—not that she's seen much of Ivory's face, which
spends most of its school life mashed against her boyfriend's chest.
Every morning before the bell for homeroom rings, he leans on a
locker, his hand massaging her butt. Once she asked them to *move
along,* but afterward she felt old and humorless.

Mrs. Cadenza is ardent on these girls' behalf. Libby Junior High's
just an hour's drive from the city, from the Atlantic, and the chance
at a wider world, but they inhabit some far-away pocket. *Fight for
your future,* she tells them, *Take good care.* They nod, they indulge
her, and yet their lives seem to be happening at another location, at
the bottom of a long tube they're assigned to squint at through a
microscope. They pretend to see, they say a halfhearted *Cool,* then
drift away, unmoved.

Ivory doesn't have any questions. Mrs. Cadenza knows she won't.
Still, Ivory's eyes are so blank and sad she feels it in her throat, and
she makes a mental note to ask around. Nothing in particular, she
just wonders.

But the next group is eighth-grade boys. By the end of the day
the bee has been whacked silly and smeared across a Women's History Month poster of Margaret Sanger, and her mental note flies out
the window into the sweet, liquor-lilac air.

four

F lorence listens outside Ivory's hollow plywood door. Sounds do travel through wood, but they are not the sounds she hopes for. Instead, a burst of laughter from the TV, fake and too loud, like the girls in the lunchroom at the blanket mill where she works first shift. Duncan's got some comedy show on a few feet away in the living room. She wishes he'd turn it down. It's important business she's about. A mother needs to listen.

All spring Ivory's kept calling Florence at work to get dismissed. The school nurse didn't want to let her get out of gym so much, and then they dragged in that social worker Ivory talks to. *Ivory tells me there are some problems in the home.* She made it sound dirty, like her dad beats her or something and there's alcohol nobody mentions. No problems in *this* house, only troubles, the kind that afflict folks everywhere but on the rich side of town where that social worker probably lives—too much desire and not enough of anything to fill it. Two teenage kids make a lot of wanting.

The social worker said, *I of course don't mean to interfere*—and she interfered enough to make Florence's stomach grind shut, what Ivory says happens to her stomach at school, can't she come home before she throws up?

At work, called away from the finishing room, blankets waiting to be folded and bagged, the supervisor counting under her breath, all she can think to say is, *Okay, dear. You be home when Dad and me get there.*

But it made her think, that call from Libby Junior. It's true Ivory keeps her feelings private, it's a family trait, you keep things protected down around your stomach, where people can't drag them out and pick them apart. Ivory's sensitive. Girls are sensitive, she guesses. She was. Dunc Jr. slams doors, that finishes it, and he stays out with his friends. But Ivory, being a girl, they've tried to take special care.

And now she listens. Ivory won't come out of her room for hours. Florence slides down the wall and sits curled up around her knees. Dunc Jr.'s out. Duncan's asleep, she imagines, letting those TV laughers laugh themselves silly, loud and lonely as some family reunion of strangers trying too hard to have fun.

Music. The wall vibrates. Some boy screeching. He keeps yelling, *Baby.* He's after some girl that's not after him. Scratchy squawks, worse sounding than the TV people you never see, who laugh just for money. She imagines hearing under the boy's misery a girl sobbing. Maybe it's a guitar gone crazy. That's what the kids like.

She wants to knock. *Ivory, honey, it's Mom. I'm here to comfort you, just one old knee to cry on.* Ivory might smile at that.

Mom, Happy Birthday. Last week, Ivory said that, *Happy Birthday, Mom, I love you.* It was a back scratcher, her gift. To feel those tiny wood fingers scrambling that spot on her spine. Ivory's a treasure of kindness to even come up with that one idea out of all the world's ideas and to get herself to a shop where they might sell Chinese stuff like that.

In the confident moment of that memory, she stands up and knocks. The music waits. Inside, Ivory waits to see if she'll dare knock again. Holding that back scratcher in her mind, she dares.

"Thanks for my present dear."

Ivory's standing there, sweatpants, sweatshirt, those raccoon makeup eyes, opening the door like Jehovah Witnesses have knocked. There's no invitation to enter.

These kids, in the dark. Ivory's got one small candle going and all that shows is the radio dial, a corner of the purple spread.

"What do you want?"

"Just saying thanks."

"You already did." Ivory talks the way those TV people talk, like they're made of hollow wire. She stares back. She's tall, well, taller than Florence. With the nice lanky chin that runs in Duncan's family. So pretty if she smiled and sent some current through that hollow wire.

"How was school?" She's running out of time. Already the door is moving. "Dad and I thought maybe you'd like to watch a show."

"I got homework."

The social worker said she's dreamy in class, pretends like she doesn't hear, hangs all over her boyfriend in the halls.

"You're forbid to see him. Remember Dad said that."

Florence can't explain why those words jump out of her mouth. On her birthday they'd had such a good time. Ivory made a box cake. And the back scratcher, the warm waters of daughter-love— the day before the blow-up about her sneaking over to Blake's against Dad's wishes.

Ivory freezes at her words. Black eyes and pale lips, they freeze. Florence feels a smoky chill. She steps back.

"You used to like watching shows."

"Leave. It's my property. Get your foot out."

The voice like her supervisor's, you're bound to obey. She glances down at her foot, the one inside Ivory's room, just an inch or two onto the shaggy purple rug. "I got hot chocolate packets," she hears herself say.

Ivory's eyes so bitter-cold you could ice skate on them the way they used to do on Horseshoe Pond. Ivory's wobbly ankles tipped so far she almost skated on ankle bones instead of blades, and they laughed till tears froze on their cheeks and Ivory laughed too after she was done being mad. The pond was shiny black with white letters skated in. Dunc Jr. was going to be a hockey star. He whizzed like he had motors for feet. They made hot chocolate and cut marshmallows in with scissors. The door shuts.

five

Ivory turns up the radio, loud, after she gets rid of her mom. But she can still feel her outside, listening through the cardboard wall. It's like her whole breath gets sucked away, her mom's lungs crave her air, that's what it feels like. *You're forbid to see Blake,* Mom says, but she's never the one to forbid, just the one to remind.

Under the mask of radio sound, Ivory unscrews the heating grate with a screwdriver she swiped from the garage. Any little noise— the scritch of metal, the lifting of the plate—and her mom might knock again. The cat helps. Her pink nose pokes the plastic book cover. Speedy likes diary time, she likes butting her whiskers in, licking off ink. "Okay, you little fur-ball," Ivory whispers, rubbing a ballpoint pen along Speedy's money-colored back. Flecks of copper, flecks of silver-gray, like coins in a piggy bank. "Little hunter-girl." Baby birds, baby mice. Speedy leaves heads behind, sometimes faces only. She can't help it, it's her nature.

Ivory cross-hatches one whole blank page, no words, just cross-outs until it's all purple, dark as a bruise. With the pen, she lightly touches her belly. Inside, the maybe-baby is a heavy dot, no bigger than the eraser on a pencil. If it's real, then with every breath she takes, it grows. Her and Blake's cells, splitting in half, right down the middle. Over and over again.

It's a miracle you want to save for later, Mrs. Cadenza says. Dying with a red scarf on, and *she's* worried about *them.* What she means: That eraser will erase your life. You won't have fun with your friends, you'll be stuck at home, no more partying late, no more talking on the phone till all hours. You'll need a job, daycare, a place to live; your one hobby: trips to the laundromat.

Outside her bedroom, the lilacs are beginning to topple. She smells them through the open window. Her mom cut her a pompom and stuck it in a mayonnaise jar. Now it's beside her candle on the radio. The shadow wobbles it's so top-heavy. A pretty thing, color like a scoop of vanilla plopped into grape juice. Her and Blake's eraser baby'd be winter-born, a future in February. Her mom'd knit a purple hat, buy a snowsuit with fake fur around the cheeks. *The season's so short,* her mom says, *and you wait the whole winter to smell that smell . . .*

Lady teachers stick lilacs on their desks at school, Mrs. Cadenza has some. *You deserve the best.* But it's up to you to imagine, yourself, what the best can be. Mrs. Cadenza sounds like a magazine, always talking about yourself, yourself. About doing things, changing things. Ivory's tired. It makes you tired, holding a future in your own two hands.

If she's pregnant, in a week or two the size of the baby will be the size of those little birds, those voles and mice. Abort, that's what Nicki would do. You can get it on the sneak, your folks won't know, just lie about your age. *Say you're eighteen, you could pass.*

You think?

No problem.

What if she said: *Mom, my period's late, I might be—I'm scared.* Her mom would sigh and push fever-bangs off her forehead. *Mom, I might be pregnant, if I am, do you hate me, it's not the worst thing—*

If I'm pregnant, I want it. Just your size, Speedy-girl. Derek for a boy, Tamara for a girl. Hair softer than kitty-fur. It kills her, how soft baby skin feels, their silky hair. *You'd be such a cute mother,* Geena says. Geena's mom's a drunk. Nobody'd say it out loud to hurt Geena's feelings and nothing against her mom, you just can't hang your hopes on somebody gonzo like that. You'd not open your trap, you'd not dare to. Her own mom listening outside. Or a Mrs. Cadenza kind of mom, talking about Choices and Protecting Your Future. You can be anything you want. Any boy who holds you back doesn't really love you at all, he's using you.

But if he says you're beautiful, you are. If he says, *You're so hot I gotta fuck you*, is that using? He's like Speedy, the hunter-girl, he can't help himself. You can be anything you want to be. Dream big. Make a list of what you're good at. Last year she got A- in art, this year she's failing for attendance, but everybody says she's still got a talent. Her friend Pammy's always talking about it, the way she can draw.

Once Pammy found a matchbook with a side view of a terrier on the cover you're supposed to copy and send to New York to see if you qualify for the Famous Artists' School by mail. Ivory did it, she sent away. It was amazing, her sideview dog better than the matchbook cover. *You can be a Famous Artist, Ivory*, Pammy said, a Famous Artist. The school wrote back, *Congratulations, you've got promise and there's a wealth of opportunity out there*, but first you've got to turn eighteen, with parent permission and $199.

Ivory closes her diary, lies back against the pillow, pressing her stomach hard to see if the maybe-baby's grown at all in the last couple of minutes. Speedy settles on her belly, purrs, eyes half-open, half-shut. It's a small dream. She can't say it out loud. She pets Speedy's back. Her future's quiet, a single cat hair.

Suddenly she lifts Speedy up and listens for kittens, her hand on Speedy's warm head. They could do it together, be pregnant. *Blake, you ever want a baby?*

Shit no.

Me neither, don't worry. She takes a shed-hair off Speedy's tail and holds it to the candle flame until it poofs. Stink-smoke to make your nose curl.

six

In the living room, Duncan wakes from an uncomfortable dream. He coughs, then shifts in the recliner and feels for the bit of whale's tooth he always keeps in his pocket. Touching it smooths over the dream but doesn't make it go away. Something about that diary of hers he found, checking the heat in her room. With a screwdriver he took up the grate, and there it was: a secret book. He read it then and reads it now.

Ivory doesn't know this of course. Each time he's careful to put the diary back just so. She tells it every foolish thing—purple exclamation points, i's dotted with open circles—how much she loves Blake, how he beat her up, how she'll kill herself, maybe get married. She's lost her head. So foolish it breaks Florence's heart—and him, he's just so damn fed up. She used to belong to him, now it's that boyfriend sniffing around. How quick a girl betrays you. The smell of animals in heat. He's read her diary, he'll keep reading it. It's some connection. Life's hard all around, and he's earned the right to more respect than he's getting from his troublemaking girl.

People on TV are selling a new kind of margarine. He dozes off, then wakes, the tooth still in his hand, and it's her birth he's dwelling on. It was not your average situation, he remembers the doctor saying that.

Duncan Jr. just slipped out in a package of blood and spit before anybody had a chance to worry about him. Florence cheeped and lowed, hissed and growled up the food chain from snake to bird, from cow to lion. If he'd had a superstitious turn of mind, it might have spooked him, her squirming on the bed as if possessed by the pains of death when in fact it was a live boy who dropped out. Thank God he didn't have to witness every second the way they make the men do now. He got her to the hospital just before all hell broke loose and the sack of waters burst.

But Ivory was a different story. She got herself tangled up even while she was still swimming inside Florence. The way the doctor explained it, Duncan pictures one of those old-time diving outfits, the baggy jumpsuit, the globe for your head—*you* inside the aquar-ium—Ivory decked out with the hose still attached to Florence. But that piece of imagination scrambled itself with the moon landing and those fellows in their spacesuits, playing golf and leap-frog like it was Sunday-in-the-park. He and Florence saw it on TV, just a few months before Ivory was born. Either way you looked at it—un-derwater or outer-space—Ivory got herself into trouble doing hand-springs, slow-motion, turning that cord into a noose.

The year Florence got pregnant with Ivory, she started working at the blanket mill. She'd come home exhausted from the push, push to meet her quota. Her legs would feel boggy, she said, standing all day, and ready to explode from the heat. It felt like everything inside her head—thoughts, memories, all that blood and water and fussing she kept inside her skull—the whole lot of it drained into her legs, her head like an empty gourd set on a gorilla's belly and elephant legs.

So the naming got dumped in his lap. Once or twice Florence murmured something about *Rebecca, if it's a girl*, but her voice was so soft and unsure, it was more the rustling of birch leaves than any name you could beat time to with your hands. So Duncan opened his ears. It was something new, this opening in preparation for a daughter's name. He listened when Al at the heavy equipment deal-ership talked about Jeannie and Thomasina. He swore he'd never heard of their existence, this wife and daughter of a man who'd repaired diesel engines beside him for fourteen years. He felt it as wonderment, this wellspring of names bubbling up—*Sally, Kathleen, Molly, Brenda, Daisy, Evangeline.*

At home Florence got birth-addled, then real calm. She seemed content to lie on the loveseat after work, counting her breaths, watching flies crawl up the wall. If he'd been a superstitious man, he'd have said it was an enchantment and he'd have called Help! to God to unravel the strange mystery of his life just then. As it was, he took care of Florence and four-year-old Dunc—Dinty Moore, Chef Boyardee, nothing fancy—but he liked the grace of her peaceful breathing those weeks. If it was enchantment, it was a happy thing. He didn't know to be afraid.

Florence liked playing with things, running them through her fingers—bits of sea glass, a pine cone—as if worry had moved from her brains into her fingers. She smiled, dreamy as a movie star, while she squeezed his milk-and-honey-colored lump of whale tooth. He still could see the bright moment when his grandfather pulled the thing out of his pea-coat pocket and dropped it into his hand. *Here, boy, see how that feels.*

A funny item for a farmboy used to practical gifts, this scrimshaw whatchamacallit his grandfather carved. He'd worked as a cook on whaling ships out of New Bedford, he said, before the family turned its back on the sea. Late that night, unable to sleep, Duncan wondered how his grandfather had thought to etch the picture of a schooner into a whale's tooth and tattoo it with ink.

Look close, you feel the storm rising, foam splashing her hull. She cuts the water right smart, don't she, Grandfather said.

Florence liked to let the ship tumble from one hand to the other, weighing it, pressing it. Those weeks of waiting on the loveseat for a child, it gave her comfort. When the baby finally came, she was sideways, cord around her neck, the doctor worried she'd breathed in her own poop by mistake—

Still no name. But then he held her, stretched out along his forearm. Her swaddled toes brushed the crook of his elbow. He thought of Grandfather's scrimshaw gift, and a name entered him. *Ivory*, he called her, that bit of flotsam tangling herself up every-which-way, good for no earthly purpose but the pleasure she gave, her head in the hammock of his hand.

Now that baby lets a juvenile delinquent run her roughshod, and Florence crouches outside her bedroom door, listening for tears.

seven

Ever since Nicki's joke about suicide, that word has vibrated at such high frequency it drives the kids crazy, but the grownups don't hear anything at all. The weather is so perfect, day after day, if your life sucks, it's just not worth living. That's what Nicki told Ivory last night, the first person she called after Howie dumped her. They'd been going out for a month and she was thinking of dumping him, but he beat her to it. They never exactly went on a date, it was going out on the phone. Still, they were boyfriend and girlfriend. Now he's probably in the boys' locker room, boasting about how often he scored off her, how she put out every night. There's that, plus the orthodontist just tightened her braces and her whole mouth kills. It's all so terrible Nicki decides to skip school.

It's hot out, the sky's a blistery yellow-blue, and she's at Roxanne's house, a two-bedroom ranch safely off the main road so nobody'll catch them. Roxanne's not a close friend the way Ivory is, but she's always up for skipping and no grown-up's ever home. Her dad works two shifts at Sargent Meats, her mom's dead.

They're sitting at the kitchen table, thumbing through *Woman's Day*. The blinds are closed so it looks like night. "I hate my hair," Nicki says. "Ivory thinks if I cut my bangs I'll get a whole new look." To demonstrate, she takes an elastic and pulls her rust-colored bangs into a ponytail, which sticks out like a unicorn's horn from her widow's peak.

"What a waste," Roxanne says. "You been growing them forever."

"Ivory says when you get dumped, you need to do something big. You know, *big*. I hate my bangs. I hate my braces. I hate Howie." She undoes the elastic, makes another ponytail low on her neck.

Roxanne shrugs. "Whatever." They down a bag of Cheeto's while they pick out the prettiest model in each magazine ad. "My dad canceled my mom's subscription, but they just keep sending 'em."

"Ivory says Howie's not up to my standards." Nicki's angling for support, but all Roxanne comes up with is a halfhearted, "He's an asshole." Nicki's beginning to regret skipping. School will call home, her parents will go ballistic, she'll be grounded forever.

About noon, they amble outside, down the dirt lane to the mailbox, past a broken wooden swing hanging from a willow. The tree's leafed out, most of it, though several branches have split, no leaves at all. Dead twigs litter the yard. As they walk, Roxanne squashes dandelions growing up through the prints of tire tracks. "I hate dandelions. My mom had a can of something and she zapped 'em. You could watch 'em kiss-off."

A couple of shopping flyers, no personal mail.

"Ivory says she'll keep the baby. If it's a baby," Nicki adds.

"My mom wrote lots of letters. She got lots, too."

"I'm sorry." Nicki really means it, but it's awkward. A whole year's gone by since Roxanne's mom died and what's there to say?

Just as they turn back toward the house, a black fly bites Nicki's forehead, under her long bangs. She screams. Next thing, they're inside and Roxanne's smearing on Noxzema to kill the itch. But the bite continues to swell. It looks like she's been hit with a baseball, Nicki sees in the mirror. They collapse together on one end of the plaid couch.

"Every morning my mom washed her face with Noxzema," Roxanne says, "then she splashed cold water twenty times. Sometimes thirty times." At that memory, her own face buried in maroon plaid pillows, she bursts into tears.

Nicki's scared. There's crying, and there's crying. She tries to comfort Roxanne, but she won't stop. Suddenly—Howie, her stupid bangs, the metal in her mouth, everything, it's too much, and she's sobbing too.

Hours later, it feels like, Roxanne gets up, goes to the bathroom, returns holding a prescription bottle. "My mom's pain medicine," she says. They watch the bottle. Then Roxanne opens it and dumps the contents into her palm. Two-tone capsules, half blue, half see-through, sixteen pills. She counts eight into Nicki's hand. They don't speak, they simply nod. With something like ceremony, they clink Mickey glasses of Diet Dr Pepper, then swallow their handfuls and wait.

At first Nicki's thrilled. It's the most important thing she's ever done. The moment of doom, the rush. But nothing happens.

Soon they're raiding Roxanne's dad's liquor supply. They start with rum and Dr Pepper, move into vodka and Orange Crush.

"Cut my bangs," Nicki says, she thinks she says, her last dying wish. Roxanne cuts. It's a little zigzag, she cuts more, it feels wonderful, this release of hair.

"I want Ivory to see," Nicki manages to say. "You know, *before*." Roxanne giggles. "Come on, we'll hitch."

Somehow they lurch down the lane and some guy picks them up. When they stumble through the doors of Libby Junior, Nicki throws up. Mrs. Cadenza spotted them first, she finds out later, and called Rescue. They're wheeled into Emergency, parents telephoned, stomachs pumped. They spend the night next to bald chemo kids on the children's ward.

When Nicki wakes up, it's the next afternoon. Roxanne's gone. Her head kills, her stomach kills and her throat. Her parents are at work. But Ivory's there, holding a blue plush girl-Smurf. Her eyes are swollen. Her hand on Nicki's forehead feels like a cool cloth.

"I wrecked my hair," Nicki says.

"Don't you *ever, ever* do that to me again!" Ivory's furious, but when she yells it's okay, a comfort somehow. She drops Smurfette on Nicki's chest. "I used the last of my babysitting money for this, you better be happy. I got my mom to dismiss me. I didn't tell her I was hitching, I said your parents were giving me a ride." She laughs.

"I'm happy."

"You better be."

"Did you get your period?"

"Not yet."

"Does Blake know?"

A nurse appears. Blood work. She pulls the white curtain around Nicki's bed, leaving Ivory outside.

eight

"Keep me company while I pack," Ivory told Pammy when she showed up, soaked, at the back screen door. "You want a towel?"

Pammy shook her head. "Just water." She wrung both braids out in the kitchen sink, then made herself a peanut-butter-and-fluff sandwich. They've been down-the-road friends that long. In grammar school they did everything together—chicken pox, head lice, pink Velcro shoes—but things changed at Libby Junior. They rode a bus and Pammy got mono, then missed three months and had to stay back. She won't be going to high school this fall, she's stuck at Libby another year. Still, Ivory told her about the scare, of course—the maybe-baby. They were in this very bedroom, listening to Led Zeppelin—late June, the day school let out—when Ivory's period finally started again.

But now, a month later, when Pammy asks, "Where you goin'?" Ivory says, "Nicki's, she's havin a sleep-over"—which doesn't explain why she's blow-drying her hair for the second time in an hour and cramming her gym bag full of clothes, including Pammy's purple chamois shirt she borrowed last month that doesn't fit any more—not that Pammy questions.

In fact, Ivory's headed for Blake's. No big deal. She could have told Pammy, but this one time, she just can't. Lately, her dad has this creepy way of catching her up. Two weeks ago, she told him Geena was having some girlfriends over, then him and her mom, in town for coffee, spotted her with Blake, sashaying down the sidewalk, right past the window of Bob & Pat's Coffee Creamer.

No matter what you do, he said, *eventually I will find out.*

Pammy snuggles Speedy, sniffs, makes a face. "Cat breath, gross!" she says, plunking Speedy down.

Ivory's checking her backside in the closet-door mirror. "Do my buns stick out too much?"

Pammy gives the Look—you-gotta-be-kidding—so big and comfy-looking in her dad's New England Patriots' sweatshirt and baggy jeans. Ivory herself frets over every pound, but Pammy's Pammy. Just right. Different rules.

Like she's flicking a sow bug, Pammy pings the pair of rollerskate pompoms hanging off the headboard, which swing and tangle and give Speedy ideas.

"We should go skating sometime," Ivory says. They used to rent skates at Roll-a-Rama every Saturday afternoon, and they got so good they could spin. One Christmas, Pammy's mom made them matching pink pompoms to tie into their laces—before Pammy's dad broke his back, before spending two bucks caused fights.

Pammy nods. She pitches the pompoms. Speedy bats them until she snags one with her claw.

Ivory zips her gym bag. "What are you doing this weekend?"

"Nothing. Me and Mom gotta cook spaghetti for the church supper. That's tomorrow all day. Tonight I got my shows."

"I think Howie's starting to like you."

Pammy stops fooling with Speedy. "You do?"

"Maybe."

"Which one is Howie?"

"Used to go with Nicki. Freckles, zits. He's a jerk, though. You're too smart for him. And pretty," she adds. With a little fixing up, Pammy'd be a knockout, but she's still a kid, not much into boys. Someday . . . The way her mouth and eyes sit—they're wide and curvy, like three sweet cradles a boy might rock himself inside.

Someday, she'll draw Pammy's face. "You could do a lot better than Howie," she says. "If he calls, don't talk."

"You think he might call?"

"He might."

"I hope."

"Just hang up."

They sit on the shaggy purple rug, backs against Ivory's bed. Two candles lit, music off, big bag of chips, and Speedy's chin to scritchy-scritch. With two fingers up for shadow ears, Ivory's hand makes a rabbit bounce across the far wall while she singsongs, *"Little Bunny Foo-Foo, hopping through the forest, pickin' up field mice and boppin' em' on the head."* Then her shadow whacks Pammy's, and they laugh. "I only remember stupid stuff like that when you're around," Ivory says.

Pammy remembers every single little thing that ever happened. It's amazing how far back she can go and what she drags up once she gets going—like she's a police scuba diver and their childhood's a pond.

"Julie's Secret Sloth"—that's all Pammy has to say, now, for Ivory to see that long-ago chapter-book as if it was projected on the wall.

"I loved that story!"

Pammy was always borrowing books from the school library. When she said this one was the all-time best, Ivory believed her. She remembers not knowing what a sloth was, supposing it looked something like the hand towels Pammy's mom kept folded in the bathroom cupboard. It was the secret-part she loved, the idea of hiding something from Dunc Jr. He hated to read. He'd ransack her bureau, swipe Halloween candy, laugh at little things she prized—a broken jay feather, a moth wing, the mold in a glass of Coke left under her bed. But a book stamped *Property of Narrows Primary* he'd never touch.

The sloth turned out to be this giant kind of guinea pig with long toenails that lived in this girl Julie's closet, and nobody guessed. He slept all day. At night he ate napkinfuls of pot roast Julie stole from supper, baked beans, chunks of cake. And he adored her so much he kept his mouth shut so she didn't get in trouble. Ivory liked that best. No talking, no singing, no tap-dancing the way most book-animals did. You could love something quiet like that.

A while ago, her mom told her that when she was little, she was a talking-bug. If she wasn't talking, she was singing. If she wasn't singing, she was humming. Her mom said, *You never was quiet.* But Ivory wonders. She doesn't remember that noisy girl. She sees herself in the dooryard, under the kitchen window, digging with a spoon. She liked to bury things—a penny, one of Dunc's cat's-eye marbles, baby teeth.

Pammy silly-talks Speedy, then baits him and gets scratched.

"Was I loud?" Ivory asks, "you know, at Narrows?"

Pammy thinks a moment while she licks the red line on the back of her hand. "Medium, I'd say."

Soon the rain lets up, and Ivory's walking down the muddy drive-way, balancing the weight of her gym bag on one hip. A black purse dangles from her other shoulder and with each step brushes her thigh. Pammy's beside her, walking her bicycle. At the road, they separate. Pammy hops on her bike and pedals toward home. She zips through a puddle, then turns, laughs, waves.

Ivory heads down the crumbling shoulder of the road. The woods are noisy with drips and dark, but she knows her way. She'd like to turn around and spend the night at Pammy's, watch shows in their pjs, drink sodas, eat junk. It's close, the thrill of riding your bike fast, water shooting up your spine. But she's alone in the dark. Even so, she begins to hum. She can't help it, she's already woozy, thinking about Blake.

nine

Soon, a motorbike shoots out of the night. After it brakes and skids to a stop, Ivory hops on. Tommy drives fast. Ivory loves that, holding her gym bag, her purse, pressed tight against Tommy's chunky back. He's Blake's friend. Sometime, maybe this weekend, she'll let him know about girls—how they might like him—brick-colored hair, fat orange freckles—that is, if he ever smiled. Compliments wouldn't hurt, either. Mostly he scowls unless he's high or stoned and then he's blank, a thick face behind a wall. Still, she's grateful for the ride.

Her house sits at the far edge of the Narrows, a little country neighborhood—*no bigger than a blink*, her dad says. Tommy whips the bike around—"Lean," he tells her, and they lean so far she's afraid they'll crash and crack their heads open—then up the road, fast, a blob of lights for TeeGee's Variety, the filling station, Pammy's house with its TV-glow. Soon they're in the woods on a shortcut path. It's only about three miles to Blake's this way. On the road, five or six.

The trees thin out, there's some lumps of grass, a snowmobile, somebody's junked fiberglass boat the color of church-wax, then Blake's house, set on a concrete slab. Tommy skids around front. Blake and his other friend, Ricky, are waiting by the picnic table, smoking and drinking beer. Everything snappy-electric, everything purple from the bug zapper light. Blake's lips are soft, his dark hair's wavy down his neck. He tastes good underneath the beer and dope and cigarettes. *I-want-you.* The beautiful muscles he's so proud of, the drum of his belly.

Ricky's pissed, as usual, a tangle of tight blond curls. "What the fuck's keeping Geena?"

Ivory shrugs. She's artful at secrets. Geena called that afternoon to say she wasn't going to show at Blake's that night, Ricky scares her to death. Last weekend she broke up with him.

They were all over to Blake's that night, and Ricky begged Geena not to leave him. His eyes bugged out, all bloodshot and weepy. Then he turned mean and came at her with a butcher knife. He chased her outside, back of Blake's house where it was dark. He tracked her by the sound of sticks breaking underfoot.

I'm gonna kill you, bitch, screwing around on me, gonna make you sorry.

Ivory watched. She felt in her purse for something sharp, a pen, gouge-your-eyes-out, no luck. She'd do it, but it happened so fast, the knife blade glinting in the porch light as Geena ran up the front steps. She screamed, her face splotchy with crying. Ricky was right behind her while she turned the knob, then Blake grabbed him and the porch light turned them all yellow.

Take the knife, Blake told Ivory. Ricky was crying so hard his grip broke. Then she hid the blade under the pup tent at the edge of the trees.

You saved my life, Geena said, *the both of you.*

As Blake pulled Ricky back to the picnic table, he yelled things, then they laughed. Ivory guessed it was dirty talk about bitches, but that's okay. Everybody calmed down. Ricky's a wildman, no question. The time she and Blake broke up and he was seeing Charity, she hung out some with Ricky. He said sex stuff, love stuff. Nothing happened. He's eighteen and done with school. Hot. Scary.

That night, Ricky took off down one of the paths that ends at

Stan's Bottle Redemption. Stan's his grandfather, so he's got the run of the place. In the junkyard out back he's rigged up an old Delmont 88 with sleeping bags, just in case. Ivory got Tommy to ride Geena home.

During the week Ricky was still berserk. He kept saying he'd kill Geena, kill himself, kill somebody and make them sorry. He wanted somebody sorry. He bugged Geena on the phone, even followed her in town. Under the rings she always wears, one on each finger, a rash broke out in the shapes of hearts and skulls, like the rings had turned to molten silver and burned her skin. And her eyes went from shock-blue to gray. Ivory understood, she knew that feeling, but in her own mind, the knife-waving was already murky, growing more like a game, a kind of teasing the boys liked to do.

Not for Geena, though. She was still nerved-up, she said, the knife blade bigger and sharper in memory. *Okay, Ricky,* she finally told him—not meaning it—*I'll go out with you next weekend. Friday, yeah, over to Blake's.*

He nicked me, Ivory. There was blood on that knife.

Don't worry, I won't tell.

ten

When it's finally dark, Ivory, Blake, Ricky, and Tommy hitch to the Barstow Pit, out beyond even the last ripples of town. It's alive with noise, headlights shooting beams, car radios turned full blast to heavy metal or country. You walk in and out of sound waves. Some knock you over, like you're caught in a rip tide of rhythms buzzing windshields they're so loud, others splash your feet, your face like a day at Christmas Beach. Each summer the pit's a little bigger, carved out a little more where sand's hauled away. Every night it's party time.

The air is humid and still from the rain. It's so loud you can't hear mosquitoes until they bite your brains. Somebody sprays Off! somebody else laughs. Smoking's the only repellent that works. They drink rum, there's plenty of grass, speed, and coke, too, snorted along dashboards. Blake's arm loops Ivory's shoulder, his hand cups her knee. Ricky gets smashed fast to blot out Geena's not showing up. Lucky, he doesn't want to talk about it. Soon he's so wasted his edgy-blond hyper smooths out, and he studies the knotty tendon in his forearm.

"That's him!" Ivory points at a guy in his late twenties—long hair, mustache, skinny neck, nice chest. That's him that came on to her a few weeks ago when Blake's mom needed him to fix her car and she went to the pit with Geena.

Your name's Ivory, somebody told me.

Yeah? He was kind of cute, kind of old. She liked that she turned him on. Blake would kill her.

He passed a joint, they smoked, then cigarettes. *You got soft hair.* He took her arm, just above the elbow where it's tender, pulled her out of the headlights into the dark.

Watch my jacket! She pulled away. She didn't like how heavy his fingers pressed, pawing her head. He grabbed harder. She shook him off, then shoved him. Suddenly, she was beating him with her fists, calling him asshole, not afraid but mad. She hit him over and over until Geena pulled her off and held her.

Fuckin' dink. I know his brother . . . Asshole family . . . Geena's eyes electrocuted the guy on the spot, not that he could feel it.

"That's him," Ivory tells Blake, who jumps off the pickup tailgate they've been sitting on to fight the guy, but his nice chest and mustache evaporate suddenly into the sticky night. A truck engine fires up, a spray of sand, he's gone.

In all the years of partying at the pit—kids to grown-ups, sometimes up to a hundred people—nobody remembers the cops ever hauling anybody off or making a bust. Even when shots get fired, the cops don't investigate. The same night the guy grabbed Ivory's arm, she and Geena watched Amber try to kill herself, no sign of the cops.

It happened so fast they almost missed it. Amber had problems, so didn't everybody. She was older, in her late teens, out of school and from another town, so they only knew her from the pit. Some nights she whined, most nights she never said a word, then all of a sudden she was standing with the loaded shotgun off the gun rack in her boyfriend's pickup, waving it around. It seemed she couldn't figure out how to hold it, where to hold it—a long shotgun for a girl with short arms. And Ricky got laughing, how she'd fuck even that up. But the gun fired anyway and echoed off the sandy caved-in walls. She hit her foot.

Ivory and Geena froze, then everybody was pushing in, staring. Suddenly, headlights made Amber glow like radiation—Star of the Show. Ricky was still laughing, Tommy was too stoned to pay attention. Ivory stepped forward into the headlights and took Amber's hand. It felt sweaty and cold. A mosquito was biting the fleshy root of Amber's thumb, which bothered Ivory more than all that blood leaking through Amber's running shoe. She smeared the mosquito, wet her finger, wiped the blood. Amber's skin pale as Indian pipes. The boyfriend with the pickup wrapped Amber's foot in an old beach towel, stiff with motor oil, and pushed her into the cab.

Shit, he kept saying, *shit, keep your fuckin' shit off the upholstery.*

When Ivory thinks about killing herself, sometimes writes about dying in her diary, it's never messy—not like Amber's bloody gunshot or Nicki's puking on herself. Her way, it's a relief, a place to escape to, a quiet room where you're safe and nobody yells or slugs and you're perfect, no matter what you do or say. You simply stop and wait. You don't care what you're waiting for, like in real life. In that silent place, you don't care why you're waiting, it just slips your mind.

After Nicki and Roxanne took all those pills, Mrs. Cadenza got going about suicide. *Temporary problem, final good-bye. Don't you see how precious you are?*

Now Amber's boyfriend's truck spits sand, the way the guy's with the nice chest did. Both gone. Ivory tucks in closer to Blake. They kiss, drink more, smoke more. His arms are polished wood. Soon there's sand inside her Nikes, her jeans, under her bra strap. She feels Ricky's wild eyes, watching, then he turns and leaves.

They're floating above the sand pit, her and Blake, above the clank of music and light, above laughter, above fighting. They talk about running away. Or maybe she only imagines they talk and it's all floating, bliss, forgetfulness.

eleven

The next morning, a voice snags Ivory awake, Blake's little sister Janet, yelling "Mom's home!" Blake's arm is a damp branch, anchoring her to his bed. Half in, half out of a dream, she pulls on last night's clothes. Her underwear's made of sandpaper, it feels like, no time to fix her smeary eyes. They run. Ricky and Tommy, two snoring blobs passed out on the kitchen floor, each get a kick on their way out.

She was dreaming about Inkspot, her road-kill cat. In the dream he was alive, and some boys were slicing him with the knife her mom uses for meat and watermelon, seeing how long before he died. She's glad not to recognize the guys. Still, the dream hangs off her the way spider silk does a few minutes later when she's first through the woods, ahead of Blake. He reaches for her hand, but she pulls away, running faster than the boys down the path that ends in the field of rusted cars behind Stan's Bottle Redemption.

Once a rumor moved through the pit, more a joke than a rumor, that Blake and Tommy liked torturing animals. Somebody said they saw them shoot squirrels, not shoot to kill, just to watch. *Lop tails off, swear-to-god, peel back skin.* They might spin crazy circles or go dead quiet while they were still alive, who could tell? Woodchucks worked best—big and stupid, more blood. Blake wouldn't do it except high or stoned, Ivory knows that, still the dream's a question and a stain. It doesn't evaporate from her skin until early afternoon.

They're back at Blake's by then, pretending they slept somewhere else and just joined up. Blake's mom has no idea anyway, last night she stayed at her sister's apartment in town and the kids had the house to themselves. Still, it's fun to play-act, more exciting to be together if somebody'd get pissed off at the truth.

The day passes. They hang out at the picnic table. The bugs are bad, close-by a chainsaw whines. In and out clouds and sun, no rain, humid still. They talk about Birch Pond, but Tommy's dirt bike won't carry them all. They smoke, drink, Blake pulls out cards for a game of Screw Your Neighbor. Ricky's up for the Speedway, he says. Nobody mentions Geena's name. He's already talking about some other chick.

"Chick?" tag-along Janet says, "that's not a nice word." She mock-punches Ricky's arm, and he swipes her head.

"Get lost, kid."

"He loves me!" Janet dances closer, chanting his name.

Ivory smiles and shakes her head. At eleven, Janet's still so teensy she's more like an elf than a sixth-grader, but with size-nine feet and that mouthy voice, it figures she'll get her growth spurt soon enough. Because of Blake's stutter, he mumbles, not to draw attention— except when he's mad—but Janet's high volume, all the time, even when she's not love-crazed. Once Ivory said, *If me and Blake get married, we'll be sisters. Would you like that? I'd like that.*

Late in the afternoon, Ivory asks Janet to call her mom with a second night's alibi. "Pretend you're Nicki." They practice, then Ivory dials.

"Mrs. Towle?" Janet says. "This is Nicki, Ivory's friend. Me and my mom was wonderin' if Ivory could come with us to the drive-in, you know, stay another night. We'll bring her back tomorrow morning."

"Is your mother there?"

Janet covers the receiver and rolls her eyes. "No," she says, "I'm calling from the store 'cause our phone's out of order." She's beside herself, not knowing what to say next. "I'll go get my mother and call you back."

When she hangs up, she's so wound up her barrettes pop. "I can't believe she bought it!"

Ivory giggles and tucks Janet's home-perm curls behind her ears. "Okay, that was good, just not so loud. And sound older." Ivory repins the barrettes. They rehearse more lines. In a minute, she dials again.

"It's Nicki back. My mom's at the store, but my dad says fine with him."

There's a pause, more eye-rolling. Janet holds the receiver out.

"Okay," says Ivory's mom, "just so long's she's home sometime Sunday."

twelve

The sky finally clears while Ivory and Blake party at the pit. Away from the headlights, it's a clear dark night. No city haze softens the sky. If you climbed to the highest point nearby—the land a gentle tumble of hills with mountains beyond—you'd see the blanket mill, a peach stain on the horizon, but at the edges of the pit, it's truly dark and the stars are throbbing.

Ivory's happy, speeding with that natural power surge she sometimes gets right before her period. She hasn't thought about protection ahead of time, no pads in her gym bag. She doesn't plan, no plans at all, only white powder and drift.

They stretch out on somebody's car hood. Blake closes his eyes. Ivory looks up at the stars. The Milky Way is almost green. It reminds her of the neon dots, billions of them, she and Nicki once saw at Christmas Beach—some kind of tiny sea creatures with built-in glow-in-the-dark, an old man told them, standing close by in water ankle-deep. She remembers those magic things, green and alive, winking and floating on the tide. She still writes about that night in her diary. It's stuck with her, she's seen so little of the world.

She misses Nicki. But Nicki hasn't come to the pit since one night just after the Fourth of July when she sneaked out of her house and hitched a ride. Her parents won't let it happen again. Since Nicki's suicide-business, she's been grounded. Ivory can't imagine being stuck at home all summer, she'd die, just curl right up and die. She's tried to call Nicki, but Nicki's mom always hangs up, like it was her fault or something, what happened.

Roxanne shows up, with some older guy. After her mom died, she started acting sluttier than Charity. Ivory could care about Roxanne, though. With Nicki she could say goopy stuff about the stars without being made fun of. Nicki would remember the ocean lit up, how Ivory got this crazy idea and rubbed shiny water up and down her arms, covering the scars left by fingernails and razor blades. It always felt good to cause pain, herself, then everything quiet. But it left such ugly marks.

Nicki had tipped her head back and whooped for joy. Her braces glittered. *Aliens!* she cried. They laughed, smearing green on each other's eyelids, lips and hair.

At home, Ivory took yellow and green markers and tried to copy that color, but it didn't look the same. It wasn't dark water dotted with Day-Glo and the hope of something wonderful splashing into your life.

Ivory whispers in Blake's ear, how the Milky Way's like fireworks, but he's too zoned to hear or maybe just asleep. The car hood feels hard under her butt, she can't get comfortable. About three o'clock, back at the junkyard, they crawl into sleeping bags in the car Ricky slept in the night before. Ivory stays awake, looking out the rear window. Only a little sky shows, no green ocean of stars.

thirteen

Sunday morning Blake wakes to crows rawking at the junkyard dog. *Knock it off*, he's about to yell through the busted driver's-side window, but Ivory's breathing so calm, so peaceful, he just lets her be. He likes watching her sleep. The shape of her bottom lip, her tits rising, falling, no bitchy words, just sleep.

He loosens her fingers on his shoulder, then moves her arm without disturbing her. He's stiff from lying too long on a car hood at the pit and sleeping tangled up. He struggles out of the Oldsmobile. His brain's sliced in half, it feels like, and those damn crows hammering his skull don't help. Still, he waits until he's crossed the field of junked cars before he lets go. "Shut up!" he yells into the tops of trees. Of course the crows could care, and his head screams with pain, but it's okay. If he yells loud enough, sometimes the words shoot out, no jerks, no stumbles, just clean and strong, like water from a hose.

Mist rises, muting the chicory and black-eyed susans blooming here and there among rusted Pintos and Darts. Everything's muted, then a blast of sun and scolding from the crows, who flap awhile before settling on a Neil's Bakery delivery truck, junked at the edge of the woods.

One crow's picking at the ripped upholstery of a blue Volvo, two rows over from Ricky's car. The passenger-side door's rusted open so it probably just hopped right in. He shivers, thinking how one yellow-eyed-mother might have brushed its wings against his mouth while he slept. Or maybe, crows being the scum they are, it sat on his shoulder, pecking Ivory's closed eyelids.

The air is close, it's hard to breathe. He pulls his T-shirt away from his neck and finds some kind of thin metal chain. He'd rip it off, but something stops his hand—last night Ivory took the necklace off her neck, then stood on tiptoe to fasten it around his. A thread of fake gold, a few bits of glass. He grumbled, it barely fit around. In fact, it cut, but she was acting foolish, acting sexy, she licked his nipples and talked about how good he smelled. He'd let her do anything.

But today, he's choking. She's sentimental. Everything means something—Miss Federal Case—everything he says or does she takes the wrong way. Like this weekend. Maybe today he'd want to do stuff with guys—nothing against her. Work on the guts of a Mustang, take parts out, clean 'em—it's beautiful—figure out how they go back in.

Ivory likes them hip-to-hip, *IvoryBlake*, like they're soldered together. She picks fights so she can hear him baby-talk and beg for her body. He gives what he can. She wants more than everything.

He keeps notes she writes him, little stuff; that's different, though. Ivory's obsessed.

When we get married, when we have kids . . .

He's scared about knocking her up, but condoms really suck, and she says, *Don't worry*, so he doesn't. *I love you, baby, come, baby*, that's what she wants to hear.

He does love her, he guesses. Sometimes, though, he'd just like to say, *Stop. Stop Now.*

He'd talk real calm, no stammer, the words marching out of his mouth in one fine long parade. But he won't say them, they won't come out right unless they're shouted, and then she'll cry and pout and he'll be back eating humble pie.

He just likes covering ground, that's all, moving fast from here to

there. She always wants to talk. About *us*. About *love*, period. Girls—
what can you do with them except get fucked and then get laid? He
doesn't mean any harm, but she hates those words. She loves him,
he loves her. He means it.

You don't mean it, she says.

He's checking out the tires on a junked Chevy wagon, deep in
concentration, when she touches his hair. With regret, he abandons
the Chevy and kisses her forehead. "H-hot one," he says. "H-how
you doin, ba-babe?"

She doesn't answer. He yanks at chicory, which comes up by the
roots. When he drops the ropey stalk, flowers and all, Ivory scoops
it up and pulls off petals: loves-me, loves-me-not.

"You sleep okay?" she asks.

"O-o-kay, h-hung-over."

"I got cramps wicked."

They hold hands.

"Ivory," he says. The word spills off his tongue, smooth and easy.
No other girl's name does that.

They make out awhile, leaning against the Chevy wagon. Sunlight glares off the hood and the word SAVE spray-painted red across
the windshield looks hot enough to blister. He shuts his eyes. When
he comes to, Ivory's picking at his T-shirt. Slowly they drift toward
Stan Carbon's house, out on the road.

Whenever somebody's folks are away, their house gets magnetized. Out of nowhere, people show up. Stan, that owns Stan's Redemption, left yesterday for two weeks in Wyoming. Word just gets
out. Him and Nonie are Ricky and Buzz Carbon's grandparents,
but same difference. The boys' folks split from each other when Buzz
was two and Ricky wasn't born yet, and the mom split three years
later—last Christmas card, Orlando.

Stan's an easy-go guy and Nonie's like everybody's foster grandmother, but even they got fed up and threw Ricky and Buzz out—
in-house theft from grandsons they raised from scratch—it didn't go
down too good. Even so, there's a king-size bed upstairs in what's

still called *Buzz and Ricky's room*. So—nobody home—the weather's hot, nice house, new red aluminum siding, new in-ground pool, the place just fills up. It's a drop-down thing, nothing you'd call a party, just something mentioned at the pit last night.

fourteen

When Tommy pulls into the wide dirt-and-gravel yard, there must already be six or seven pickups and cars, mostly ones he doesn't recognize—relatives of Stan's and Nonie's, plus Buzz, his wife and kid, Ricky, Blake, and Ivory. People come and go, drinking beer at the kitchen table, playing cards, hanging out by the pool, though nobody's taking a swim.

Tommy's out of grass. Last night, he gave too much away. Somehow, Ivory ended up with his bag, she was passing joints out to everybody in sight. He just can't help himself, that hot feeling he gets when she rides his dirt bike and her arms slip 'round.

Ricky said he'd have dope this morning, stop by Stan's, but it turns out he's empty-handed. Tommy wants some now, he's got his mind set, especially after what just happened at Spangler's Store, where he'd pulled in for a pack of smokes.

There Tommy was, lighting up in the parking lot, when a gray BMW backed up and almost ran him over. He's ripshit—not so much the almost-run-over part, but the driver not seeing him. It was Zack, who—first-off—was inside buying the Sunday paper and cut in line, like Tommy's invisible. Zack, one of those funny smart kids everybody loves, who lives in a mansion near school, and his mom's a long skirt-granola-type that's gonna inherit half of down-

43

town when her dad kicks—the drugstore, the hardware, probably the bank. Zack's president of something at school, student council, a brown-noser all the teachers eat up, too.

Zack used to see Tommy, you can bet on that. He used to be scared shitless. Sixth grade, Zack waited for his mom after school—couldn't walk two blocks by himself—and when she drove up, she'd push the passenger-side door wide open like she's letting in the glory of the sun. While he waited, Zack had a circle of kids around him. This one time, he was showing off some little lead soldier thing—boasting how he got it off his great-grandfather that fought in the Civil War or the Revolutionary War, some war, all the kids yipping and yapping.

The circle's tight. Tommy's watching, under the basketball hoop. Then suddenly he walks over and shoves Zack's friend, the one holding the lead figure. He's soft as a girl, that kid, soft like some stupid animal. When he falls, Tommy swipes the soldier and leans back to heave it onto the school roof.

Zack yells *Asshole!*, like that's gonna do anything—watery tears, it's disgusting. In a second, Mommy'll kiss him all-better on the front seat of the station wagon, she'll call the principal, get Tommy suspended . . . Something better than the roof jumps into his mind.

He jams the soldier in his mouth. With that circle of kids staring, he chews it, his teeth on fire, his gums and tongue. Then he spits it on Zack's new Reebok shoes.

But at Spangler's, when Zack backed up the BMW, with his little learner's permit and Mom beside him, he didn't see Tommy at all. It just makes him boil. So dope's a good idea and Blake's willing to go look, except Ivory's bitching how she hates being left behind. Blake says they'll be right back, quick trip to town, quick score, and she's not invited.

"H-here, Ivory," Blake says. His neck's red where her necklace cuts. "G-get it off me."

He bends over, she undoes the clasp. She looks so pretty, bright red and pissed off, with that little bit of gold and sparkle swinging

off her fingers. When they drive away—Blake's sitting behind—
Ivory's still jawing, and he's wicked steamed.

In spite of the bitching, Blake's one lucky shit. If Ivory'd gave
him that necklace, he'd save it, not throw it right back in her face.
He'd stuff it in his mouth and chew it, swallow it down, if need be,
just to keep it safe. Still, he's happy to leave her, happy it's just him
and Blake.

fifteen

It's so humid that maple leaves hang heavy and still along the path. The smell of exhaust from Tommy's dirt bike still clings to Ivory's jeans jacket, to the necklace Blake made her take off him. It's the only beautiful thing she owns.

You don't have the right to give it away. Not to him you don't, her dad would say. Mom wouldn't say, but her mouth might fall, the way in November a jack-o-lantern smile decays. It's not fair, showing the insides of your disappointment like somebody'd drawn an empty hole.

Scratch my back, will you, dear? her mom would say, after. Always trying to push bangs off her forehead, to touch and pat. So she'd take the back scratcher off its kitchen hook and fire those wooden fingers up her mom's spine, and her mom—*Thank you. Thank you, dear.*

Blake hated the necklace around his neck. It cuts, he said. Take it off.

Gold chain so fine it feels creamy in her palm, gold heart edged with five glass stones and a red one, no bigger than the head of an ant. She's deep into the trees now. Walking toward home. Dirt bikes, snowmobiles, ATVs—they've widened the trails, but animals came first. She smells them. They don't show themselves though, only the buck did, once. The path cups her footsteps. She passes the old pine where she and Nicki left notes sometimes.

He's with Charity, she knows it. Last year, she stole a dollar out of Charity's wallet. She'd left it open on the dashboard of her cousin's pickup—a packet of guys behind plastic film, all of them backed up to painted clouds and fake blue sky, grinning for Charity's sake. And Blake's face fell out, so it was only right to swipe the bill, tucked in behind him, touching the back of his head if a picture had hair and a nape-of-your-neck. The dollar stank. Charity probably pawed it off some older guy at the pit.

The path splits. One trail winds back toward Stan's junkyard. One leads toward home. She can run it easily. Today, though, it's too far. She'd like to stop and wait for Blake. But he won't come back this way. He and Tommy took the road and won't be back. The air's so heavy it presses hard against leaves, and bright green drips into puddles of moss. Lichen, smeared on the north side of trees, still looks lit-up after Friday's rain. Once, her dad showed her how it worked, that brightness on the north side.

It's truly a wonder of nature, he said, using his pocket knife to dig some off the trunk of the maple by their dooryard, which he placed in the palm of her hand. *It's two things*, he said. *A fungus does the climbing, but it's a parasite, like your Indian pipe.* With the toe of his work boot he rooted out what she called a ghost flower in the cavity of a rotten log on that same north side.

The lichen does the holding, he told her, pulling apart threads in her hand—*it's strong as all get-out—makes a net, you might say, for your green stuff, the algae, that's chock full of chlorophyll.*

She liked how gently he talked with his lesson.

When it rains, he said, your *lichen sucks up water like you'd do through a straw and it goes all transparent—letting your green hum its own song.*

Today it's a harmful green, not climbing up but dripping down. She hesitates, deciding on a path. She won't walk home, it's too far. *Call me any time*, her dad always says, but she can't. He'd catch her up for sure in the stories she'd told to be with Blake. And her gym bag's still in Ricky's junked car. Her blow dryer, Pammy's purple chamois shirt. One of the boys finding her diary. She won't imagine that shame. Her stomach kills, and the sky tilts. She kneels, lifts a soft fist of moss and drops her necklace underneath. She hides it, the way she hid Charity's dollar, hungry to take a thousand glass hearts and bury each one. It's her necklace, she can do what she wants. But her stomach kills, and the sky tips to harmful green. *Take it back*, she tells herself, *it's yours*. She crouches, knee pressing on a pine cone, lifts the moss like it's a lid on a jewel box, curls the necklace in her palm. Then she turns and walks back toward Stan's.

sixteen

In spite of the heat, Ivory's still wearing her jeans jacket. She's uncomfortable, everybody's pretty old, except for a girl, Rhonda, Lisa's thirteen-year-old niece, who's supposed to babysit later so Lisa and Buzz can go out. Rhonda's got a flat moon face, but her lips are nice and full and if she wore bangs and eye-shadow, she might look decent. But Rhonda's keen on bumming cigarettes and leaves when she finds Ivory's out, too.

Lisa is the only other person Ivory kind-of knows, except for Buzz and Ricky, but they disappear somewhere—the garage, Lisa says. "They got car-stuff they're working on though they've lost their license, the both of 'em." Lisa laughs.

Buzz is Ricky's brother, older by a year or two. He's got Ricky's same yellow curly hair and smart-ass smile. Lisa's married to Buzz, she has his baby girl. In spite of a cold, the baby's sweet and lets Ivory bounce her while she sits with Lisa at the edge of the pool. It's hot and steamy, the smell of chlorine smarts her eyes.

Lisa's wearing yellow short-shorts, her legs so tan and smooth-shaven they're shiny. Her hair's shiny, too, just washed and blow-dried, a nice taffy bottle blond. She's like a movie star, not a care in the world, everything perfect. Ivory wants to ask Lisa what it's like being married—she heard the wedding was a few weeks ago—and to somebody as handsome and risky-tempered as Buzz, but it's so private she doesn't dare.

"You get a honeymoon?" she asks instead.

"Not with her." Lisa tweaks the baby's pink macaroni ear. "She's colicky, this little girl. You ever babysit?"

"Sometimes. Her I would." She touches the baby's forehead with her palm. She feels hot. Her temples are blue just under the skin, where her pulse beats.

"I might call you," Lisa says.

The baby stuffs a pebble in her mouth. Lisa scoops it out, then splashes her hand in the pool. Ivory's period starts, cramps like stabs. Her insides are falling out. Still no sign of Blake. "You got any pads?" she asks Lisa, who shakes her head and offers toilet paper.

An hour passes, then two. Ivory's stuck. Lisa, so clean and pretty, kissing her baby's temple, dangling her hand in the water.

"I might break up with Blake," Ivory says. She's so pissed she can barely hold it in, but she's shy in front of perfect Lisa. In her head, though, she's ballistic. Blake already knew she felt bad when he left, she hates him. The minute he shows up, she's dumping him. Then it strikes her, a gut wrench worse than cramps: maybe he's back with Charity for good. The thought's scary enough her ribs collapse, and she digs her nails into her jeans, digs and digs.

"Geez, you must be boiling." Lisa swipes the baby's nose with a paper towel. "She don't know how to blow. Want to borrow a shirt? I got some things upstairs."

It's a pale blue sweatshirt, a homemade cut-off number, cropped at midriff and sleeves, the neck cut down to a V. Ivory changes in the bathroom and uses toilet paper instead of pads.

seventeen

By early afternoon even more people show up, and some guy, Farris, who says he's Stan's cousin that runs the bottle redemption, makes noises about clearing out the house and the yard. "Don't seem like nothin' Stan would like," he says, half to Lisa, half to the aqua tile in the pool. Lisa laughs and pats water on her baby's toes. Just when some other relative of Stan's starts yelling, "Party's over!" Blake and Tommy drive up, stoned out of their gourds.

In the dirt and gravel dooryard, Ivory screams at Blake, then bursts into tears. At first he's quiet. His eyes are droopy and red. In a moment, though, he shouts, "Shut the fuck up!"

Ivory stops crying. Every terrible thing he ever said or did suddenly jumps into her mind. "I'm breaking up," she says.

The words slip off his shiny arms. He shrugs. Just then, Buzz and Ricky walk out of the garage. There's back-and-forth yelling between them and Farris, but Ivory doesn't listen.

"I gotta get home," she tells Tommy, her hand over his on the seat of his bike. Then they're off, Ivory in the middle, crushed against him. From behind, Blake's holding so tight she can hardly breathe. Her belly tumbles with anger, with cramps, with awful desire.

In a moment they're deep in the junkyard. Tommy's driving too fast. Light and shadow bounce off the windshield of the Chevy wagon, a blur of red and green. Then Tommy veers into the maze of trails.

"My bag!" she yells, but his wide back swallows her voice. The air's clogged with engine sounds. She leans, an inch is all she gets before Blake's arms squeeze her straight. She can't move. "Go back, my bag!"

They won't stop. The bike's screaming. Tear leaves, spit mud, rip moss.

eighteen

Late that afternoon, Florence is folding laundry at the kitchen table. It's a little old-fashioned Formica piece with aluminum edges and legs, her only inheritance when her mother died. She's always loved the color, a light-hearted rose, like the deep insides of a foreign shell.

Folding blankets at work, folding laundry at home . . . Sometimes at the mill her fingers get cut, forcing blankets inside plastic cases and zipping them up, fast as you can to meet the quota, eighty, ninety a day, some girls can do a hundred. You're paid by the piece and fired if you don't keep up. At home there's no rush or bloody cuts, nothing but clean black dirt the men grind into their knees and grease from heavy equipment. This summer, Dunc Jr.'s mowing lawns and clearing brush for the town so his Levi's, grass-stained and stuck with clippings, smell good-and-outdoors. Ivory's little tanktops don't smell like a body wore them at all. She's so picky, though, she washes things so often they fade quick and need replacement.

The phone rings. It's a woman's voice, a young woman's voice. "I gotta take my husband to the hospital right away," she says. "Ivory's babysittin', she wanted me to call, I'll bring her home tonight, it's an emergency."

Okay. Florence hangs up. Out the window by the table, some red-topped birds lift seeds from Duncan's homemade feeder. They don't seem to mind she's there. "Hello, little fellas." They startle off.

She opens red-and-white checked curtains at the other window. Duncan's been weeding the vegetable garden most of the afternoon. Now he's scratching lines around tomato plants. They've already bloomed and the fruit's set. Always a race to pick your tomatoes before the first killing frost. It takes time, pinching off new growth at the crotch, he says, but it helps send energy into the fruit. He moves quick and nervous, like one of the kids. When she's got four piles folded on the kitchen table, she steps outside.

There's the smell of turned soil and the sharp bite of snail bait, wet from the rain. Overhead, a lid of high thin clouds, then a cardinal's whistle. Duncan straightens up for a smoke. "Hear it?" He leans on his hoe.

"The cardinal I hear."

"No, rifle shots. Somebody blastin' woodchucks."

Living at the edge of the woods, you get rabbit, woodchuck, sometimes deer that wander by and help themselves. New lettuces, tidbits of broccoli, flower buds, but Dunc Jr. keeps track of garden pests. They're not a problem anymore.

Florence tells Duncan about Ivory babysitting, the hospital emergency.

"Who was it?" he asks.

"Don't know, they didn't give no name."

Later, while she's browning hamburg, the phone rings again. Duncan's sitting right there, the phone on the wall beside the table, but he hates talking, so she answers.

It's Pammy. "Some lady just called, said to let you know Ivory's okay and babysitting late."

"Same thing." Duncan shakes his head. "Stories." He pushes folded clean clothes off his placemat, which Florence gathers up. It's Ivory's pile, little things, a hundred little things that don't add up to half a man's stack.

nineteen

They wait for the sound of Ivory at the door. They're used to the way she rushes through the kitchen and tiny hall into her bedroom, the sound of her door shutting them out, her music. Worry is a nest of nettles that coffee and cigarettes and toast with grape jelly only rile up more. Florence can't sleep. She sits, her back to Ivory's wall, hoping the radio man will moan *Baby, Baby*, but there's nary a whisper of singing or talk. She thinks to call Nicki's house, then remembers her phone's out of order. Duncan smokes Pall-Malls, coughs, snaps them into his ashtray.

About two a.m., Dunc Jr. shows up.

"You think she's run off?" Florence asks him.

Dunc gives the look that's traveled through Duncan's side of the family—something they all know that she's outside of, something so clear to them you'd not speak it in words.

"If you want Ivory, I'd check under Blake Parady," he says, like Blake's a stone in the garden and Ivory's some slimy thing. She doesn't like that disrespectful tone of voice. Well, he's almost a man, turning eighteen, a senior this year, going to graduate and Ivory'll be at the high school, too. He can look out for her.

She sees Ivory, first day of kindergarten, holding her brother's hand down the road to Narrows Primary. Such a battle to make him hold on. *It's what you do in a family*, Duncan said. From behind they both looked so slight, bones growing soft and fast, like the suckers on a willow.

Later, walking by herself as far as Pammy's house, Ivory was one proud child. Miss Grady's second grade, hair braided so tight she had Chinese eyes. It was all new to Florence, fooling with hair. Her mother didn't touch, didn't hug, didn't fix pigtails and plaits. But Ivory insisted. She made Florence practice on the doll Rose Marie's head till she got it right.

Florence walks the short driveway to the road. No cars go by. It's quiet in the Narrows, houses dark, one fuzzy yellow street light, the air still boggy and strange. She expects Ivory to come walking up the gravel shoulder. Maybe in a car.

Duncan's dozing in his recliner. He's got a late-late movie on, black-and-white war, men with muddy faces and bright teeth. He likes the old cars, the old tanks and Jeeps, just men, fighting for America.

She waits at the kitchen table. Ivory's cat Speedy yowls to come in. Drowned-rat of a thing. She herself is not partial to cats but they make Ivory happy. It's Ivory who cleans Speedy's throwups, mistakes he makes on the floor. And he sheds something fierce.

They say girls get through the worst of it quicker than boys.

Fourteen's the worst, somebody at work said.

Yup, fourteen's a bugbear, somebody else agreed.

Remember yourself at that age? the first one said. *God, I was one holy bitch.*

Ivory's a good girl, Florence told them. *For my birthday she gave me a back scratcher.*

But tonight she's glad fourteen will soon be over. Herself, she doesn't remember that year. Junior high, most likely. She tried in school, teachers moved too fast, though, and her sister died. Girls need special care. But how, she wonders, when they hate your touch? After fourteen, maybe you get your child back.

twenty

Monday, early evening, there's a knock at the kitchen door. Clean, dry air's blowing through. Duncan nods. They got here quick, the police. She introduces herself, a nice firm hand. "Sally Gregg," she says.

She sits beside Florence at the kitchen table. Himself, he leans over the counter. She's new to the force, she says, did something helpful with kids before joining up. Makes sense they'd send a female, it being a girl who run off, and she's kindly with Florence, touches her here, touches her there like they knew each other before. A woman talks to a woman better than a man.

He wonders about the police side of things, the hard questions, the knocking of sense into some fool head, but Sally's enough all-business that he takes to her himself. She's short like Florence, but made of sturdier stuff.

Florence wanted to call the police last night. He said, Wait. This morning, when Ivory still hadn't come home, she was so wrought up he had her call in sick. Him, he was just damn mad. No sense losing two days' pay so off he went, didn't mention Ivory at work, there being something shameful in the father of a sneak-behind-your-back girl.

Sally's got a missing person's report, right there on her pad: *girl about 5'5", 105 pounds, brown eyes, dark brown hair, fair complected, two holes in each ear.* Florence knows the particulars.

"Kids have changed since I was a boy," he says. "I come up on a farm, chores at four a.m. and four p.m., hell or thunder—she's hiding at some friend's house, no doubt of it, that boyfriend of hers, Blake Parady, he knows something. I'd check with him first."

He holds his tongue about the diary he reads, how she straggled home with bruises, saying she took a spill off a motorbike, how she claimed—hang-dog written all over her—she'd walked into the streetlight down by Pammy's or tripped on some tree root in the woods.

"Just your basic spoiled and willful teenage girl," he tells Sally. She pats Florence's hand, all ears and sympathy. He's thankful for that. She's too young to have teenage children herself and know that heartache, but she's had some sorrow firsthand, you can tell. Those pockets of sleepless nights under her eyes, they're too dark for somebody scarcely beyond girlhood herself.

"Tell Sally here what he said. And maybe she'd like a mug of coffee."

At his prompting, Florence remembers hospitality, offers coffee, Hydrox cookies, some crackers on a plate. But she's got herself worked up, anybody can see that. When she fixed his lunch that morning, it was bare-bones peanut butter without the margarine he favors or the jelly. Nothing sweet or a piece of fruit. When he left, she was staring out the kitchen window, doing something fussy with her knuckles. Sally declines, but you need to offer.

"My girlfriend up the road drove me 'round." Florence crumbles the edges of a Hydrox.

"They went to Nicki's," he says, just to speed things up. "Course that was fabrication—Ivory never went there all weekend—then they drove over to Blake's. Tell Sally here what he said."

"He said nothin'. He said he'd not seen Ivory yesterday at all, didn't know where she was, nothin."

"Didn't even put on his T-shirt when he come out to the car,"

Duncan adds. "Before Florence left, she told him, *I know you're lyin'*, right to his face. That's what she said."

"Do you have any recent photos?" Sally asks. Florence fetches the eighth-grade school picture off the mantel, the big one with a brown cardboard cover you get with the packet of wallet-size. Thank God, Dunc Jr. didn't need the frills.

Sally opens the photo like a hymnal. "Pretty girl."

Duncan snorts at that. "Last year's looked better, not so down-at-the-mouth."

"Must be the style," says Sally. "Eighth grade, you wouldn't want to look too satisfied."

"Where you keep the towels?" he asks Florence.

She disappears, returns clutching something light blue with fringe, which he wraps around the picture, then fastens with twine. She's talked about a frame, but so far it's not happened. "You'll not scratch it," he says, offering the package to Sally.

"No, we'll make photocopies and get this right back to you."

"Florence is one tough customer when she's riled," he tells Sally, "but you got the long arm of the law on your side. I'd drive right over to that boyfriend's. She's hidin' over there, I bet, afraid to show her face at home 'cause of her tall tales."

Upon Florence's face the smallest smile, like the hopeful shadow of those songbirds she prizes so highly. She's not slept or ate, keeps talking about that phone call with the sorry edge of regret. She tells Sally about that and Pammy's phone call, too.

"Any problems that might have caused her to run away?" Sally's hands are folded, tanned and smooth-jointed, on her police notepad. She listens first before she takes things down. But they're outdoor hands, sizable enough to handle a gun.

"We forbid her seeing him," he says. "Par for the course, I imagine, with kids these days. When I got home from work and Florence still hadn't heard a word, we drove all over, her and me, before we notified you. We had her brother out, too, checking the lay of the land. Those kids—they'd not seen or heard nothin'. It's not right, how close-lipped they get."

Florence nods her head, but she's gone. What's left is that scaredy-cat empty look that scours his throat like metal filings.

Sally shakes his hand and squeezes Florence's shoulder. "If she's around, we'll find her." She's got the good grace to add, "I'm sorry—your having to wait like this," not some fool thing like *Don't worry*, for which he's grateful.

twenty-one

When Geena hears that Ricky's gone to Lawrence, she comes out of hiding and heads back to the pit. Of course Ivory's disappearing sits tops on her mind, on everybody's mind, including the new lady cop, Sally Gregg's. Geena likes her and wants to help with the search, but other kids act like she's sticking her butt where it don't belong. You're having a smoke in somebody's kitchen, they complain—parents away, there's some pot, some beer, no big deal, until Sally busts in—one-woman SWAT-team. It's close to midnight, but she'll still be wearing her uniform, navy-blue shirt and pants, big holster, black tie shoes, like it's Halloween, and they wonder, *Where the fuck does she get off?*

Sally sneaks in back doors, trying to catch Ivory by surprise, she beams her flashlight inside the cabs of trucks, inside mosquito-proof tents, practically shoves it down your throat. Sally's everywhere, the talk is, and she's pissed, figuring Ivory's run off just to yank some chains.

Have you seen her?
Anybody else said they've seen her, heard from her?
What's the talk?
Like they'd tell.
At the pit, of course, at TeeGee's Variety, in front of LaBreque's

61

Drug, rumors do fly. Somebody's seen her walking along the road past Mosey's farm. Somebody's seen her hitching, watched her climb into a two-door green sedan. Somebody's partied with her right here at the pit, swear-to-God, somebody's heard her voice on the phone. Somebody else claims the Towles get calls all the time, but the tips are anonymous, the voices disguised.

Word has it Sally and her buddy Andy Smith, another new cop, are all over Blake and Tommy, in particular. But they've not seen Ivory since Sunday afternoon, the story goes.

Geena hears it all at the pit, staring out the windshield of a Camaro, eyes fixed on Orion's belt. Some guy, Russ, whose car it is, turns out to be Andy Smith's cousin so he has the inside poop. Tommy'd said, *Yeah, Ivory was p.o.'d Sunday afternoon, but it got settled after some hassle. We smoked dope, I fell asleep in the tent behind Blake's. When I woke up, she was gone.*

According to Blake—says Andy Smith's cousin Russ—Tommy was the one rode Ivory home to clean up, to get money off her parents, said she'd be back. Ricky said he saw her walking along the road that afternoon, he thinks he saw her that afternoon, it might have been night, and sometimes he scrambles his dates. Geena's careful not to hear it direct from him. The butcher knife he threatened her with still glints sick-yellow in the foreground of everything she pictures. *Assholes, all of 'em,* Geena repeats, to shoo worry away and the knowledge Ivory'd not do anything important without telling her first.

twenty-two

A few days later, still no sign of Ivory, and Geena's sitting on the windowsill of her mom's apartment, three stories up, catching a breath of air. Heat wave, last couple days, you feel coo-coo, inside and out. Kitchen chairs sweat, stick your head in the fridge, wake up sopping, your ankles roped to the sheets. Her fingers swole up so bad she had to twist her rings off with Crisco.

She's having a smoke. It feels good and spicy down her lungs, then calm. She's blowing smoke straight out over the sidewalk, where it hangs like a cartoon word-cloud, when down the row of four-story frame apartments a fat kid comes walking. He looks up at her, waves like he knows her, then ducks into Dave's Package Store across the street. It's too hot to give him the finger.

A few minutes later, she's got her eyes closed, just drifting. Then out of the blue, somebody starts beating on the door. Her mom's zoned out on the couch, *Dallas* on TV. Before Geena can get herself back from nowhere and off the windowsill to answer the door, a fist shoots through plywood into the hollow space. It's Ivory's brother Dunc's fist, Dunc's face, Dunc's yelling.

He pushes past Geena, toward the open window. "Ivory!" His eyes sun-red, his skin white under dark tan. "I know she's here, Darryl seen her in the window."

Six or seven of his friends crowd through the doorway. A tumble
of boots and black T-shirts, sweat, alcohol, vigilante swears. She tries
to protect her bed, her small corner of things, but when the fat boy
Darryl shoves her and her shoulder knocks the shelf, her silver rings
spill every which way and her blue china horse teeters and falls.

The boys yank off sheets, tip beds over, kitchen chairs, they ransack the closets. Dunc's calling for Ivory—behind the shower curtain, in kitchen cupboards, under the TV, and Darryl won't quit.
He's pawing her private stuff, so she swings. She connects with his
forearm, whipped in front of his face. He grabs her wrist, but she
pulls away. Her blue china horse—broke to bits.

Then Dunc's there. "Darryl, whoa," he says. It's like he snaps
awake. He holds her arms, gently now, more like protection than
attack. He's her size, eye to eye. The commando-stuff—gone.
What's left is Ivory's brown eyes, long chin, stuck onto the shoulders
of a man.

By now, her mom's off the couch, retying her orange terry halter
and tugging at her shorts. Her face is pillow-lined, but already she's
figured out what happened. "It's okay, Dunc. We understand." She
cups his face in her hands. "Ivory ain't here. Whoever thought they
seen her, they seen Geena on the windowsill, not Ivory. There's no
Ivory here," she repeats like she's telling a story to a grandkid.

Before Dunc, Geena did guess Ivory'd run away. They talked about
doing it, and she's taken off herself a couple times. But after Dunc,
she changes her mind. It's a sureness in her guts, each night bigger
and harder. At dawn it wakes her, sobbing the way her mom does
when she thinks she's alone. But she doesn't say the feeling into
words; there's still hope.

Not after her dream, though. That she tells out loud, since it won't
be silenced. And it spooks everyone. In the dream, she's asleep when
there's knocking. Her and her mom and her grandma who's dead
and her Aunt Rita who lives in New Jersey, they all crowd into the
hallway that's bigger in the dream than in real life so everybody fits.

She's the one to turn the knob, to open the door. It's Ivory. Black mascara tears, white-white skin. *Help me*, she says. *Help me.*

But Geena's froze to the doorknob. They're all froze. Before they can move their jaws to comfort or lift their hands to touch, Ivory turns to go. It takes Geena forever to cross the space between them, though it's only a few feet. It's like she's trying to run through deep water, her heart knocking, her arms and legs, but she's moving nightmare slow. When at last she reaches the narrow landing where Ivory stood, her hand clamps vacant air.

twenty-three

Stuck at home, Nicki tries to find out what's happened to Ivory, but the phone's off limits and she can't go outside by herself. Still, she knows something's wrong. A whisper in the house, a congestion, she overhears her mom and dad talking. Whatever's happened, it's nothing good. *No doubt she brought it on herself. That boyfriend, those parties. It's time you found more suitable friends, young lady.* She hates them.

Nicki spends hours on her bed. All morning she'll play with the Spaghetti-O-sized rubberbands she's supposed to wear on her braces, rolling them onto her pinkie finger. Afternoons she'll brush her bangs. They've grown back from when Roxanne cut them—a thick, rusty hedge she hates, *but no haircuts till you learn some responsibility.* Her room is pink and little-girl pretty, disgusting to the woman she feels herself to be. She packs up stuffed animals, then peels Rainbow Brite stickers off her mirror. Only one stuffed anything stays on her pillow, and that's not an animal but a girl: the blue plush Smurfette Ivory gave her in the hospital. Only one thing at the edge of the mirror: Ivory's wallet-size school picture.

Let's sneak out, the photo tells her, but she can't.

Out her window, she watches green worms turn tomato leaves into skeletons. They grow to the size of ponytail barrettes and still she keeps her mouth shut. But her mom finds them anyway. Nicki watches her pick worms off, drop them into a coffee can of kerosene, toss a match in. Smoke rises and flames shoot up. Her mom smiles, lies on her back in the dirt, finds more worms, hiding on stems and the undersides of fruit. More smoke, more smell, more flame.

Nicki tries starvation. Once in social studies they read about hunger strikes, but she's got nothing to do now except eat. Besides, before you die that way, your teeth fall out and fistfuls of hair, and your breath smells like road-kill.

From behind the window-screen, she watches cars pass, August pass, her whole life pass. It's a comfort then, sliding bare heels along the satiny pink bedspread, to imagine her own face, traded for Ivory's, off on some adventure inside Ivory's purse. That is, when she thinks Ivory's up to something good, like hitching to New York City, which mostly she doesn't.

In early August, Sally Gregg tried to interview her, though her dad did all the talking. At the end, though, Sally asked Nicki—and told her dad she wanted Nicki's own words—*Any chance she might have committed suicide?*

Course not, Nicki said. After she and Roxanne took all those pills, Ivory yelled at her—in a sweet way—gave her Smurfette, made her promise not to do anything hurtful like that again.

Still, in all the long hours since, Nicki has relived their days, second by second, and now she wonders. It's not something Ivory would do, but she can't get Christmas Beach out of her mind. At night, it hovers there while headlights walk like clowns on stilts across her ceiling. That wonderful hot night replacing this sucky one, and Day-Glo plankton, tumbling on the surf. Her and Ivory, the boardwalk behind them, the Ferris wheel, the Pirate Ship, kids squealing, flashing neon lights, but only the two of them—girlfriends, best friends—calf-deep in shiny water with their toes dug hard into sand.

Ivory looked so pretty that night, scary how pretty she looked, like some outer-space queen. They waved and blew kisses at all the cute guys across the ocean in Portugal, then Ivory knelt down,

scooped handfuls of sea water, and splashed her arms and legs like a
kid in a wading pool. After that, though, she got quiet and strange,
kind of comatosed, and with her fist she scrubbed hard at the BLAKE-
scar on her thigh.

part two

twenty-four

You think you've looked over the edge and down into all that's possible, Sally told herself, but she now felt differently. This was her first live homicide—she held on to the joke, the language of the joke, as if her throat were full instead of empty. You could get caught up in the excitement, the sheer weight of what happened, not to mention the machinery—the metal detectors, the insides of the forensic van, disgorging important steel. They'd lit up the woods— spread wide yellow plastic tape, issued latex gloves, posted security at the perimeter

As a girl she'd loved floor plans. She would plot out room after room of a dream house or a castle. She learned the draftsman's symbols for windows and doors, the landscaper's jagged-edged circle that said plant a lilac here, a juniper there, beside the flagstone walk.

Odd now, she thought, she had never pictured people, never drawn them in her plans, never imagined even a child for the playroom or the indoor swing-set she made with a protractor and compass. She dwelled on distances, the number of graph-paper squares that might create a sunken living room, a basketball court, an apple orchard with scalloped circles for tree canopies and fruit like dotted Swiss.

If you could sail your mind out from this woods clearing, never looking over the edge into the depths of the well, Sally thought, you might be safe. Already Charlie Bergeron, the state police detective in charge, had her gathering measurements—yards, feet, inches— rendering round things flat. To prepare for this first live homicide, she'd watched crime-scene videos, talked to veterans, read police reports. They trained your eyes, they trained your hands. Cordon off, sweep the ground for spent shells, a discarded knife or gun. Look, look. You are nothing but eyes.

Other things caught you unawares. Smells entered through your skin, your blood inhaled them and they traveled directly to your stomach and your heart without first registering in your mind. You didn't have a chance, Sally tried to tell herself, holding onto words, safe words.

A couple of kids were walking their black Lab out behind Mosey's farm. Their dog had caught a scent and barked. He ran off the trail, he barked and he barked. The kids found her—kids magnets to other kids. She and Andy Smith had gotten there first after the call. The Sumner Road was off Ballard, about six miles from town-center, old county roads no longer maintained, all but impassable to anything but ATVs. Their squad car bottomed out a few times and the oil pan scraped on exposed roots. Moments later Detective Bergeron had driven up, two state police cruisers behind him, an hour later Dr. Cooper, the state medical examiner, ready, after the Polaroids and on-site testing, to collect the remains.

Bergeron wouldn't let her scream or throw up or run away, all that would be human to do if you looked over the edge. His tired eyes calmed her, his weary voice, so deep it seemed to rise from somewhere below his chest. She wanted to learn, he needed to talk as he went, maybe it was easier like that. He was a compact man, somewhere about fifty, with thinning red hair, cut short. Maybe heart trouble, maybe just high metabolism—he'd made an effort to keep fit. His eyes were pale gray with whites the color of parchment, as if he suffered from insomnia or a touch of liver trouble.

"You've got to figure everything here is important, every twig, every piece of bark." He was taking notes on a yellow pad. "Useful information may extend out twenty-five feet or a thousand—we don't have any idea." His tone detached.

"Bodies hold a lot of evidence—what they last ate, if it's female, whether or not she's pregnant or had recent sexual intercourse. There might be fibers, bullet holes through flesh—here it's too late for that—but through bone, that's good. Whoever did this—their lawyer's gonna have plenty of time to pick us apart. We've got a few hours, max, to get it right."

Tree roots, lichen, moss. It was moving toward fall that day, early September, the crickets crazed, day and night, one or two startling smears of red at the crests of swamp maples—otherwise a green world. But sunlight, so lemon-like all summer, suddenly tipped toward blue and the air was so dry Sally's lips cracked.

Bergeron called her name. "You'll be doing these yourself soon enough." He handed her the homicide report, then leaned against his car, arms crossed, staring over her head into the tops of trees, while she read the paragraph he pointed to:

The body is badly decomposed and appears to be that of a young girl. She is resting on her back, fully clothed with both legs extended. Her right arm is bent, extending above the shoulder. Her left, although removed by decomposition and wildlife activity, appears to have been extended out to the left. Her skull from the same conditions is separated and rests beside her left hip. She is wearing a pullover top beneath a blue denim jacket, Jordache blue denim jeans, and purple Nike sneakers. A black leather pocketbook rests by her left shoulder with the shoulder strap around her upper left arm. Feathers on the ground indicate probably large birds have interfered and fed on the body for many days.

Yes, a purse found—she'd found it—a wallet and address book found—she'd found those, too, and feathers . . . so that all the time since, she'd talked to herself, clamping square teeth hard on her bottom lip to control some kind of painful noise. Think of lines, think of right angles. Don't swirl the torn hank of hair into a ponytail, the melting address book into phone numbers, girlfriends, whispers.

Make a grid. Make a possible timeline, a plausible map. Don't make a diary or an angry gunshot. The point was she was now flat, almost flat—a round child, rendered two-dimensional after a summer in this clearing. An old cellar-hole nearby, green with moss, a juniper, an apple tree, split by lightning, still alive, so old it was the color of a granite cairn. The damp ground was cratered with fruit, hard as glass. If you kept your mind steady, sealed off what you smelled that you couldn't even speak into words, if you held your flashlight, your clipboard, your pencil, it was possible not to touch the edge and reach over.

You couldn't read the names and phone numbers, the rain had washed them away, except the memory of purple ink, the rounded letter-ghosts, dotted with open circles and hearts. But in spite of yourself, you had to look down into that empty well. Down your eyes went and down. And what you found at the bottom was Ivory Towle.

twenty-five

Back at the station, it was decided that Sally should notify the family. She had interviewed the Towles for the missing person report. Mrs. Towle asked for her whenever she called for news. Besides, what everyone knew about Sally but nobody would say to her face, she had the feel, the weighty gift of empathy, and for all she was new to police work, she'd done this job before—kids, accidents, support services. But unless you'd lost a child yourself, you didn't have any idea what it was like.

Baby Jack, a crib death, seven and a half months old.

At dusk, Sally parked in the Towles' dirt driveway, behind a small brown sedan and a snowmobile draped with black plastic. Six weeks since Ivory disappeared. Dark green fronds of forsythia, looping the walkway, cried out for pruning shears, and marigolds, packed in close to the cinderblock foundation, had burst into full rusty bloom amid the dead heads. Beside them, lilac blossoms had gone to seed. Amongst the tumble of leaves, they looked like fists of buckshot. A house suspended, but they were trying, she saw that: two china cats climbing blue shingles beside the TV antenna wire—new, she thought—a red whirligig that wasn't spinning right now, two homemade bird feeders, low enough for Florence to fill.

She liked this neighborhood, the Narrows. If things had worked

out with Brad, they'd talked about finding a house, good value for
your money back from the road, its own primary school. But that
was that.

She knocked at the side door. A pause, TV hushed, then Florence
appeared. At the sight of Sally, her palm flew to her mouth. Her lips
turned gray. Sally stepped inside, regretting the gun at her hip, hard
pressed against Florence's side when she tried to touch the sorry
bones in her shoulder. The screen door banged shut. *I don't know
how to tell you this.*

"What, Florence, who is it?" Duncan's voice.

God, please cover my ears, Sally prayed. It was always the same, the
parents' reaction. She knew exactly the look of that particular agony,
the trapped wild-animal cry, the steel jaws of your child dying before
you.

twenty-six

Wild dogs. The beaks of birds. *Help me*, Florence cried. Teeth. Claws. The tracks of crows across her face. Sun burned her cheeks, the ridge-line of the fine Towle nose. When Ivory was born, the space between her eyes was all of a china-blue saucer, her life beating so close to your fingertips. *Little Thump. Little Flounder. Come settle here.*

She'd rubbed witch hazel under the criss-cross straps of Ivory's gingham sunsuit—ducks wearing bonnets for a bib—her shoulder blades soft-soft and deepest pink, little angel wings. Sunburn, sunstroke, bug bites. Sun burned the back of her left hand, the white crescent scar from the woodstove, *My Smiley-Face Tattoo.*

You look at that, Ivory, and you hear it say, "Careful!" and "Take good care!"

Scars don't talk.

This one does.

I love you, Mom.

"The crows—would they step—before—"

"Don't think that." Duncan's ashy voice. "We don't know."

We know. She mouthed the words. Without sound he heard them.

Sharp things flew about the kitchen. Paring knives, carving knives, scissors. The birds had grown bolder. They'd hopped, they'd

pranced and pecked. The teeth of wild dogs ripped her bones—an
arm, a leg—their jaws feasted.

Duncan sat beside her, the edge of the bed, the edge of the world
falling at their feet. His head dropped into his hands. He couldn't
breathe. His inhaler was out, he couldn't speak for the shock inside
him. Crows pecked her skin. She was sleeping in the woods—her
cheek upon a pillow of moss—she looked asleep. The sun burned
her. Mosquitoes, no-see-ems. She couldn't swipe, they bit, she
burned, a line of ants.

Dunc lay his grown head in her lap, dry sobs. She was the one to
cry the tears.

"Blake. Had to've been." Dunc's words a fist.

"She might've taken ill, no one there to hear—she was talking
about a sore throat, that stomach—"

Sharp things circled the room. Nail scissors, needles. She could
reach out, a Swiss army knife, shards of mirror if you slammed your
head.

Through the open window the night circled. They sat at the night
edge of the world. A moon and a planet almost touched, that close,
before they got swallowed by the lilac's bitter seeds. *There's an important event in the sky tonight*, a girl at the mill said. *My boyfriend's big
on astrology*, she'd said.

I'm Sagittarius, Mom. Pammy's got a book.

What do they do?

Shoot arrows and they run fast.

Like you.

Like me. Her cheeks high-colored.

What am I?

A Bull.

Stubborn. What do they do?

Ivory'd laughed. *You're silly, Mom. They paw and they stick you.*

Florence had made horns—index fingers to forehead—and she
snorted and she chased. For a cape she'd swiped a red terry dish
towel. When she stopped to paw her tennis shoe, it stuttered on the

linoleum, and Ivory squealed. Florence stuck the best she could, but Ivory got away, she could always get away.

"One shoe off, Sally said, like Ivory lost it, running."

"A gun or a knife." Dunc's fist beat the floor.

Birds had pecked the fine pink line of her nose. Claws, the soft tearing of beasts.

"Are your eyes open—when you go—or do they shut?"

"Don't think that."

In the morning, Halliday's Funeral Chapel. A box. *You'll have your remains back, but not now, you can't have her, not now, after.* The medical examiner was doing his job—clean hair the ants tunneled for a nest. She was gone. What did a body matter? All of them dead-feeling now in a quiet dawning room.

We'll find out who did this. We'll get them, Mr. and Mrs. Towle. I am so very sorry. My heart is an empty well. Sharp things flew. Knives flew, needles, a pair of scissors.

Duncan held her, his spine the taut stave of a barrel. No thing inside her moved, she'd burned to the ground. *Little Flounder, beating soft and blue upon my lap. Little Sniffle. Little Trouble.*

The birds stirred, the songbirds, the crows. They crowded the feeders, their wings and beaks. Out the window in the shadow of lilac leaves—too much night, still, to feel the glow of the redtops—they swarmed. A crow tore the screen.

Ivory, help me.

The crows would have seen it first, in spite of raindrops, the spatter of paws and teeth, a sparkle, a glitter of barrette or bobby pin. They stepped. Onto the back of her hand. No movement. Overhead, birch leaves rumbled a warning. They must. Don't step. Still it caught the crow's eye. You could crack your head into the mirror of that shining eye and it would still have stepped, still pecked, still feasted.

Outside, a chaos of beaks, flax seed, thistle seed, a spray of cracked corn—the feeder Duncan had taken such pains with burst apart at the weight of feathered wings. But the redtops, they didn't scare off.

One of Ivory's cats had disappeared one time—not the money

one, the one before it. Pumpkin, she called him. No trace one long summer month, like this—until up by Pammy's the crows started in, the smell—

She reached up. The hope of scissors. A thousand redtops, she'd skin them alive, dip their feathers in her own life's blood, then feed them to the crows herself if it would bring color back to those pieces of child. A thousand redtops—Instead, a pillow. She cradled it, humming *Little Flounder, Little Trouble*. Then she gored. Clots of down and ticking, a zipper's gleam. Feathers floated, they pranced, they swarmed. And sharp things flew.

twenty-seven

Dr. Cooper and his assistant conducted the autopsy. Cause of death: three gunshot wounds from a .22 caliber gun. It took hours, the meticulous examination of shattered bone, the bullets' entry and exit points—her back, her head. So much flesh had decomposed it was difficult to draw conclusions. She was fully clothed. They couldn't determine if she'd been raped—too much rain, too much decomposition, too much animal tampering to detect traces of semen on her underwear or skin. Something of interest about the sternum—some kind of round puncture. Raccoon, coyote, wild dog?

Anthropologist Ed Mosco, an expert on the skeletons of New England wild animals, agreed to take a look, if the bone was sent up to the University. Because of its tapered shape, a tooth left a larger entry than exit point, and he'd recognize the maker.

This puncture, however, turned out to be of uniform size, top and bottom, he reported. It was almost perfectly round, and there were faint traces of metal around the hole, in keeping with a wound made by an ice pick or an awl. Maybe a screwdriver. Dr. Cooper concluded the puncture was *periterminal*—around the time of death—meaning before or after, they couldn't determine which, but not too far in either direction.

To establish approximate time of death, he sent insect samples

to an entomology professor he'd worked with before. By examining
insect parts, live specimens and their tissue host, this fellow was adept
at establishing how many generations had reproduced themselves—
taking into account weather, season—and therefore the number of
weeks, sometimes days, since the subject had died.

In addition to the catalogue of clothing already in the homicide
report, Dr. Cooper added:

> *white athletic socks, black underpants, a white Cross-Your-*
> *Heart 'slightly padded' bra, size 32 C, style #73. Through*
> *the right side of the right cup, there's a ragged approximately*
> *one-inch hole—one of the bullet exit sites—leaving portions of*
> *outer lace fabric in this area missing and torn.*

twenty-eight

"Catch a Falling Star" played through the new music system Calvin Halliday had recently purchased for Halliday's Funeral Chapel. He hummed along, *sotto voce* of course. No words on the tape, just soothing instrumental, still the lyrics ran through his head. There was such a crowd he'd had to pull back the wooden room dividers. Even so, every chair was occupied, people lined the walls, some had even spilled out onto the lawn. Good thing, it turned out, that the cursed crows had woken him at five o'clock pecking at the new tin flashing around his chimney. He'd run the sprinklers long enough to bring the green back up and still shut them off in time for the grass to dry before the service started.

It was one o'clock now, a hot, bright day with building clouds, gold filigree where they touched the sun. Though it was just past Labor Day, Ivory Towle's girlfriends wore pastel dresses and white shoes. They looked so young, new to grief and disbelieving still, their necks adorned with colored strings, their wrists, their ankles. They sobbed and embraced. Girls' foreheads rested on other girls' shoulders. The men glistened with discomfort.

Calvin himself rarely sweated. In his profession, that was unseemly. All he could give—besides the logistics of burial—was kindly formality, the respect of manicured nails and expensive charcoal suits. He was thirty-five, and it had been twenty years since his first client. He'd grown up here—only a short hallway separating the living room from the embalming room, and it never seemed out of the ordinary. He remembered sticking his head in the door to shout, *I need a ride to Little League!*—his dad busy with a cadaver.

But now, the fact of it—Death—waited, rowdy and disheveled, at the center of his days. Ten years ago, when he'd buried his grandfather's cronies, he could still relax against the cushion of generations. Then had come his dad's contemporaries. Now he was seeing people his own age, occasional high-school classmates, their children sometimes. Children caught him up short. They exploded decorum, they wreaked havoc with the tidy rightness of things. And something like this—a girl missing for weeks, found murdered—it was difficult, knowing the families, remembering the child if only from the grocery store, once, maybe a third-grade play, a softball game.

Reverend Hornby moved briskly toward the casket, the lectern. He was an imposing fellow with black-framed glasses and a full sheaf of white hair—master of the nondenominational service—but even Hornby seemed a little nonplussed at the size of the crowd and the commotion outside. Not living in town, he hadn't realized the notoriety, the shock. When he spread his wide hands flat, Calvin brought the lights up a little until the Reverend's hair glowed. The high windows in the chapel were shrouded. People liked it this way, he'd found—bright sunlight unwelcome at such a time. Behind the casket, in the alcove, new dark paneling and a mural of autumn leaves turned deep red, lit by a spotlight buried in the floor.

The notes of "Catch a Falling Star" were scarcely audible except to him, standing in the back, but he shut the music off. Storing a star in one's pocket—what foolishness. Thinking of Florence Towle, however, the idea pained him. Because the Towles had no church affiliation, they'd chosen *Popular Favorites* over *Sacred Selections* three mornings ago at his office, but he doubted they remembered discussing music at all. The small particulars of choice had overwhelmed Florence. She wasn't speaking, poor dear. Price range for the casket, type of lining, the kind of wood, the kind of service, cemetery, flowers, refreshments, any special words you wanted to include. Out of habit, it appeared, Duncan had done the deciding. Florence kept her eyes fixed on her lap.

This morning, after he'd turned off the sprinklers and instructed his young helper to unfold chairs, he'd called the Towles. Florence answered. Thinking she might prefer it, he asked for Duncan.

But she'd said, *He don't like talking on the phone, Calvin. You can tell me, it's okay.* And somehow he'd felt ashamed.

Her remains won't be back in time for the service, he'd said.

He heard Florence repeat his words to Duncan. *But we do it anyways?* A kind of question.

I thought I should call you, it's only right. Because of the nature of what's happened, of course, there's no question about the casket's being opened or closed—so nobody else will know, not even the minister.

Florence silent on the line, then repeating for Duncan. *No burying today,* she'd said, *just the funeral.* Words speaking themselves without a living voice behind.

I called the medical examiner's office twice every day and they kept telling me there'd be no problem having her remains back in time. But apparently there's been some kind of hold-up with the autopsy. Maybe more tests . . . To himself, he'd sounded like a kid, blaming a playmate for some horrible lapse of judgment, some falsehood he now regretted but couldn't yet own up to. But Florence hadn't pressed.

He dimmed the lights over the rows of folding chairs, brightened Hornby and the casket, nodded at the rookie police officers, a man and a woman, assigned to what—keep peace? look for murderers? Thank God, somebody'd had the decency to put them in plain-clothes.

The service was short and by the book. Hornby spoke of youth's flower abruptly plucked, the wonder of God's ways. He knew little about Ivory, her life as great a mystery as her murder. Then he closed with a line from a poem Calvin didn't recognize—*Remember me for a while, but not for long*—as if Ivory Towle herself were speaking from beyond the grave. An odd sentiment, he thought—now, today, so soon. He walked down a side aisle and stood behind the casket. In case. Beforehand, he'd worried about the kids not being respectful and the two officers lending a threatening tone, but so far, everything seemed right, proper and dignified.

In the front row, between her husband and her son, Florence sobbed quietly. There were no hymns. Duncan didn't want hymns. And then Reverend Hornby drew them all to their feet, his face florid, his white hair flowing in the light. Girls rushed forward. Calvin shaped them into a line. The grown-ups followed, family friends, a number of teachers, neighbors, co-workers, they all filed past the casket to pay their respects.

A brunette with startling blue eyes held three red roses. Their closed bud-heads drooped like they'd fallen asleep, chins on their chests. The girl kissed each one, then set them down where Ivory's head might be. One little blond thing threw herself onto the casket, the way a shipwrecked swimmer might, finding the capsized hull of a boat. Before Calvin could reach her, she was coaxed off by a tall woman in a purple turban, while other girls passed by, bending to kiss the cherry-stained pine.

He gathered that Ivory's remains wouldn't be more than a small bagful—some bones, her skull, some scraps of hair and flesh—but knowing she wasn't there with them, even a portion of her body, and all this outpouring directed at an empty box—to even imagine the family's distress . . . He watched Florence's hand stray from lap to mouth to throat.

It was time. Calvin helped her up. The men followed in their black suits: Young Dunc, dark-tanned, tight with rage and grief; Duncan, no more than a pile of cinders and a cough. As if leading blind children, he guided them out a narrow paneled door into the hallway, through his family's kitchen.

In the parking lot across the road, a swarm of reporters, photographers, TV cameramen. Before the service, he'd chased them off his lawn. But they'd been waiting, smoking cigarettes, lounging against the cortege of numbered cars. Now they'd clustered around car number one, he saw, as he rushed the Towles down the flagstone walk, across the road, and into a green Buick sedan, marked number four. They wouldn't get their pictures today. At his signal, his helper started the engine. Florence, lost in the center of the backseat, seemed not to know where she was or why. Instead, she fumbled with the misbuttoned pearls on her cardigan, pushing one finger through the last empty hole.

twenty-nine

Two weeks ago, maybe three, a woman had telephoned Pammy. *Call Mrs. Towle,* she'd said. *Tell her Ivory's okay, she's being fed.*

Who is this? Pammy had asked. *How do you know? What's your name?*

But the woman had hung up.

Now, standing in the hot sunlight on the wide front lawn of the Halliday Funeral Chapel, Pammy listened for that voice. In groups of twos and threes, kids with kids, grown-ups with grown-ups, people were talking, crying, laughing.

Was it old-sounding or was it young? Florence had asked her when she biked down the road with the message.

I couldn't tell. It sounded like she was trying not to sound like herself.

The voice hadn't asked for money so it wasn't kidnap. *She's being fed,* Pammy and Florence had repeated, but was that comfort or torment? Kids, must be, fooling around. But still. They'd fallen silent at the mystery of such cruelty.

Inside, when Blake had showed up, the lights over Ivory's casket flickered—like Ivory herself was upset. Pammy'd seen it with her own eyes, swear-to-God, and her dad, too. And with her own eyes, she'd watched Blake's mom hug Florence, and Florence turn to stone, her arms stone, her back stone, her face stone gray. Girls kept rushing up to Blake. Charity all over him, *Poor Blake, Poor Blake, it's so terrible, poor Ivory, poor you* . . . Charity throwing herself on the casket, like she was dying herself, and leaning way over so Blake could see her red underpants. He killed Ivory, him and Tommy Slack. Everybody knew it.

Remember Julie's Secret Sloth? They'd been sitting on the floor of Ivory's bedroom, candles lit, eating chips, making Little Bunny Foo-Foo shadows on the wall.

At Narrows, was I loud? Ivory'd asked. A funny question, but it sounded like something she really wanted to know.

And Pammy had said, *Medium.* Maybe, though, if she'd just said, *Yup, the loudest, I loved it,* Ivory might have changed her mind, not sneaked to Blake's house, not thought she had to lie. She'd have pulled her bike out of the shed, and they'd have pedaled side by side up the road, one-handed, the gym bag swinging between them. Watched stupid shows all night. Woke up alive.

There was no shade on the lawn, just prickly green heat, and across the road, reporters with cameras. Sweat dripped down the backs of Pammy's legs. *Wear pantyhose,* her mom had said. The waistband dug at her stomach. She felt hungry. High-school kids, mostly girls, gave comfort, wiped tears, shared Kleenex. She wasn't part of that. A tall lady from school saw she was alone and walked over. It was embarrassing, a teacher trying to be kind.

"I'm Mrs. Cadenza."

"I know. You talked at the assembly."

"Second day of school. I had no idea what to say. I'm so sorry, Ivory was your friend." She didn't know that, she couldn't know that, but it sounded like she did.

"Best friends."

Mrs. Cadenza's eyes were red, she blew her nose. This might have been creepy, like Charity falling on the casket, but it wasn't.

"I helped her pack, the last night, before—I live just down the road."

Mrs. Cadenza waited.

"I might have stopped—"

Mrs. Cadenza waited some more.

"That scarf thing's nice."

"Someone told me purple was Ivory's favorite color. I had her in class, but I hardly knew her."

Mrs. Cadenza was very tall, like a genie, in that scarf and a long, loose gray-and-purple dress.

"A couple weeks ago—" The phone call, the voice trying not to sound like itself, Pammy needed Mrs. Cadenza to know that too, but her dad was signaling from the parking lot.

"Ivory was so picky," she said, "about how she looked. If she gained one pound, she'd pitch a fit. That night—she hated how her hair stuck out, *beagle ears*, she called it—after she'd already washed and blow-dried it once—so she did it all over again."

Mrs. Cadenza touched her forehead.

"When school got out, she gave me a drawing, a Mustang—the car not the horse. I don't have a single horse she did, not one."

Death looked like blank paper, just then, where a drawing would want itself to be—a foal, born that morning, steamy and hopeful, a ballpoint palomino leaping the blue lines of a composition pad like they were fences made of string.

Before opening the door of her dad's pickup, Pammy looked back. Blake—standing by himself, hands in his pockets at the edge of the lawn, staring at his leather shoes. He'd got a suit on, just had his hair cut—sharp black sideburn lines, like the Devil at church school. He looked up, away. Charity was gone. The few girls still left whispered and tossed their heads, clean hair haloed in sunlight. They were still checking out the reporters, who'd almost finished loading their camera equipment into vans.

Mrs. Cadenza called Blake's name. Pammy heard that. He turned, acted lost, then confused. When she wrapped her billowy lilac arms around him, he cried. At least his shoulders moved up and down like he was crying. He made noises. And there was water on his face.

thirty

During the next few days, Dunc and his parents lived at the police station, it felt like. His mom told the lady cop that while looking through Ivory's school bag, she'd found girlfriend-boyfriend letters that upset her so much she'd burned them—love-note types of things was all she'd say about that. *But I've not dared go into her room.*

One evening, the state cop in charge, Bergeron, was interviewing them at a desk, piled with file folders and photographs, phone messages and paper coffee cups. He talked fast, but he wouldn't let himself get caught saying what was fact: Blake and Tommy murdered his little sister. The whites of Bergeron's eyes were yellow-colored, his lids drooped like he was barely staying awake, but the rest of him was hyper, like his speech. Marine buzz, Marine ring. He was middle-aged, somewhere. *Did you see anything, hear anything.*

When Bergeron got up for a moment and left the room, his dad pushed a paper aside, nonchalant so his mom wouldn't notice, but he noticed. It was the Polaroids the cops didn't want them to see. *Her remains*—isn't that the word they kept using?—her remains scattered on dead leaves, under a tree, her skull, her skeleton fingers still wearing all those rings that girls will wear.

·   ·   ·

That night, Dunc went out drinking with friends and didn't come back until late. Toward dawn he was still awake. At least the night had turned, he'd made it home. Home to what would be morning if he lived that long, if the sun made it over the wall of pines beyond the garden, if he could still breathe without jabbing a knife in his guts, if he could stop seeing the cop's Polaroids.

Close-ups, taken in the woods. She'd been found by kids, fooling around with some dog that smelled her—a girl he couldn't stand most of the time, spoiled, sneaky, always spying on him, stealing stuff out of his room, out of his jacket while he slept—dollar bills, dope—like some dog sniffing it out. His kid sister.

A kid's skeleton, picked at by birds, coyotes, who knew, maybe that dog. Her head—her skull—wasn't stuck on her backbone anymore, it was down by her jeans' pocket. His mother hadn't seen, him and his dad wouldn't have let that happen for love nor money. Her face was ashy, the flesh color gone since Ivory's body was found.

He sobbed, dry gulps. To look at your own sister's decomposed body. Fourteen years old. Knowing that someone shot her three times. No details, but lots of close-ups. Her black pocketbook, her wallet. You could see it spilled open on the path—damp leaves, blueberries—and one of those Smurf pencils she'd liked so much, unsharpened. She liked Smurfs—Smurf cartoons, Papa Smurf, Smurfette, everybody blue, and Snorks. She liked those, too.

They'd had a fight over which program. He hated Smurfs. She'd hit him, he hit back, she cried. She always cried and blamed him.

The sky was lighter, maybe. His bedroom window sat low and played tricks with natural light. So maybe it was lighter out, maybe not. Five fifteen. He lit a cigarette. It was something anyway, something to hold between your fingers when you'd lost what you hated, what you loved, and saw all night behind closed eyes. He pulled on his pants, then stubbed out the cigarette.

Dunc, give me a ride in town? Give me a buck? Come on, don't be a creep.

Swing me around? Play Candyland?

Dunc, you be Papa Smurf. I'll be Smurfette. You start.

· · ·

The TV was on in the living room, his dad asleep in the recliner, the inside of his mouth blue, like he was dead. He coughed, woke, squeaked the recliner to upright, and narrowed his eyes, a faint dip of his chin was all for greeting.

I got a knock-knock joke, Dunc, you start.

Okay. Knock, knock.

Who's there?

How should I know? It's your fuckin' joke.

That's it, that's the joke! She'd barked like a seal, clapped and barked, she was so pleased with herself.

He'd groaned. It was dawn then, too, she never slept; even as a little kid, she practically never slept. He cuffed her head. Her hair was soft and clean, she loved water, took showers so often it was weird.

" 'Morning," he said to his dad. He boiled water, then mounded two teaspoons of instant coffee into two mugs and added sugar. He took one out to the recliner. There was coughing, some labored breaths.

"You sleep, Dad?"

"Naw. You?"

"No."

"Sure wish those coroner fellas would let her go. Maybe today. It's hard on your mother."

Smurfette. Sneaky Smurfette. Back in the kitchen, he stirred sugar up from the bottom of his mug and stuck the spoon in the pencil jar, that stupid pencil jar Ivory made out of an orange juice can and pink yarn for Mother's Day. He took a pencil out, the lead ground down to the nub from Ivory drawing horses. Horses, cats, dogs. It was a knack in their family that had come to nothing. His father had it, Ivory'd had it.

He slid open a drawer, took out a paring knife, and nicked the shavings into the sink. He made a rough point, then refined it until the point was sharp and smooth. The sun was about up, he was alive, but it was a dead knack, he could see that now.

thirty-one

A few days after the funeral, Florence was sitting at the kitchen table, holding the stack of condolence cards, not reading them, just idly glancing at crosses and Jesus's sad smile, bouquets of flowers, lambs, billowy clouds with rays of sunshine peeking through. Neighbors tidied things in the bedroom, two fussed with the refrigerator. She looked out the window at the bird feeder, hung on a cherry branch, just beyond the pane. A little bird was hovering close by, almost beating the glass.

"They've let her go." She said out loud what the little bird had just told her. A moment later, Duncan, in the living room, saw that same bird at the front feeder, near the window by his recliner. "Ivory's at peace," he said. For a moment his heart lifted.

Minutes later, the telephone rang. It was Dr. Cooper's office to say the autopsy was finished, all the tests done, they were releasing Ivory's remains. Florence knew that Duncan couldn't have heard her from the living room. That bird had come and told them both the news, one at a time.

Dunc Jr. didn't see the bird, what she called a finch, Duncan a wren, but the same creature, they were positive. The next day they buried her. No stone yet. There wasn't money enough for that. Dunc said he'd make a plywood cross, but for now just a metal tag, advertising Halliday's, stuck in the hard September ground, and the words: *Ivory Marie Towle.*

thirty-two

Tommy'd wanted to go to the funeral, he really had. He was dying because Ivory died, but his mom forbid it. *They think you killed her,* she'd said. *Imagine you wipin' your nose over the coffin and them goin', "That's him!"* His dad hadn't said, one way or the other, but he was ripshit about Romaine being hassled at Libby Junior. She'd gone two days and wouldn't go back. What's it feel like, killer for a brother? some kid said. And her the family whizbang. Got the science prize at sixth-grade graduation, and on "Star Spangled Banner" she'd played her clarinet. His dad called the principal, called the cops. *You keep my girl out of this.* And he went nuts about them dragging Tommy in for questioning after they found the body. No parent notified, no Miranda Rights. *He's not a suspect,* Detective Bergeron told him. *My fat ass,* he'd said back. When it came to family, even Tommy, his dad was big on rights.

But today, he wasn't going. *I wash my hands* is what he said.

For Romaine's graduation, Tommy'd been bought new shoes, leather ones you polished. Himself, the morning of, he made them shine brighter than ever they had at the store. Romaine'd got nylons, first time. She tootled her clarinet till her face turned blue and she squawked bad on *Bombs bursting*, still his dad cried. Brightest star in the Slack family firmament. His mom had looked his way.

Later, at the party, his dad blew up. Saw he'd got shoe polish under his nails, on his knuckles and palms. *Jesus fuckin' Christ. Looks like you play in shit for a livin'. Can't you do anything right!*

That was before they'd cut the six-foot Italian and he'd got into the rum and Coke.

It's a party, his mom had said, *he's just a boy.*

I wash my hands, said his dad.

So today, the juvenile hearing, it was just him and his mom. It was nothing. Him and Buzz Carbon had gotten wasted, broke into Dale Griffith's camp and lifted some guns—.22 Ruger semi-automatic pistol, .22 revolver, 410-gauge shotgun and a hundred rounds of ammo . . . He remembered that.

What guns do you associate with Blake? the cops kept asking him.

He wasn't sure what they meant. He thought maybe the .22 Ruger'd went to Blake for a couple joints, but who knew? You had guns and you let them go. That end-of-July weekend the cops kept bugging him about—*when you and Blake rode off with Ivory on your dirt bike for the last time*—couple days after that, him and Buzz had done the break-ins, seemed like a couple days, seemed like after, but might have been before. Couldn't have been much after since Buzz spent August in jail for the time he escaped the Youth Development Center.

They couldn't keep that guy in. He'd just said, *Fuck you,* and run off. Cops couldn't catch him. Six months he was free—time enough to knock Lisa up, get married, string of girlfriends besides, and those break-ins, they'd done those right before he'd started the month of time the judge slapped him with. More or less. Incredible guy. He'd got it all figured out—cops, girls, he was that smart. They'd gave him a month, but he was free and clear for six. *You do the math,* he'd said the night they'd took tire irons to Dale Griffith's picture window on Carter's Mill Lake.

Buzz had asked him to. Buzz wanted to do those break-ins, just them two. Buzz—nineteen years old, him—sixteen. Doing stuff with Buzz spined him up, made him feel important. Not that it mattered after, only while you were doing it. Take the guns they'd stole. He could hardly remember, he was so fucked up, except the adrenaline kick when they'd forced a door, you couldn't forget that, the sound of glass breaking, the just plain glee.

Today, there was no glee in sight. Melody Something, the lawyer they'd gave him for free, said, *Buff yourself up.* That's exactly what she'd said. *Take a shower, use deodorant, shave, wash your hair, shine your shoes.* She'd meant, Wear the kind of shoes that can take a shine, forget boots. Melody was pretty. She wore soft blouses. Girls he knew were soft everyplace but their mouths, like that bitch Geena, who'd said to his face she hated him. Melody looked like a kid carrying a briefcase, hair pulled back, zits on her forehead, eyes that never blinked. But she was smart. He thought he might be her first case, though he was shy about asking, it seemed disrespectful some-how. He'd not want to embarrass her, pretty Melody, butt-up against some sicko judge.

So he found the shoes from Romaine's graduation. Just three months old. But his foot had spread. The toes killed. His dad laughed at the way he hobbled. *Sure, wear my shoes, go ahead,* he said. Since he wasn't going to this event, he could care. He didn't say *son* or *Tommy.* Himself, he never said *Dad.* They didn't call each other anything.

Tommy swiped dust off the tongues with his thumb, then rubbed them clean. Melody was skinny and quick-moving the way Ivory was. He'd loved it when Ivory held him around the waist, riding fast through rain on the back of his dirt bike. Her tits pressed his back, her smell, the girl perfume, he'd wanted just to touch her once. She screwed every guy in the world but him . . . Ivory's arms never quite reached around. Melody's wouldn't now. Ivory had a bitch-mouth and it killed her, he knew that much. Melody hadn't asked him, none of her business.

They polish up good, his dad said, *if you're willing to provide the elbow grease.* Tommy flipped open the Kiwi can. In just three months, it was about dried up. He took a washcloth—one of the pink-and-white-striped ones his mom bought—and dug in anyways. The smell grabbed his brain. The bite of lead, the bite of school.

Mr. Slack, please come to the board and share with us the results of your labors on word problem number five. Kids had laughed. Mr. Preble laughed.

Retard. Freckle-ass. I wash my hands.

His dad's shoes cramped his heel. Hard to walk straight. He roughed the polish in—black shoes, brown polish—and rubbed them till they shined. *Remember to brush your teeth,* Melody said. He did, twice. Nice mint-flavored paste. She'd be glad. He wanted her good and glad so her arms fit around when they rode through rain. In his mouth, the taste would ride with them—lead and spearmint and bitter things, spit out.

thirty-three

Three weeks into September, Detective Bergeron asked Geena to show him the roads and woods paths she and Ivory had used back-and-forth to Blake's house from the Narrows. It was fall now, clearly fall and cool. Bergeron picked her up at school in his state police car, everybody gawking. It got her out of Grief Group. Everybody'd pushed her to go, but she'd already punched out one girl, Jennifer, who lied about missing Ivory. *I loved her so much*, she'd said, but they hadn't even been friends, she was a Prep, just wanting attention and a break from Earth Science. Geena wouldn't ever let Jennifer or any of those girls know what she'd lost. They kept saying, *I'm scared walkin' outside alone, I don't sleep, if it happened to her, it could happen to me.* Out of their mouths, it would have pissed Ivory off so bad. Herself, she stuffed her tears.

They walked for almost two hours. A few trees were turning—stains of yellow and red. It wasn't these exact woods where they'd found her body—she'd heard they'd still got the spot sealed off, cops guarding it twenty-four hours a day—but it was woods like these. She'd not have walked there anyway, but Detective Bergeron was Top Banana.

He asked her questions, took notes, drew a map. She skipped the real reason she hadn't been around that weekend—no mention of

Ricky waving a butcher knife, acting crazy enough to kill her for breaking up. It was cool in the shade, she'd not thought to wear a sweater. Sometimes, when they hit an open patch, she felt sun on her hair, but it was blue sun, bright as metal, too weak to warm your scalp.

"Tommy maybe, but not Blake," she told Bergeron. He nodded, she thought, and his eyes went yellow-white like you'd scramble an egg, but he didn't write down anything.

"Make sure you take this left fork," she said, "or you're screwed." He wrote that. She scuffed leaves where the trail divided. Not many yet, but the sick ones had already started to fall. They'd used to rake big leaf piles, then jump, her and Ivory. They'd be horses and count with their hooves.

You're Blaze, I'm Midnight—shiny-black, not one single white hair.

No, I'm Midnight—you be Blaze, white mane and tail, white star.

I was Blaze last time.

Midnight.

Okay, see these sticks? Long one's Midnight, short one's Blaze. I put 'em behind my back, you pick.

One time, Ivory'd climbed the tallest pine tree back of her house, then jumped into the leaf pile they'd spent all afternoon mounding up—like she was some champion stunt-horse flying off a ladder into a glass of water—and she'd sprained her ankle. She hadn't bitched a word, though, just a brave neigh or two. They packed moss around it—still not a word—they wet it with spit, then wrapped it with cattails instead of tape. Ivory flared her nostrils, she turned the whites of her eyes crazy-wild the way horses trapped in fires do, she snapped her hair like a real mane so it rippled when she jumped. And over-night, her ankle healed.

"Did you witness any arguments between Ivory and Blake?" Bergeron wanted to know. "Was it Ivory's habit to hitchhike?" "How well did she know the Carbon brothers—Ricky and Buzz?"

At home Geena punched another hole in the hollow plywood door that Dunc had already put a hole in, the door Ivory'd knocked at in her dream, crying, *Help me, Help me*, before she'd disappeared. Her knuckles killed. "Ivory," she said, "Ivory."

What was it like getting shot? Like sprained ankles, like butcher knives? You ran, didn't you, and the guy holding the gun, you smacked him good with your hooves.

Pain, she dwelled on that, what she pictured Ivory felt, second by second, hot sun, red leaves, the hateful smell of blood.

thirty-four

Three times Florence printed *STORM* at the top of a page in one of Ivory's junior-high doodle notebooks that started out with words like *Language Arts* in fancy purple letters—the L and the A spackled with dots—then trailed off into sketchy horses' heads and ponies with French-braided tails. Just the rump of a horse on the last page, trotting out of the lines and into summer vacation with Ivory's morsel of a joke. Her doodles took up maybe seven or eight pages, plus the horse-butt at the end, if you were counting. She was counting.

What do you suppose she was learning, Florence wondered, those days that left such a poverty of marks upon a page? She'd dared to open Ivory's door, dared to step her foot onto the shaggy purple rug Ivory'd chosen herself. *Leave, it's my property,* Ivory had told her once.

What if she'd not kept out like Ivory insisted? Back then she hadn't thought to disobey a command, though it came from a child. The wind had been high and sharp that night. Ivory might have turned down the radio boy crying, *Baby, Baby,* to sit and hear Florence sing them both a windstorm lullaby. She had no voice such as they'd seek for a church choir, but a few songs had come true and sweet as maple sap on a warm March afternoon. And the lilac had rubbed the window that night, like a fool playing a rubber band.

There was nothing sweet and true now, no joke of a horse's ass that, for all its life, resembled Mr. Hargrove the language arts' teacher's face that favored cheeks to eyes or forehead.

Ivory could make a pen and paper smile with the lines she drew. They'd gone to parent-teacher conferences. And every time the vanilla cream cookies they served on tissuey blue napkins had lumped in her throat. Duncan heard, *She's not applying herself.* She herself heard, *She's dreamy, I don't know how to reach her, can you help me?*

You had one chance. This room that had scared her with its whiff of grape candle under the door, its long-haired boys on posters above the bed. They still banged their drums and wore studded tires for clothes. How far a child traveled without you along for company.

She made herself not look at the rest—Ivory's small, lonely things—only listened to the windstorm that other night in lilac time sweeping the drum of the window with a soft brush. Ivory had accepted a mayonnaise jar of lilacs after supper. Somewhere close to the house a wire had torn from its pole and it sparkled and smoked, but the lights had kept on anyways.

Three times, sitting on Ivory's tight-made bed—a neat and orderly child she was, is what she wanted to be—pale lavender spread with worn-out nobbles—three times she wrote *STORM* in Ivory's Language Arts' notebook. *DEAR STORM.* It was the start of a letter she was writing to nobody. She didn't write letters. No one was out there to receive. Seven pages drawn on—one hundred eighty-eight pages empty. She made a point to count. And then she wrote something on every single page left blank—a line, a circle, a sweep, the words *Language* and *Arts*, the letters *IMT*—Ivory Marie Towle— but no dates. What had Ivory learned those days? Something, Florence made something on every page, front and back.

thirty-five

When the phone rang Detective Charlie Bergeron was sleeping, just off a week's worth of nights. The deputy on the line said it was important, something about the Ivory Towle case, which was why his wife Sunny woke him. Mid-morning, mid-November, the sky overcast, like the land. No snow yet, no banner-blue overhead, the kind you got on cold dry days. It was all the color of khaki, any sunlight brackish with tannin, like the depths of a leaf-choked lake.

At dawn, when he'd driven home—he'd spent the night reading the murder file through whole—trash blazed up in his headlights: crushed soda cans, sticky cellophane, the treads of blown-out tires— disorder that flowers and red-turned leaves usually distracted you from. November was the season for noticing structure and the messes people made. But order had prevailed along his own short driveway, vacked clean of maple debris and bordered with cedars wound tight with burlap and string.

He picked up the phone in their bedroom, then walked to the garage—bone-cold it felt—so as not to track criminal behavior across Sunny's new Congoleum floor.

It was a deputy calling from jail, the next county over. He'd got Buzz Carbon locked up on some assault charge, who all night boasted how he knew who murdered Ivory Towle but wouldn't talk to anybody except Charlie Bergeron himself.

"Buzz had his thumb out," the deputy said. "Some poor fella picked him up, claims Buzz robbed him. No gun, but he forced the fella over, pulled him out of his little Honda-car, turned him upside down and shook him."

Nutmeg, Sunny's year-old Pek-A-Poo, scratched and whined on the other side of the door. "Anything come out?" Charlie asked.

"Couple quarters, pack a gum—not what Buzz had in mind, so he beats the crap out of the fella, even takes his wedding ring. And the whole of last night he's right full of that girl's murder—can't shut the guy up, got the gift of gab."

"Give me an hour."

The storm door into the kitchen banged, which set Nutmeg off again. He'd promised to fix the latch today—a little sleep, monkey the spring, then Sunny'd got something planned that night, he'd forgotten what. Their boy, Roger—a football bottle drive, starting at eleven, he'd promised that, too.

The kitchen was hot, bright-white and yellow, like you and your cereal bowl just parachuted into a wildflower field. Daisy mugs and napkins, daisy magnets on the fridge. Since Marta left for college, their first-gone, Sunny had turned to crafts with a vengeance. Late last night she'd sprayed gourds and armloads of Indian corn, she told him with coffee. He smelled fixative underneath the flower smells she squirted from a can.

"Noon, I'll be back."

"They'll already be out collecting."

"I've got a felon, dying to tell me who murdered Ivory Towle."

"He knows?"

"I believe he does."

It made sense he would, though Buzz's two previous statements were contradictions. Landing in jail churned up his memory, he said. You couldn't fault the guy for creativity. One of Youth Development's prize graduates—just a dimestore country con if you'd seen even one morsel of the world, but to the likes of Tommy and Blake he was something pretty special.

Right after the body turned up, Buzz had said he'd heard some guy named Small Runyon killed Ivory. Small had been camping in the woods back of Stan's Redemption, he and some albino character with long white hair. According to Buzz's sources, Small shot Ivory when she'd walked by on her way home that Sunday afternoon—motive unclear. In early October, arrested for the burglary he'd done with Tommy, Buzz had fingered Ricky Carbon, his own brother—motive: *Ricky was pissed off. He's a wildman*, Buzz added. *Ivory came on to him out by Stan's pool, then she wouldn't put out.*

While Charlie backed out the length of cedars, Sunny stood on the stoop, wiring Indian corn to the front door. For Halloween, the door had been painted black and glommed with angel hair, and she'd tacked up one of those cardboard skeletons with joints that swung on brass paper fasteners. Now the door was painted a color she called *gourmet mustard*. The house faced north, so those cobs would rattle and thump when the wind blew hard, but the door was important now that Marta had gone. It occupied Sunny's time, just the spraying and arranging, the marking of holidays until Marta came home. Better a door that turned into a three-by-seven haunted house or a vertical Pilgrim's table than one like Geena Winter's.

The day after Geena had showed him the trails she and Ivory used walking back and forth to Blake's neighborhood, Geena's mother had called the local police chief, all upset, but it had to be Bergeron himself she talked to—which hadn't sat too well with the chief. The next morning Charlie had driven out and woken Mrs. Winter up—cat smell in the hallway, two holes in the apartment door, punch-outs nobody'd bothered to mend—*somebody else's fault, somebody else's problem, the landlord shoulda fixed it*—when it had most likely been her own fist or some boozeman companion's that busted it.

I got to thinking, Detective, Edith Winter had said, *come in.* The same lean, carved-out face as her daughter, same flat hair—late thirties probably, but looking like fifty, with pointy overlap teeth. *My cousin Buster, he come over close to July Fourth, bombed out of his mind. Him and some other guy. They were braggin about pickin' up some fourteen-year-old girl, beatin' up her boyfriend, havin' sex with her all night. In the morning they dumped her someplace, scared her into not filin' a complaint.*

Edith had patted a sticky kitchen chair for him to sit himself down on, which he'd declined. *At the time, I just shook my head, not hardly believing 'em,* she said. *Geena's about that age, and Buster's an asshole, I gotta keep my eye on him, but then I got to thinkin'*—

Geena had just listened, bare feet, fidgety blue eyes, smudged black underneath, chin buried in the Smurf pillow she'd hugged tight for shame. Poor kid, the day he'd picked her up at school she was dressed like a hooker for want of a mother at home saying: Not on your life, young lady.

It just got gnawin' at me, said Edith Winter, *and I started piecin' things together the way you do after something terrible happens. I figured Ivory must of known Buster since he was stayin' across the road from Blake's house. Ivory must surely have been introduced. My mind just kept steamin'. Buster's my cousin, but think about it, Detective.*

She'd waited, lighted a cigarette. *Ivory was fourteen, same as the girl in the story. The dates are wrong, I know that—but there's somethin' creepy about that coincidence, maybe it happened again, serial-type-a-thing.*

He'd just nodded and taken names.

Sally, the lady-dick, I told her Tommy had a fresh mouth on him—a red-head temper—as a tiny tot, he did. I wouldn't put it past him. Blake, he did HeadStart with Geena. Nice-lookin' little son-of-a-bitch back to the age of four, lady's man type-a-kid.

The smell of sour milk; by the ashtray, two bowls of Sugar Pops, bloated as ticks. The hollow plywood door with two splinter fists through, no sign of a man around.

When he had Sally follow up, the Buster story had evaporated. The file was full of cockamamie theories like Edith Winter's. And meanwhile the local chief demanded action, and the weekly newspaper was up in arms. It took time, it took patience. You listened and you waited and most of what you heard was more gossip than fact. But in the absence of a weapon, a confession, or witnesses, what was your other choice?

Neighbors had described the Towles as salt of the earth. *Nice family*, said a catty-corner woman. *They kept to themselves. Those kids ran wild*, another one claimed, *just left too much alone. The minute their folks pulled out of the driveway, cars'd wheel up, making all kinds of noise, a red Chevy with a white vinyl top, I remember that one in particular.* Another: *the sounds of fighting comin out of that house early in the morning, five thirty, six o'clock—after the grown-ups left for work. Ivory and her brother, goin at it fierce. But brothers and sisters, they're like that—cats and dogs.*

Though these statements weren't directly relevant, they did create a climate, a life-and-times, and the adults, at least, took their best crack at truth-telling, even the Edith Winters. But the teenagers— so used to lying to parents, to teachers, to boyfriends and girlfriends, not to mention cops, they didn't think a thing of it. The Blakes and Tommys, the Buzzes, the Geenas, they were all sitting on infor- mation, one kind or another, he was certain of it, but they could stare you down and deliver falsehoods, time after time.

His own two—they were good kids, but did he trust them? No- sir. They took the car, he read them the riot act, and every night they came home late, he hugged them, one sturdy girl, one burly boy, and you bet his Breathalator nose worked overtime. When he was on nights, they had to knock on their mother's bedroom door, go in and give her a kiss—that was how it had stood before Marta left. Now poor Roger, she stayed up till all hours, fussing with Indian corn, until he was safe in bed.

thirty-six

"The guy says I bashed his head in." Buzz rubbed a callus on his thumb, then smiled. "Fact is, I did."

They sat in a small interview room, cinderblock walls, no windows. Buzz was a blond-headed, wiry kid about Marta's age, eighteen, nineteen, with a kind of macho speed-hype the younger ones went for, boys and girls.

"You got information about Ivory Towle?" Charlie asked him.

"He come on to me, Detective. Jesus Christ, fuckin' homo, it was disgusting. This is how it was." He leaned forward, wiped his face, slid his hands through his hair—high drama. "This guy stops his Civic, I get in, okay, then he starts sayin' how good-looking I am, can he fuck me. I sort of flip out. I tell him to pull over, let me out, I can't take that stuff, but he won't let up. Finally I just lose it."

If Charlie wasn't so tired, he'd have appreciated Buzz's full-of-shit entertainment value a little more—if Sunny wasn't waiting—the storm door, the bottle drive—if a girl hadn't gotten shot and stuck with an ice pick, then left for birds to eat . . . But Buzz himself was in no hurry. He had plenty of time and no commitments.

"Summer before last, maybe June-July, me and Lisa—that's my wife—we was hitchin' outside Virginia Beach. Nighttime, this semi picks us up—truckers. They separate us, me in back, her up front,

110

then they rape her. They bang her right in the cab, me watching from the back. I flashed to that with this homo guy, this pervert. I beat the crap out of him, sure, he deserved it, but I never stole nothin' of his. You know about the wedding ring?"

"Yeah, I heard about it."

"He told you I stole it, isn't that what he's sayin'?"

"That's what his statement says."

"You're not gonna believe this, Detective—he's fuckin' in love with me, this guy. He's got blood gushing out of his mouth, he spits a tooth and his brain's jangled—not that he didn't deserve worse— he *gives* me his wedding ring—like he fuckin' loves me, the pervert. I felt like chuckin' it in the bushes, but you know, I figure if I get cash for it, I can buy somethin' nice for Lisa."

"So this defense of your manhood sort of joggled your memory about Ivory Towle, is that right?"

"Something like that. All this time alone, nobody to talk to, nothin' to do . . . it makes you think back."

"I see."

"Well, I got to thinking back on July. Everybody keeps asking me what happened to that girl, like I'd know. Well, in June some-time, I bought a twenty-two off some guy that I turned around and sold to Small Runyon, everybody knows that, and they're saying that's what killed her. So after that, after she died, Small goes around boasting how he did it, him and that weird albino. I forgot this until last night when that pervert came on to me."

He spread his fingers out as if to part the very walls. "I remember talking to Small this one time. I can see it in my head, clear as day. *Small*, I said, *why'd you kill her?* Small, he laughed real hard.—She was walkin home by herself, right by the spot they were camping, and she was all pissed off at Blake and Tommy—he'd already told me that part.—Then he says, *She wouldn't fuck, so we pumped forty, fifty into her*, that's what he said."

Buzz leaned close in, confidential, tawny as a tiger cat. "Small's crazy, Detective. But that albino kid that helped him, he's fuckin' sawed-off."

"So let me get this straight. You're saying you lied when you told me your brother Ricky shot Ivory. A month ago, remember, you said he was mad at her, too. Apparently she did a whole lot of not putting out that day."

"Yeah, well, I got confused."

Ricky was no saint either, but his alibi checked out—he'd spent that Sunday night in a van with some underage girls who swore it was the truth. He had freaked at his polygraph and tore out early, still he was no murderer. Small Runyon was drunk twenty-four hours a day and the albino had turned up in some other statements, including Buzz's first one, but nobody'd been able to locate him or even give him a name.

So—what Charlie'd gotten for his trouble was one sawed-off phantom albino and a hundred-pound psycho drunk. Still, in spite of his weariness, he couldn't hide the corner of excitement he felt. Buzz knew something, Charlie was sure of it, he just wasn't quite ready to deliver. Maybe by the time Sunny had covered the front door with gold foil and criss-crossed it with a red bow, he'd have what he needed to make an arrest or two. Maybe they'd scour up the gun and get a confession. More likely, Buzz would finally roll over and say Blake and Tommy couldn't wait to mouth off about what they'd done. Maybe by then Edith Winter might patch the punch-holes in her door, so cigarette ash and snowflakes wouldn't blow into Geena's Sugar Pops.

thirty-seven

It was never truly dark at Youth Development. Blake latched on to that, not to freak out. One little thing that upset him: they kept light bulbs on day and night—fluorescent tubes—and those airport lights close by.

He'd used to be scared of black nights, he'd say terrified. Walking in the woods with Ivory—from his house to Stan's, even all the way to her house—she'd felt loose, easy, like she'd had eyes in her feet, she'd run down the path without making a sound, not even snapping twigs. No sound at all except a whispery laugh at him crashing along behind. He'd knocked against dead branches, tree roots.

Shit, that goddamned thing poked my eye.

Give me your hand, Blake.

What's so funny? That damn thing just about gouged out my brains.

Give me your hand.

Hers had felt cool, dry. He'd forgot how strong her fingers could hold.

She was a night creature, one of those deep-woods animals with eyes that shine yellow-green. She wasn't quite human in the heavy way he had, himself, of setting down tracks wherever he stepped, of letting a place know he'd been there and changed it, made noises, killed something quiet underfoot.

I didn't do it, he kept telling them, but they were all over him, had been for months, poking under rocks where they didn't belong. They'd found out about the guns he'd moved from one place to another, no connection to Ivory—he'd barely touched them—but he happened to give them to somebody for a couple of bucks, they called it weapons trafficking. . . . So they'd sentenced him to six months, and they were still jawing about Ivory. It was terrible she died. He'd loved her, he really had, but she was gone and they still wanted him to cry every day for the rest of his life. A beacon from the airport sliced his patch of sky and moved on. He followed that sick, milky light.

What do you think happened to Ivory? Sally Gregg kept asking him, almost panting she was so eager to catch him in a lie. What a bitch.

Cops didn't understand how Ivory was. Not human. At night in the woods, she'd taken care of him, though that sounded kind of funny. She was a small-size girl, not much here-and-now to her. When he'd picked her up and swung her—he'd seen it in a movie and she'd said he didn't show his affection—she weighed so little, the same as a log you tossed in the stove, but longer, softer. Not human at night the way he was.

It was never dark on his wing. And never quiet. Ivory knew quiet, how to listen and wait. *If you die, it's absolute, total quiet*, she'd told him once. If you made that happen, you could just float, just drift, like all the dope they'd smoked, lying on a truck hood at the gravel pit, looking up at the stars. She'd meant better than that—he hadn't been able to stay awake—she'd meant wide awake and noticing things, night smells, walking down a dark and narrow path in your mind without knocking into branches or roots and fucking yourself up. That was how she'd been at night in the woods, easy and quiet, maybe laughing a little but silent, always waiting—no matter if she was running or standing still—waiting but not worried about what for.

I didn't do it, he said.

They stuck guys in the restraint chair, days and days strapped down, and they went crazy, they shit their pants, they'd puke and cry. Sometimes he heard their mewling, he thought he did, and he got small as death inside. It was another building, the place was soundproofed one guy told him. You couldn't hear the chair. He heard the chair, he heard twigs snapping, the brush of animals. He'd just like one thing—no searchlights, no cop questions—real darkness, a no-moon night, and the chance to run.

thirty-eight

Night is hardest, people told Florence. You felt loneliest then, and grief would choke the very idea of sleep. But for Florence, this wasn't true: noon was hardest.

Midday usually found her at the mill, standing in the finishing room while the conveyor belt growled, *Hurry, Hurry*. Sweat prickled her scalp, even on cold days when the building was drafty, nerves made her sweat and the frantic folding of blankets, some days yellow ones, some days baby-blue, and the zipping and the folding of cardboard boxes to load the blanket cases into. At noon, for half an hour, she sat down, every day the same corner seat at the lunchroom table, and she opened her paper sack to the same sandwich—iceberg and bologna. She'd stopped tasting things when Ivory disappeared. All of her senses just shut right down.

First thing in the morning, there was so much to be done— Duncan looked after, his breakfast and Dunc Jr.'s, lunches. It rode her through. By noon she was exhausted. This December day, close to Christmas, it was blowing a gale, you could see it out the lunchroom window, and she felt panicky about getting stuck there, trapped by the snow. It was a midday kind of terror. The sky had tumbled onto the road. The snow was blowing sideways, falling up instead of down. You couldn't even call them proper flakes they were so small, more like grains of sand, hissing against the glass.

It occurred to her she could just walk out the Exit door, past all the signs telling you Don't do this, Don't do that—all the safety messages nobody heeded. She could just walk out and sit down in it and that would be that. The snow was pretty. She'd always liked snow—something different, something fine and clean and new, like that necklace she'd given Ivory. Cut glass with a drop of red, ordered from Fingerhut for Christmas last year. It had sparkled at Ivory's throat, such a pretty place to nest, that little hollow. Of course Ivory was too skinny, that hollow was deeper than it ought to have been, more like a little uncovered box.

Ivory'd been partial to little boxes, little knickknacks. It popped into her mind, a Christmas present Duncan once made—a stool, really, but shaped like a box—so Ivory could stand high enough to look in the bathroom mirror. Even as a little girl, she'd liked that. *Brush my hair, Mom*, she'd said, and wanted to watch, watch and count, as if some magic lay in the strokes leading to a hundred. She'd come home from kindergarten with a story—a fairytale, she'd said, though Florence herself had never heard it—about a girl who lets her hair down and it's so long a handsome prince grabs hold and climbs up it—

Ivory's hair, tangled with forest debris, walked on, shaken loose by animals. Torn, chewed, spit out.

It was these things that haunted Florence while she ate. The girls across the table—scarcely older than Ivory'd been—they'd never have believed what went on in her head.

At night, not so much. All that holding things together during the day—the dam broke at night, she cried and cried, sorry tears she knew wouldn't bring Ivory back—then sleep, no dreams. Everybody dreamed about Ivory but her—it made her feel a little jealous—still, she was grateful even for empty sleep. *One Day At a Time*, said those AA bumper stickers. At noon, a day was only half over.

Sometimes she saw herself as clear as a body in front of a window—all light and shadow—she saw herself brushing Ivory's hair, long as that girl's in the story from school. With each stroke it got a little longer, and then suddenly—while she was still looking—Ivory stood holding the brush: *It's your turn, Mom.*

Florence's hair was short and gray, growing out from a home perm so it looked both crinkly and straight. But in the night, it grew, too, like Ivory's—long and dark and bountiful as winter sleep. *Good for you, Mom,* she'd say, *you got through another day.* They'd wrap each other up—so much hair, an abundance between them, the plenty of a waterfall. It smelled like summer, all that hair made a robe, a comfort that rocked her in its embrace.

Now, though, it was only noon. Her sandwich felt like Cream-o-Wheat in her mouth. Her back itched a fury. It was snowing out, the radio in the lunchroom forecasted "a blizzard of major proportions." The girls snickered and whispered behind their hands. They had a whole life of cracking jokes and gum and fooling with each other's hair.

Up at the cemetery, the same blizzard. She pictured wind devils whipping Ivory's plywood cross. Dunc had cut it with a jigsaw, the way he'd promised, and painted it gold, then he'd set a red jigsaw heart in the center with Ivory's name and dates painted black. But now you'd look for that cross and not find a thing. Snow must have stuck, turning the gold arms white, if they even showed above the drifts.

part three

thirty-nine

Though a whole year had passed, you could still touch Ivory's absence. Duncan knew Florence needed more Ivory-talk, little memories, and how he was feeling. Himself, though, he just couldn't. The lonesome business of day-to-day rolled along, no matter how it sat. Most days that summer, after he picked Florence up at the mill, they headed for Hilltop Cemetery. It was something he could do. Slowly, driving up one of the rutted dirt lanes, they passed granite monuments and bronze plaques set in the ground. The grass was growing fast now, hanks of wild lawn that burst up no matter how many times they got mowed.

Ivory's grave sat toward the back, close to a waist-high chainlink fence marking the cemetery's border with the woods. Beyond the fence, a brook had almost dried up. On the other side of the road, somebody's fields looked ready to hay if the bright weather held. Other families planted flowers. Florence favored artificial roses. They lasted longer than the cut ones, she said. The way those living heads drooped right after you bought them upset her—he saw that—too much death right there in your fist.

Memorial Day, Florence had picked out some purple posies at True Value. Since then they'd gone milky, day after day in the hot sun. The girls at the mill took up a collection a while back so Florence could buy a Madonna. She was three foot high, white plastic, with her arms spread low and wide beside Dunc's homemade cross.

Once, they'd found the statue tipped on her elbow. In the process of righting her, Duncan saw a key chain pushed under the base, one of those clear plastic gizmos, stamped with a curlicue letter R. He'd picked it up, stuck it in his glove box, and wondered what it meant. The police wouldn't pay attention even if he drove it over to the station—some evenings he found a litter of beer cans, tossed around the grave, but do you think they asked what that might mean? When he told them he'd heard three gunshots late on the afternoon the day Ivory died, they said at that distance, he couldn't possibly of— he'd imagined it, the father, desperate to rush the investigation along. But it wasn't that far, he knew, through the woods, the way sounds traveled when the air was still. And Pammy's dad, over at his house, he heard the same thing, same time.

Dunc Jr. graduated high school at the beginning of June, smart as a whip, that was one good thing. Hard to believe Dunc'd been able to see it through, what with Ivory's death-shadow five times longer than she was tall. Along about March, there was some talk at the high school about Dunc pursuing drafting next fall—he was good that way with his hands—but one thing and another, he needed time to get his sea legs. In *his* day, boys joined up after graduation, that's what you did, that's what he'd done, but Florence couldn't abide that idea. Just too much to ask right now, Dunc understood that; besides, he'd not shown much curiosity about the future.

Somebody up at the school decided to dedicate the Stallions' yearbook to Ivory, a girl who'd not made it across the ballfield to senior high, though they talked about her like she was a freshman anyways. The dedication page had a blow-up of her eighth-grade school picture, and a friend of Dunc's named Joey wrote a poem they printed underneath her face. The poem seemed more about the evils abroad in the world than about Ivory herself. Still, it was a tribute, they agreed, in spite of the printer's screw-up with spelling that called her a *rainbow angle* more than once.

forty

One evening, middle of summer, Duncan had the ball game on—Dunc was listening too—Sox behind, Florence ironing in the kitchen. Out of the blue, Dunc fetched his yearbook, then opened it on Duncan's lap. "Joey that wrote the poem—Detective Bergeron's turned the heat on him about his drawings. Look at this one." He flipped to a page labeled *Activities*, the word in big scrawly letters down one side. Next to it was a pen-and-ink drawing of a teenager, cross-legged on the steps of a ramshackle cabin, strumming a guitar—rosebushes blooming, a big tree with a split crotch.

"Bergeron says, '*Kids are talking about your picture*'—that's what Joey told me Bergeron said. '*They're saying you know what happened to Ivory*' "—Dunc's voice swagger-imitated—" '*like she got killed at that cabin, there, like those shingles sticking off the roof, each one's a tooth of hers, and the roses, those were her favorite flowers. You got angels with wings everyplace in this yearbook—you drew them all—and that's her, right? And then they're saying the murder weapon's hidden inside that tree.*' " Dunc pointed the way he imagined Bergeron pointed.

"'Joey said he just shook his head. " '*You know how kids talk,*' he said. '*Besides, wasn't me drew the tree, some other kid did. I just felt bad she got killed, that's all.*' "

123

Dunc slammed the book shut. "That's how the investigation's going." His jaw worked, tight under his tan.

It was eating him alive.

Back in November, Dunc knocked down the wall between his room and Ivory's to give himself extra space. Because Florence didn't have the stomach for it, Dunc packed up Ivory's animals and clothes and took them to Goodwill. Florence squirreled away a few things in a shoebox, otherwise, not much sat out. Duncan himself wasn't one to moon over knickknacks, no point to it. Still, an old photo caught him up short. Late August, he was checking his tackle box, looking forward to a fishing trip, him and Dunc, when he found the picture by chance, under a tangle of filament and lures.

There she was, in the palm of his hand, rowing a boat at Bear Paw Lake—Florence had taken it, they rented a camp for a week one time . . . Ivory was still out there, splashing, funning around to begin with. Of course she had to take the boat out by herself—no lifejacket—she was that stubborn. He said no, she went anyways. They exchanged some words. Scarce above a whisper he spoke across the water—words stood out, sharp as hooks tied to a line. *I—want—you—back—here—now.*

She laughed, he remembered that, a snorty laugh, pretty-sounding—to think, this daughter of his—though he was ready to cuff her quiet just then. By that point she'd rowed herself away from shore. She wasn't getting the rhythm right, how you push your arms out straight, then pull that whole big lake right into your chest, then glide. She was facing him, not looking where she was heading—she had that much right. *It's all in the breathing*, he'd told her, and she wasn't but sipping air.

Florence called the police station every chance she got, trying to get Sally on the line. Sally was different, but that's only one cop. *No word yet, we're close*, the others said. Detective Bergeron never called. Too busy. Too important. Himself, he often stopped by the station on his way home from work. *Nothin' new, Duncan, but we'll contact you when something breaks.* It was a lie. They knew who did it, he knew who did it. He wanted them in custody, in court, behind bars for the rest of their days.

What is it that you want, Mr. Towle? one of the new rookies finally asked one day. The fellow was all exasperation with him hanging around, making everybody nervous. There's that old expression about looking into your own soul—he was talking churchwise—and finding you've come up wanting. What is it that he wants? The rookie wouldn't follow.

The rowboat leaked, she got all foolish showing off. Way out in the middle like she was, she dared to stand up.

I want you back here now! he yelled.

In the course of that maneuver she knocked an oar into the lake and the boat rocked like crazy. He kept yelling—neither one of them could swim worth a damn. She got herself going in a circle—nothing he could do but stand on shore and shout directions. But his words flew right by her, then came back and slapped his face.

What is it that he wants?

Those boys, dead. Dumped in a lake, say, nibbled by fishes—something painful, something slow.

But of course what he really wanted was to dive into that picture, pull her out of the rowboat and drop her back on solid ground. He longed to give her what-for, nice and leisurely, sitting on the split-log bench in front of their cabin. She'd cry, he'd end up guts cramping he felt so bad, but she'd be safe again.

If he could, he'd kill the boys himself. The Chief caught wind of that and talked him down. That same night he had a coughing attack so bad Dunc drove him and Florence to Emergency, couldn't catch a breath and keep it.

He'd been found wanting.

He thought Florence might like the picture, she had two more of Bear Paw, that week they rented a camp. She kept things in a scrapbook—condolence cards, pictures. Him, he didn't care for it much, he was waiting for a detective's call.

forty-one

The day after Halloween, Charlie Bergeron had another investigation dumped in his lap. No relation to the Ivory Towle murder case, he told Man Grady, editor of the *Yankee Times Weekly*, just by chance he'd been put in charge of them both, but in his own mind, he saw connection: Buzz Carbon was involved. Buzz, who'd been serving an eight-month sentence at the max for bashing the guy's head in and stealing his wedding ring, he'd expected a deal—information about Ivory Towle in exchange for reduced time—but Charlie'd said no way, Buzz's memory was still too vague.

As soon as he could, Buzz had applied for a transfer to the minimum facility closer to home. Guys at the max beat on him, he said—*hostile environment*—and some idiot granted his request. If anybody'd asked Charlie, he'd have said, *Forget it, you got a runner on your hands*, but nobody asked. So Buzz was moved only twenty miles from Stan's Bottle Redemption—only a matter of time before he took off, which was just what happened.

Based on what he had learned, Charlie pictured it this way: Halloween evening, Buzz and his cellmate Simon Tordoff sat polishing off platefuls of American chop suey in the dining hall when there was some trouble at the far end of the table, one guy talking trash about another guy's girlfriend—something. Usually Buzz took sides and egged on somebody's low punch, but that night he looked out and away, through a window that wasn't there.

After supper, he and Simon lined up to return to their cell, same as always. Simon was up for burglary and theft, four years, he was twenty-two. Suddenly though, instead of sticking with the other inmates they bolted, taking off across the wide mown field. It was cold and clear that night, planets so close they jumped into your hand. Charlie saw them himself that night, the planets, not knowing yet that Buzz was out and about. He walked their dog, Nutmeg, while Sunny dumped Bit-o-Honey into trick-or-treaters' bags, kids drawn like moths to the blacklight rig she'd gotten up, the front-door cardboard skeleton swinging in the wind.

Outside the prison wall, grass crunched underfoot, and Buzz's boots pulverized the few dry leaves not blown to kingdom come. In a moment they were scaling the fence, twelve-foot-high chain-link topped with razor wire. Buzz, the artful dodger, scrambled up and over, no problem, before Simon even reached the top.

An hour later, state police tracking dogs followed their scent across the Clarion Tool & Die property, then lost it at a nearby intersection. Most likely, a get-away car was waiting, though enough high-school-age kids were out roaming that night, Buzz and Simon just might have slipped through on foot. Before dawn, a break-in was reported at Stan and Nonie Carbon's house, four hundred dollars stolen by their own grandson.

From there, Buzz and Simon headed north and apparently broke into the Pompano residence, where they stole a .30–.30 rifle and two handguns, as well as some camouflage clothing. Witnesses, fingerprints—Buzz and Simon without a doubt. A few days after their escape, it seemed they might have split up. It looked that way to Charlie, who stuck pushpins into a topographical map after each sighting.

In any case, Buzz, acting alone, circled back and hit an optometrist's house on the prosperous side of town, near the high school. It was about two thirty a.m. He forced a garage door, no challenge, then two thousand dollars cash stored in the cookie jar practically shouted his name. He was rifling a mahogany desk in the living room when suddenly a woman appeared and stood watching him. It was like a dream, she said later. She watched him, fascinated, drugged by the strangeness of the scene: this beautiful young man, wild hair with glints of gold, tearing at letters from her grandchildren, yanking out drawers only her hands had ever touched. When an inlaid corner ripped, she screamed.

Buzz grabbed a chair, raised it chest-high, then took a step forward. *I'll break your head,* he told her. His voice was *soft and seductive*—the words she used. At that moment, the optometrist himself rushed down the stairs, waving a pistol. Instead of breaking the woman's head, Buzz crashed the chair into a plate-glass window, which didn't even crack. The man fired at him and missed. Again the chair heaved against a window, and this time, thinner glass shattered into diamonds. Buzz vanished through the hole, leaving fingerprints behind on the chair.

All quiet for a week, no sign of Buzz or Simon. Then, in mid-November, hunters in Day-Glo orange, out tracking deer in a steady downpour, found a man's body instead of a six-point buck. Unlike Ivory's, this body hadn't been dead very long, maybe only a day or two, and because the weather had been cool, the remains were intact. The man's face and tattoos corresponded to those of Simon Tordoff—full lips, brown curls down to his collar, nose squashed by a fist—he was wearing camouflage gear, believed part of the take during the Pompano robbery, and he'd been shot through the head.

Early reports claimed suicide, but nothing conclusive. Charlie told Man Grady it would be premature to speculate whether the death was suicide or murder until after the autopsy. According to several correctional center guards, Simon was a water-runs-off-his-back kind of guy, not the type to kill himself, though Dr. Cooper did rule it a suicide. Still, a person couldn't help but wonder about Buzz's involvement, if any.

A story surfaced that in the joint Buzz told Simon he killed Ivory, boasting the way guys will. Later, afraid Simon would snitch to the cops, Buzz cooked up the escape plan, invited Simon in, then killed him, making the shot appear self-inflicted.

A week later, Buzz turned up again. At about midnight, a new town patrolman named Thornberry spotted a stolen Dodge pickup, heading east on the highway, not too far from Stan's. Thornberry gave chase. Siren, blue lights, gallons of adrenaline. The stolen truck veered south, then screeched around a corner and smacked into a barn. Buzz scooted out of the cab and took off. Dogs tracked him across a corn field, where he disappeared. Sometime before dawn that morning, he stole an Oldsmobile, parked out on the street.

Close to Thanksgiving, Thornberry, still on night patrol, was turning back toward the station when he caught sight of the Olds. Another chase. Thornberry got close enough to identify Buzz in the driver's seat before he floored it at the top of a hill. The Olds went airborne, sailing across an intersection, no brakes at all. *Damn, what a thrill*, Thornberry said later. He couldn't help himself, he loved the meteor shower of sparks when the Olds bottomed out before crashing into a snow fence. He was too far back to see it himself, but witnesses claimed they saw one person tear into the woods on foot. Another passenger didn't run. He'd simply stood outside the car, stunned by alcohol and excitement. He was a hitchhiker, picked up heading for Boston, he claimed, and didn't know the other two. Amazingly, his story checked out, and they let him go.

Later that morning a new red Audi was stolen from another driveway in town. It was recovered that night, hidden under some hay bales, its paint job scarred with a key. After the Audi episode, Buzz vanished—no sightings, no spoor of burglaries, nothing. A short time before Buzz's escape from the minimum facility, his wife Lisa had left her sister's house to live with some guy at Christmas Beach, but it only lasted a week. Soon she moved back into Stan Carbon's house. She claimed not to have had any contact with Buzz, but rumors flew. He was somewhere out West, Washington State, Alaska, maybe Florida . . .

forty-two

One evening in early December, Charlie sat across the kitchen table from Sunny, who was writing notes on Christmas cards. Marta was due home from college in a week, Roger'd made the All-State football team. Charlie was looking through past issues of the *Yankee Times Weekly*. Man Grady was all over him, greedy for Buzz Carbon's latest exploit. His readers loved it, Man said, you couldn't blame them—he ran three or four Buzz columns every week.

Charlie was furious about the escape, but Buzz would show up again, he felt sure, eager to trade freshened-up memories for reduced jail time. Buzz knew what happened the day Ivory died, Charlie still believed that. Blake and Tommy had no real alibis—a little sister's recall, a mother's inability to pin down that afternoon. Witnesses saw them argue with Ivory, saw them ride off into the woods on Tommy's motorbike, Ivory between. He just needed Buzz's coherent story—details, lots of details.

Nutmeg wagged his stump tail and yipped to be let out. "God Rest Ye Merry Gentlemen" was playing on the radio. Sunny's kitchen looked like a field of daisies, and the woodstove cranked the heat. "Okay, you little rat-ball." Charlie pushed his chair back, a joke between him and Sunny, this grousing at her drop-kick dog. He doted on Nutmeg, they both did.

Suddenly, Charlie thought about Ivory's parents, how he'd love to give them an arrest. Blake. Maybe Tommy. But you couldn't just arrest, you had to make it stick in court. He opened the storm door, leading into the garage. Just as Sunny slid a card across the table for him to sign, Nutmeg yipped to come back in. On nights like this, the damn thing wouldn't go through the dog door, he circled and circled by the steps, then peed on the garage floor. Sunny claimed she didn't mind cleaning it up, she was a terror with bleach. It was well below zero outside.

forty-three

For the month of December, Mrs. Cadenza worked over at the high school, teaching a unit on sexually-transmitted diseases for required freshman Wellness. It was a mixed group, last period, three days before vacation started and time for a quiz.

"Okay, test formation." The kids groaned, and Mrs. Cadenza herself winced as she said it. But the truth was: almost everybody cheated. "Nothing personal against you," sweet-faced Pammy in the front row told her one day. Even in test formation, two or three kids would have *gonorrhea, syphilis, vaginal warts,* and *herpes simplex* inked on the pads of their fingers.

"I like your outfit," Pammy said. Mrs. Cadenza was wearing a silver lamé turban and a flame-red Indian print dress that swooped around her ankles. She smiled. "We're having the teachers' Christmas party after school today."

It was a standardized quiz on mimeographed paper, though Mrs. Cadenza hated fill-in-the-blanks. The school board bought the whole package before she was hired, or—as the principal so delicately phrased it to a group of concerned parents—*came on board to put the full court press on casual sex.*

One-armed bandit desks scuffled, lots of noise, but little actual movement.

"Spread 'em!" barked Rob, a tall boy with helpful instincts but an awful mouth. More scrapping, seats pushed a few inches apart.

The last seat, second row, was empty and had been all week. "Anybody know about Callie?" Mrs. Cadenza asked, opening her attendance book. A few kids smirked.

"She dropped out," Pammy volunteered. She tugged at the sleeves of the baggy sweatshirt she wore every day.

Mrs. Cadenza pictured Callie's gap teeth, her ash-blond hair, skin translucent as fine china and that same color. A nail-biter. "How come?"

"She got knocked up," said Philip, nicknamed Pork.

"No, she didn't," snapped Mia. "They wanted to get married." She jabbed his back with a pencil.

"You were there?"

"They eloped."

Mrs. Cadenza listened, back and forth, as Pork and Mia wrangled over details. Yesterday, Pammy told her they just broke up.

"Yeah, Ricky Carbon said he'd kill her if she didn't stop sluttin' around, so she married him." Pork puffed up, important with flat-toned calamity.

"A love match, I see." Mrs. Cadenza didn't even try to mask the horror she felt. "You're not just saying this to get me going, right, you know—test formation?"

"No, swear," said Mia. "She used to live down the street from me, but her and Ricky just moved to Massachusetts."

"Her dad disowned her."

"You're an asshole, Pork. He's my uncle, she's my cousin, that's a lie."

"Okay—" Mrs. Cadenza raised her arms, the wide gauzy sleeves of her dress calming the waters of discord. "Remember, spelling counts," she heard herself saying, down that long tube she imagined the kids stared at their lives through. But it was herself she wondered about, how her own life had deposited her here, a week before Christmas, insisting kids spell gonorrhea right to get full credit.

She handed out papers. "You have twenty minutes," she told

them, but in her mind she was running over what Pork said: *If she didn't stop sluttin' around, he'd kill her, so they got married.*

Mrs. Cadenza might have let Callie's story slide, maybe asked a couple of teachers about her and did they know anything about a Ricky Carbon—in January, after vacation, once things settled down. But Ivory haunted her, the picture in the newspaper, the black-ringed eyes. And Pammy, after the funeral, who'd stood alone on the lawn at Halliday's. I don't have a single horse she drew, not one. And Callie's nibbled fingers.

In the guidance office, she looked up Callie's phone number and called. Her mother sounded curt—from sorrow, embarrassment, mistrust, Mrs. Cadenza wasn't sure. "Callie has a job now, she's married," Mrs. Viola explained. A pause. "She's sixteen."

At the faculty party, Mrs. Cadenza drank more than her usual glass of white wine and bled her heart about Callie, one of her best freshmen, could you believe it, until Art Lundgren, Social Studies, patted her shoulder. "Buck up, Ruth. You of all people ought to know what these kids are capable of."

forty-four

All winter long, the phrase *We're a phone call away* plagued Ivory's family. Detective Bergeron used it when talking to the papers and to the Towles. *A phone call away*—cryptic and unsatisfying, it still felt like the close ring of hope. But a phone call to whom, Duncan wondered, from whom and about what? Bergeron wouldn't say. A roll-over, wasn't that what they called it when one guy ratted on his buddy? Or maybe a confession was what they were waiting for. Dream on . . . So many phone calls, all of them painful, the disguised voices, the false clues, and that moment when the young dispatcher down at the police station recognized his voice.

Over Washington's Birthday, it was the family's habit—minus Florence—to travel up north for a few days of ice fishing and snowshoeing, maybe skating if the lakes were clear of drifts. How he and Dunc used to laugh at Ivory's first attempts on snowshoes. One foot acrost the other, she'd drop in deep powder, tangled like nobody's business—her own worst enemy and funny, too. Given a choice, he'd live fifty miles from nowhere up in Canada, way off from civilization. Dunc would like it, too.

This Washington's Birthday they still went, without Ivory. One day they hiked out onto Chaney Pond, sawed holes in foot-thick ice, set down fishing lines. A friend let them use his icehouse for a

couple of days—about the size of a privy, without the holes. Inside
its rough pine walls, they kept the woodstove red-hot. Hours they
sat, smoking and worrying lines.

Dunc Jr. opened the door of the icehouse—its rusty hinges shrieked
with cold—and his boots slipped out from under him. In a flash he
sat sprawled on his behind, eye to eye with a pickerel, quick-froze
in the ice—poor devil, too slow or sickly or stupid to swim deeper
down while it had the chance. Some old guy out on the lake once
told them the story of the Birdseye fellow—that was his real name—
who made a fortune in frozen foods, how he was ice fishing and
noticed the way his catch froze up solid at well below zero—quick-
as-a-wink—and how fresh it tasted later. Quick-freezing kept the
puncturing of cell membranes to a minimum when the creature
thawed, the fellow told them, and it made sense.

Now Dunc's hands felt numb. He pictured ice daggers popping
cell walls at the tips of his fingers, leaking into nothing when they
warmed again. He had Ivory's hands, artistic and crafty, not big thick
men's hands. For a long time it shamed him, small hands and feet.
Now he looked down and imagined what she'd do with those
hands—draw a horse, maybe a fish like the one staring through him.

I got a knock-knock joke, you start.

The bowl of blue sky tipped everything blue. His dad called him
back.

Snow fleas hopped in the footprints their boots made as they hiked
out to the road. Ivory hadn't freaked out about bugs like other girls used
to, friends she brought along. She liked the small stuff—ants, beetles,
snow fleas. He stepped in his own purple footprints, crushing a peppery
bunch of them. Strange how they lived in snow and swarmed at the
taste of cold. His thin features were hers, more so since she died. She
was like that fish, staring up, watching him from the frozen lake, looking alive as could be, but once you went to thaw it, all the cells busted
open and it died. He was so keenly aware of her now it burned him the
way below-zero did—what a pain in the butt she'd been sometimes,
the joy of a live kid-sister he'd chop his own hand off to get back.

forty-five

That same long-weekend, at the start of the February school vacation, Blake competed in a high-school j.v. basketball tournament. He was a sophomore. The coach took a shine to him, and at the end of the season, he was elected captain for next year. He was a new boy, a different boy, almost unrecognizable from the person he'd been two years ago. Since spending time on Youth Development's drug and alcohol unit, he'd been clean.

All that winter and spring, he felt a cushion of faith around him, pieces of it anyway, so that he almost forgot the cops breathing down his neck, that bitch Sally Gregg, the cold stares from Ivory's friends, her brother, the snubs in town. They were trying to stick him with the murder, the way you'd pin a butterfly to fiberboard. But mostly, he didn't let them get him down.

Blake credited Mr. Cook, a man who'd stepped forward and taken his part. Mr. Cook owned a construction business and grew vegetables on the side, which his family sold at a farm stand. He'd hired a string of teenage boys to help in the fields. Even before the trouble with Ivory, Blake had worked for him after school.

While Blake roto-tilled, fertilized, and planted peas, he quietly watched April Cook, who hovered like she was magnetized, wobbly but transfixed, at the edge of his chores. He'd asked Mr. Cook's permission to take her out, not wanting to upset anybody, but he was naturally flirty and exuberant with girls, he couldn't help himself. In his own mind he'd put the Ivory business behind him.

He was respectful of April. Sweet, her parents agreed, and old-fashioned somehow, this Blake-April thing unfolding softly as fiddleheads along a stream bank. It was the season for attraction, and Mr. Cook gave his blessing. Blake was no murderer, he knew, just a boy caught up with the wrong crowd, a boy who'd taken a few wrong turns. The first time he found his daughter in Blake's arms, though, it knocked his breath out, but it wasn't because of the murder stain—April was his little girl, and she was just fifteen.

Only once did Mr. Cook ask, "What happened?"

Blake looked him in the eye. "I-I-I d-did some things I'm not p-p-proud of." It was painful to speak of those days, to own that long-ago boy as himself. "I-I-I left her, w-we'd had a f-fight. B-b-beyond that, I d-don't know." He couldn't bring himself to speak Ivory's name. Mr. Cook waited, laboring each word with him, but still waiting, intent on an answer.

"I-I'm s-sorry, what happened—" Blake paused. Mr. Cook's sun-bleached eyes pulled his own back from driftiness. "—W-what hap-happened to Ivory, I'm s-sorry. Sh-she hitched a lot, s-s-somebody come along, m-maybe. I c-called her h-house l-later that day."

April stood outside the circle they made, watching them talk. He could feel her, the wild gyroscope of his desire, the cloud of black flies he waved away, and her dad's gaze tugging the vagueness out of him and the dope-haze of that far-away July afternoon. It wasn't good enough, he felt that, his *I'm sorry*, his *I called her house later*. Why should Mr. Cook believe him?

April continued to watch, shifting her weight from one sneaker to the other and flicking her hand at the flies. She wore a tight new-green T-shirt, he saw out of the corner of his eye. Overhead, an airplane, on its descent toward the airport, over the grounds of Youth Development.

"I s-smoked so m-much mar-marijuana I don't ruh-remember much." In a moment, his words would break down. He couldn't ever quite get a rhythm going, where talking took on a life of its own, separate from his tongue and throat and lips. Then Mr. Cook's big hand spread wide and hopeful on his shoulder. "T-Tommy Sl-Slack and me, w-we r-rode her on his d-dirt bike into the woods, b-but she made us dr-drop her off when we cr-crossed B-B-Ballard. Sh-she was so m-mad at me, she s-s-said sh-she'd rather hitch. T-Tommy took me h-h-home. A-about three. I w-wouldn't h-hurt a g-girl I cared about."

He had cared. A long time ago. In a nighttime, shadowy world. Far from the sun on April Cook's coppery hair and leaf-green T-shirt.

Mr. Cook let out a deep sigh and lifted his hand off Blake's shoulder. He was a tall man, even taller than Blake, thick at the waist and through the shoulders. The black flies hovered in an angry swarm but didn't dare to bite. "Okay, boy," he said. Two words is all, but Ivory's name wasn't spoken between them again.

forty-six

Geena saw Tommy at parties, but only once in a while. The minute he'd turned sixteen, he'd dropped out of school, even before he got sent to the Y.D.C. Since January, he'd been back living with his parents, and pumping gas in town. He acted jittery and tried to stay stoned, waiting for something to happen, which made sense since he and Blake were still number-one suspects. As much as Geena hated Tommy, though, he didn't creep her out the way Blake did. Blake had gotten to be Mr. Alligator Shirt and he went with the goody-goody Cook girl, but he'd still murdered her best friend.

Sometime in late February, Geena bought a half-priced calendar with pictures of horses. Soon enough it was May, but she hadn't flipped the months forward, the calendar stayed on January, which showed Ivory's picture—Ivory as Midnight, the black mare with nostrils red as heart valves, black mane, black tail. In the calendar photo she was rearing up, hooves striking the men who shot her.

Whenever Geena imagined that scene, the men's faces took on disturbing shapes—her dad, her two stepdads, Tommy and Blake. She puttied their features, insisted they wear masks. One shot Ivory. The bullet struck her shoulder, a splatter of red and satin flesh, her wonderful neck swiveled, her teeth glowed, her tongue. She stomped them, red bubbling down her legs, and Geena stomped, too. They crushed the guys until they were flecks of foam, spit, bone, blood—nothing human—and if it was winter she pictured and there was still snow in the woods, the white shocked pink for a day or two until snow fell again.

Then the deer found that ground and slept there. A sacred place, a hushed and holy place, not the scene of murder. Midnight lived there, drinking rainwater pooled in rocks, and Geena visited every day. In the other everyday world, Ivory seemed forgotten. But she was alive in the grove of cedars and birch. A stallion got her pregnant. It was okay, though, she wanted it and had her foal. She was a tender mother who kept herself clean, her foal clean, more like a cat than a horse. It was so quiet Geena heard her own blood rushing up her wrists. And when Blake hugged her at school like some kind of old friends, she spit him out and trampled him, then lugged his heart to the place where Ivory stood waiting.

forty-seven

That spring they were still a phone call away, but the Towles didn't talk about it much. Duncan spaded his garden, harder work than last summer or the summer before. He felt increasingly short of breath. He'd gasp but couldn't keep down more than nips of air because his lungs felt already full. Emphysema, one of the doctors said. Himself, though, he claimed it was just the asthma kicking up. Dunc Jr. helped, he kept helping. They rarely spoke Ivory's name. They didn't need to. She was the air he couldn't let out or take in.

Still no leads concerning Buzz Carbon's whereabouts since he had escaped the minimum-security facility last October and begun his crime spree. But a new rumor circulated, at the gravel pit, in the parking lots of country stores, that Lisa had joined him in Florida. She was bartending at the Doll House Lounge in Miami, so the story went, the same place Buzz's real mother worked. But in summer, rumors burst into bloom, so many petunias in a window box. You didn't set much store by them, thought Duncan Towle.

forty-eight

It started off good, Buzz thought, getting it on with this couple. The man was doing himself, Buzz was doing the wife while the guy watched, their apartment looked out into the arms of a palm tree. They still gave him a kick, palm trees. The first time he saw one, outside the Miami Airport, he was just a kid, nine years old, and Grampa Stan had sent him and Ricky down to visit Tina, their mom. She was late, very late. Him and Ricky waited, checking out the palm trees and the women—ladies in sky high heels and tight polka dot dresses wearing mink coats in that heat. Even then they made him sweat—black eyebrows, candy blond hair, everything big—diamond rings, butts, boobs, pocketbooks. The wife at the bar was one of the ladies from that boyhood airport, at least he was smashed enough to think so when her husband first bought him a drink.

Back at their apartment though, looking out the window through rusty palm fronds to a parking lot and sunlight blasting off car hoods, he could hardly breathe. *Turn up the air, Jesus.* The woman had big ones, muskmelons, pale blue-green, and she liked showing them off, dancing in her underpants, wiggling her hand down and coming up sticky. Her husband had his dick out, stroking himself to beat the band. Then the guy stuck his tongue in Buzz's mouth and kissed him.

He jams his finger up my hole, Buzz told the cops later. I hit him just to make him stop. "I can't have you doing that, get the fuck off." I knock him around a little. The wife freaks but she's still horny as all get out. I'd have gone back and done her some more and kept doing her, but he was spraying blood everywhere, like some fuckin' garden hose.

She goes ballistic, the mess, and up close she's a lot older than she looked at the bar—he had hair on his back, and the bitch, gray roots, I hate that. I tell Lisa, do it so you don't show roots. He came at me with blubber lips, I was just protecting myself. On their coffee table, they had orchids floating in a bowl—they looked like human organs, it was weird—white carpet, white sofa. The guy's blood fucked everything up.

Buzz got out of there fast. The minute he left, they called the cops, who took fingerprints off a glass he'd used—the couple had even got his license-plate number, like they were out to nail him from the beginning—and they traced his car to Tina. He was borrowing it that day, she let him every once in a while so she could see her granddaughter.

He was sitting at Tina's kitchen table with Lisa and his daughter, eating breakfast, out of nowhere the door got blasted off, windows burst, broken glass all over the place, SWAT-cops swarmed like termites, knocking things over, pointing their guns, they came out of the sky, out of nowhere. Flying glass might have cut his little girl's face all up to hell. They said the asshole couple was pressing charges—like they hadn't enjoyed it, like they hadn't begged him to do them. They said he landed the man in the hospital with a busted head. Lisa was swearing, his daughter screaming—terrible thing to do to a kid, he should sue them. And then of course those Florida SWAT guys already knew—cop computers—that he'd jumped the fence back home and was getting fingered for a string of auto thefts and break ins he did not do.

So, in light of this heat, Buzz remembered—details clear as snapshots in an album—what happened to Ivory Towle, who did it and how it went down—what was told to him, what he saw. He made a statement to the Dade County guys, who didn't know shit, but they figured things out enough to contact Charlie Bergeron.

But it was only mid-June. It would take another month before ripples of action washed up to New England. Meanwhile, Buzz was singing again, this time over the phone, and Bergeron kept nodding, you could hear him wetting his pants he got so excited—the call he'd been waiting for, his big case and Buzz himself the star witness.

Buzz fought extradition, a matter of honor, but the couple ended up dropping charges—they wouldn't have come off smelling too sweet some lawyer must have told them—so Florida had nothing on him and New Hampshire was thirsty for his blood.

forty-nine

Down the road from the Towles' house, Pammy was busy preparing for a boyfriend. It took most of her time. She hadn't visited Florence since before school got out, and now it was the middle of July. Pammy had left her bike behind and caught up in other ways. She'd shucked sweatshirts in favor of V-necks that showed some cleavage—at least she was trying—Ivory would be proud. All morning Pammy had fiddled with her bangs, they just didn't look right. She felt like Ivory herself, washing her hair, blowing it dry, styling it, then, when it looked queer, starting all over again.

She took last year's yearbook off her shelf, it opened by itself to the dedication page. *In memory of Ivory Towle*—and some other kid who'd died but she didn't know him. It was not that great of a picture—Ivory had looked much prettier in person—but her bangs were inspiring. Pammy touched them, studied them—separate strands with space between. They stayed. *Use a lot of spray,* Ivory used to tell her, *that's the secret, gunk it on, just tell your boyfriend keep his hands off.* She didn't have a boyfriend yet, but eyes zoomed in on her chest, so there was some interest, some hope.

Underneath Ivory's picture was the poem Joey wrote, angels and rainbows. Pammy knew it by heart. Folded and slipped into that page was the drawing of a Mustang Ivory had made for her. It was done so carefully, pale pencil strokes, hundreds of them, curving fenders, door handles, windshield, tires, headlights. The car wasn't on a road or anywhere else, just speeding through white space. But even in Ivory's hands, a pencil car had so much personality you wanted to give it a name and slide behind the wheel.

Pammy felt hungry. It was almost lunchtime, but she was thinking about skipping if she could stand to. She was on a new diet, one her cousin had told her about from a magazine, you only ate meat and cottage cheese and you got bad breath but it worked fast and just took weight off where you wanted it taken off.

Suddenly she remembered the purple flannel shirt she had lent Ivory because it was too small for her then. Now it might fit—what Ivory was wearing when Pammy had biked up the rainy road, turned, laughed, and waved that last time. She'd like that shirt back, it was a good color and it had touched Ivory's skin, but maybe it got buried with her or maybe it rotted, lying out there in the woods all those steamy days. Or maybe—this idea freaked her out—the murderer stole it and kept it for himself, or maybe gave it to his girlfriend.

It overtook her then, a wave of missing that was as hungry as a crocodile down a well, a huge mouth and sharp teeth. She missed Ivory's advice, how she could make every little thing you thought or felt important because she listened. With that same overtaking, that same hunger and the bright burning of Joey's poem in her mind, an idea grabbed her. She forgot her bangs, her flannel shirt, her own self, empty of talents. She picked up a pen and wrote.

> *We're alone walking in a fog, just the two of us, it's dark but all-white at the same time, and we're tired because we've been walking a very long time. At first we were laughing and joking, then the fog got thicker and swallowed us up. My voice disappeared. I tried to catch it with my hand. I could see it slipping away, right through my fingers. All of a sudden I can't move. I'm lying down in the fog, screaming but there's no sound. I was so scared. I didn't know why you left me there, trapped*

inside my stiff body. Then you come back, everyone comes back, you're all crying. I want to comfort you, but I can't. I have to leave. The fog blows away and I can see again, and I walk up the slope of a rainbow. I can talk and I'm calling you from the highest arch of the rainbow. The angels are pretty and nice. You'd like their hair and their wings, all covered with satin feathers. They know my name. I keep walking, it's easier now. I'm not tired or sad and nothing hurts. There's no pain. Paradise is everything I ever hoped for. I'm happy but I miss you.

Pammy felt happy writing this. Once during Wellness, she had showed Mrs. Cadenza one of her poems and Mrs. C said she was a good writer, she ought to take a class over the summer. Maybe she could send this new thing to Mrs. Cadenza, maybe it could go in the yearbook next spring. But she didn't know where Mrs. Cadenza lived, and somebody said she was back dying of cancer again—she was bald and you ever noticed how her cheeks puffed out? That was what cancer did, it puffed out your cheeks, all those chemicals they shot into your veins. She hoped Mrs. C held on long enough to read what she wrote. She could mail it, but she didn't have an envelope or a stamp.

More than anything, Pammy wanted Ivory to read those words, Ivory a person with a talent, a kind person with a talent, who'd cry and shake her head and say, *You made my eye makeup run*, then, stroking the paper, *This is so good, Pammy, I'm jealous.*

But the truth was, for as long as Pammy lived, her friend wouldn't ever read that page. She never, never would. This was the first time Pammy understood the *always* part of Ivory's death, and it was so terrible it parched the need for tears. She closed the yearbook and returned it to the shelf, her small story on the back of Ivory's Mustang, folded inside.

fifty

That evening, Pammy walked down the road to the Towles' house, swinging a Diet Pepsi bottle by the neck. She knocked, banged the screen door behind her. Florence hugged her and wouldn't let go. Dunc held up his hand in greeting, then ducked into his bedroom. Florence squeezed Pammy's hand. After that, she set out a plate of Hydrox, not part of the diet, but there was special dispensation here Pammy hoped God would think. The back scratcher on the wall, a Smurf by the refrigerator, ashtrays, that pencil holder Ivory made. Everything the way it always had been.

"You're skinny as a fashion model," Florence said.

"Not fat like I was," Pammy qualified. Speedy, Ivory's money cat, rubbed her leg. "How you doin', Little Miss Speedo?"

"She's been tom-cattin' something terrible this summer." Florence opened a Hydrox and licked the frosting, such a kid thing to do, Pammy smiled, but her heart bloated with dread. Ivory wouldn't ever breeze in again, pick Speedy up, and duck into her room.

"Remember the woman that called you when Ivory was missing—said she was being fed?" Florence asked. "You ever hear her voice anywhere since?"

Pammy shook her head.

Duncan appeared in the doorway. "Soon as they know something, they'll call, that's what the police keep telling us. They won't, though, I know they won't." His mouth a flat line.

Pammy stayed, they watched some TV. She felt pampered and paid attention to but deeply sorrowful in this house, guilty for things she couldn't even begin to picture, let alone name.

part four

fifty-one

When her husband cried out, Doris Slack was bleaching the cutting board Tommy made for her in the shape of a strawberry. He'd sawed it himself in shop class, a machine saw, but he'd sanded it by hand. And he'd oiled it himself, vegetable oil, low cholesterol. She was chopping soup bones on it—they showed on TV about germs, how you were to bleach your surfaces once a month, religious, to keep diseases down where you worked with food.

She was wearing yellow rubber gloves and scrubbing when Harvey yelled. It sounded like he'd been shot, then a string of swears. She dropped the board, which clattered to the floor. Her back was to him, working at the sink, but he was close by, over the open countertop, watching TV before he went to work. Usually she sat beside him for *As the World Turns*, a habit they had. It was foolish, it didn't mean anything, he just liked her there.

But today she'd got it into her head to make stock for tomorrow. The bones were hard to break apart, they just wouldn't give at the joints, and she was nervous about leaving beef germs on the board for the next person coming along and fixing a peanut butter sandwich, laying the bread out and having it suck up deadly poisons. Funny the things you worried about that didn't really matter, you saw later. A crazy day for soup, cool that morning, soup weather in the middle of July, but now it was heating up.

So Harvey shouted, she dropped Tommy's strawberry and spun around, her hair spilled out of a twist—all one fraction of a second. He was pointing at the TV screen. There, on television, a newsbreak flash—her boy.

—Arrested for the homicide of Ivory Towle, a fourteen-year-old girl found shot in the woods—

"My God" was all she said. Harvey was silent now, too. Her boy handcuffed, his head ducked for him as he was getting into a sheriff's car, looking young and scared. Too pale-skinned, all orange hair and freckles, you'd think a boy would tan up in the summer.

—A juvenile accomplice was also arrested today at his job site, on suspicion of murder in that same homicide—

"Where was he at?" Doris whispered.

"Someplace in Vermont, I didn't catch it."

Blake, that must be the other boy, but no TV pictures of him, only Tommy because he was just a few days past his eighteenth birthday. Harvey turned the sound off. They sat watching TV actors pretending to have problems, terrible problems—then back to the story, more ads for floor wax. Her boy in shackles, unnatural pale, like he'd not slept for a night or two. The police thought he'd murdered Ivory. They used to play together. She'd drive over and help poor Mrs. Towle pass the time—two kids and she didn't drive—stuck home all day. They thought her boy killed Ivory Towle.

He was eighteen, but of course he was a toddler still, flopping himself down for a tantrum on the linoleum, his arms and legs so soft and round they were her pride and joy—not a cut or a bruise—those perfect plump thighs and spongy elbows. She'd loved to bathe him, show him off to friends, her beautiful, beautiful boy. He was eighteen but she saw no whiskers on his cheeks—so smooth they looked, snowflakes would slide right down them, quick as tears but leaving no trace.

He'd missed his birthday. She still had his present waiting, but he visited Mother's Day, the last time. No murderer was ever that sen-

timental. The pink card—shiny as his boy-self after a bath and just
that color—it had everything a mother could wish for on the outside—a wicker basket full of carnations and bows, even a kitten—
all that painted onto the shape of the earth, turning in space with
full sun, shining a glory. Inside it said—she still had it up on the
refrigerator—*You mean the world to me.*

"Where'd they take him?" she asked.

"County jail, I'd say, or Youth Development." Harvey leaned
over to tie his boot laces.

"We've got to find him."

"I got work."

"I'll go."

He frowned. His back had kicked up lately, lifting too heavy loads
at Sargent Meats. Now his son—arrested for murder. She put her
arms around his neck, his own arms hung limp. He was in shock,
his son accused of shooting a fourteen-year-old girl. She was still
wearing rubber gloves, the smell of bleach sharp as pins.

"I'll call you on break," he said. "You be home."

"I'll find him."

"He needs a lawyer, not a mother," he said, but there was kindness at the bottom of his gaze.

He backed the truck down their driveway. Dust hung in the air,
then floated away.

"Help me," she said to the people on TV who shared her problems, who must know what action to take. Call a lawyer, that was
what they'd do, but it was always some friend of theirs or a member
of their family. Her family didn't run to lawyering.

She rinsed the strawberry under good hot water and soaped it
down, then a little vegetable oil. It helped her not panic, the hot
water, the soap, the oil. Maybe she'd find him if she drove around,
he'd be thumbing a ride the way he used to, just to get her goat she
worried so. If she could just find him—

The phone rang, some fellow from the *Yankee Times Weekly.*
"Mrs. Slack, did you know your son was under suspicion in the
Ivory Towle homicide?"

At the time, she didn't think to hang up, what Harvey would tell her to do if reporters called again. "The police talked to him when she first turned up dead. But I don't know." Then, not sure if she spoke out loud or only to herself, she added, "He's innocent, my son, but I'm not to tell strangers."

When she hung up, her fingers felt hot enough to explode. She shucked the gloves, quickly pinned her hair into a dark knot, grabbed her pocketbook and car keys.

fifty-two

◇

Early afternoon, and the sun beat fire-yellow and red. Muddy sweat covered Blake's face and bare chest, his muscles taut from physical labor. He was making decent money, everything was good, Mr. Cook had promoted him from weeding vegetable rows to construction work for his new company, Cloud Nine Septic, and he was helping to install a leach field for somebody's new tank. He dug and lifted most of the day, no driving of heavy equipment yet, but Mr. Cook promised soon.

He was wiping sweat out of his eyes, thinking about the pink tanktop April wore last night, when two sheriff's cars wheeled into the site, boiling clouds of dust, and there came a sudden clatter of crushed rock pouring out of the truckbed into the trench, it was deafening and the stone dust and the cop dust blinded him. He'd been caught in an avalanche, it felt like, his eyes weepy, his mouth dry.

"Blake Parady, you're under arrest for the murder of Ivory Towle."

They read him his Miranda Rights, two sheriffs he could barely see. They didn't understand that those rights weren't really his because it wasn't him they let splash his face clean or pull on a T-shirt before they snapped handcuffs on his wrists, it was some other fellow they'd come for, one who looked like him, one who'd stole his name, maybe killed that sad dead girl he only vaguely recollected holding in his arms. She'd kept after him, he remembered that, fingers always picking at his skin. She loved him, she kept saying it, twisting it tight around his throat. It had to be a lifetime ago he'd been fifteen and somebody else shot Ivory Towle.

The two sheriffs didn't understand this. One was old and wrinkle-tanned with a white spot on the top of his head from a recent buzz. The other one young, somebody he swore he'd seen at the pit, out of uniform, in the dark. They acted like he shot that girl point-blank on his way to work that very morning, they didn't understand he loved April, he had a job, he'd be a junior and she got good grades.

While they rode to county jail, he stared out the window without seeing what passed by. His brain had delirium tremens the way one of the kids had got it at Youth Development. His brain was zagging out of control when he was just able to grab hold of the thought of April. Her skin last night, like a bolt of satin his cousin had unrolled for her wedding dress and made him stand on a chair—*You're my mannequin*, she'd said. *Pretend to be a girl*—and she'd draped satin off his shoulders, the material so smooth and cool.

Ivory had been leaner, sharper-boned, more edges. He tried not to hate her for getting herself killed but it was hard, with his wrists shackled in his lap, as if he'd just said his prayers—if anything, though, they were prayers of hate. When he'd felt scared at night, hearing animal noises out behind Stan's, Ivory had showed him how to walk down the dark and narrow path in his mind to safety, but that was never where it led, really, it led to this avalanche of stones that had buried him alive.

They allowed him one call. He picked Mr. Cook, who'd phone his mom and find him a lawyer and comfort April who'd be crying herself inside out that very moment, no doubt, eyes swollen shut, skin soft enough you blew on it and your breath made a fingerprint.

fifty-three

By the time the six o'clock news came on, the Towles' phone had rung so often they took it off the hook. But not one of those calls was from the police. Duncan in his recliner, Florence on the old loveseat, they watched Tommy's arrest. He sure looked like a killer, mean, scrappy red hair, rumply like he'd just woke up—in the middle of the day.

The next afternoon, home from work, Florence called the police station, Duncan at her elbow. The dispatcher put Sally Gregg on the line.

"They got 'em, didn't they, Sally! I knew it was them. Sure took a long time."

Sally sounded happy, too, but remember no jury'd said they were guilty yet, lots of water would flow over the legal dam. "They were arraigned today in District Court," she told Florence, "and there's to be a certification hearing next month. The State wants to try them as adults even though they were under eighteen at the time of the murder. If they're convicted as juveniles, they'll only get sent to the Youth Development Center until they're twenty-one, that's it."

Florence agreed it wasn't enough, then relayed what Sally said to Duncan in short pieces, asking again about a certification hearing and what happened at an arraignment. Sally was kind, she repeated things and explained them, but it was still hard to follow.

Since Ivory's death, Florence had struggled with fuzziness. Things went in one ear and out the same ear, Duncan sometimes teased. She still lived in a dream, the kind where you heard and saw yourself but what you did wasn't really yourself at all. You felt hungry and every time you tried to pull that apple off a tree, it just drifted farther out of reach. People seemed that way now, ideas, words.

Duncan came back to life at the news of the arrests, though the excitement kicked up his cough. "Ask her what's the chances of nailing them as adults."

Florence asked and listened. "Good chance, she says, a crime that terrible, they got lots of evidence, which is how come they waited so long to arrest them."

"What broke things open, can she tell us that?" He turned away, hobbled by a second attack.

"She says it's Buzz Carbon, they captured him down in Florida and he talked."

"He knows something, I'll bet."

Florence's mouth chewed while she listened to Sally again. "She says one of the detectives will be in touch. We might need to testify when they do the certification. I hope not," she added.

fifty-four

That evening, after the sun drained the day's heat into the wall of pines behind the dooryard, the Towles drove to the cemetery. In the pasture across the road, two draft horses were grazing, plagued by flies. Their tails flipped across their rumps, their hides twitched, but the flies wouldn't budge. Those poor souls must itch a fury, Florence thought. The air was still.

Somebody'd put in a new grave three down from Ivory's they saw, two marble bunnies, crouched on the grass, someone's baby boy. This time they found no discarded cans on Ivory's plot, no key ring. The grass was dry. Their tires kicked up dust that settled over the Madonna and muted the white veil over her head. While they sat side-by-side in the front seat, drinking 7-Ups, a breath of air stirred. Cloth flower petals lifted, then fell. The wind picked up and blew through the window. On the horizon, slate clouds exploded upward, like fireworks, and they saw the silver backs of leaves. Suddenly, the wind tumbled through branches, tearing greenery and dropping it on graves. As Duncan headed down the rutted lane, back to the road, big drops splattered the windshield, making sudden clear bursts on the glass. Thunder boomed behind them, they heard a crack. Ha! Duncan slapped the dashboard.

"I don't want to testify," Florence said. "I won't know what to say."

"They get you ready, that Detective Bergeron, he knows. They probably won't want you to anyways."

He turned on the wipers, which smeared the windshield so he could barely see. A few more big splats, but no steady rain. The windshield washer button had broken. He hunched down until he found a clean spot to peer through.

At home Florence filled a milk jug with water at the sink and carried it out front, where Duncan had planted her a red geranium next to the house. It could have used a good soaking rain. Everything was thirsty, the geranium, the lilac parched outside Ivory's window.

Inside, Duncan was still coughing. "You got your doctor's appointment," Florence said. She was worried about him, the way he'd lost weight, the way he took quick breaths like a child does when it's just stopped crying. She wet a washcloth and hoped to put it on his chest, but he pulled away. He didn't like being fussed over the way Ivory had when she was little. It popped into her mind, the pleasure of brushing Ivory's hair, the little box she stood on to see in the mirror. *Am I pretty? Am I pretty? You will be. You will be.*

She wondered about the baby's mother, the baby who'd died, only two months old, one marble bunny for each month. So little time that mother'd had with her boy, but maybe it was a comfort knowing she'd held him his whole life, sung to him, rocked him in her arms. Ivory grew up, shrank from her touch, and told lies.

Florence wished now she'd had more chance to spoil Ivory. They'd tried not to, Duncan especially, you waited for grandchildren to do that, but just a little, just a dime's worth of spoiling might have felt good, remembering. Men didn't want spoiling, they shook it off like those horses tried shaking off flies, but a daughter . . . Ivory loved hair brushing, the strokes leading to a hundred.

"Yup, they got 'em," Duncan said. "Let's hope it sticks." Florence nodded. It was a cup of broth they shared between them, enough to keep them alive, but no cause for jubilation. She wrote *certification hearing*, those new words, on a scrap of paper by the telephone. In bed, tears dripped into her pillow as they always did. Finally she dropped off, still wishing for a gravestone and Ivory's waterfall of hair.

fifty-five

At the arraignment—technically a juvenile detention hearing since Blake and Tommy had been fifteen and sixteen at the time of the murder—the boys pleaded innocent, and their lawyers fought for bail. They argued that Blake and Tommy were good risks: why would they run now if during the previous two years, knowing they were prime suspects, they'd stayed put? And Blake, a kid who'd turned his life around, deserved his junior year of high school, just like the rest of his classmates, instead of untold months in jail. But the judge denied their request and ordered psychological testing and evaluation—useful information for the certification hearing scheduled for the end of the summer.

Don't cooperate, the lawyers told the boys. *They won't let you have legal representation during the testing.*

Tommy wasn't sure what they meant, and he never saw Blake in county jail to ask what he thought. *Don't cooperate*—like yell during the whole test or spit in their face or pretend you were deaf-and-dumb?

An older inmate, Orin, helped him out. Orin was small and sharp, most of his face taken up by a shiny black mustache which he called the Machete. He was in his mid-thirties, somebody who'd bounced around the prison system, even went to college for a couple of years. He'd done construction, been a chef, then head bellhop at some fancy hotel. Now he was working on a law degree—correspondence. Since he was already a jailhouse lawyer, might as well get the paperwork.

Tommy first met Orin in the little hole of a room they called the library. Orin had been bent out of shape about some D.W.I. screwing up the Dewey Decimal System. Tommy felt glad he hadn't touched any books, just showed up to smoke and flip through magazines.

Orin had a vocation, it turned out, bringing along the younger guys. Soon he took Tommy under his wing. "When they show you the ink blot," Orin told him, "say you see roses even if it looks like a pile of shit. Roses and butterflies, they love that."

This made Tommy smile and feel in on something crafty—just the opposite of how he felt in the company of his court-appointed lawyer, Bill Davis. Tommy wished he could have Melody back, Melody with her sweet face and ponytail, her black briefcase and soft girl-eyes. *Remember to brush your teeth*, she'd told him, and that'd be all it would take for her to get him off, that's what she seemed to think, though it hadn't worked out that way in court. So? It didn't matter—she believed him. Bill treated him like a cheap con. Nothing exactly he said, just a feeling. Bill wouldn't have cared if he'd come to court looking like some bum alkie, green moss hanging off his gums.

Your buddy Buzz Carbon's sold you out, Bill had told him at their first meeting. *He says when he got back from Maine that Sunday night, somebody told him you wanted to see him, had something burning you up you just had to tell him. Buzz says you confessed, says you told him you and Blake murdered Ivory, you were boasting about it. You've got to level with me, Tommy*. Bill had put his hand on Tommy's arm, some kind of man-to-man thing, but his water-green eyes and stiff white shirt said, *I don't believe you*.

"The stakes are high," Bill kept telling him. "Felony murder if they certify you as an adult." In front of Bill, Tommy puffed himself up, a frog gulping air. At night he felt terrified. They'd locked

him in a cage, a real cage with bars, two cots, a toilet. In the basement
of the sheriff's office, no daylight. He choked on his own breath.
The cage he was in, it gave him the creeps. Somebody locked up
before him must have kicked the bars, smashed his head until it had
bled and the bars gave a little.

Bill kept reminding him of the other shit he was in, the arson
charge still up, and that cock-and-bull story Toni Sparrow'd been
telling, the last girl he fucked, perfect, wouldn't you know. She was
a cokehead, couldn't even tell it was him, and afterward she'd said
he could sleep the night in her bed. Sexual assault, right . . . Toni'd
been to rehab twice as often as he had, which was just the rock
they'd drug her out from under to cry Rape.

"I've got this impression you're holding out on me," Bill said,
then a stream of big words. Tommy felt intimidated by those words,
by the power of the stream turned on him full blast, by the way Bill
got all excited and waved his arms, sweating through his starched
lawyer shirt, and his cheeks went from red to purple over nothing.
You've lucked into one of the best defense lawyers in town, a state
cop told him, but he didn't believe it and longed for Melody.

"It's a poker game," Orin said at supper one day. "You're only
the ante. Blake's the raise-you and see-you and call-you, all rolled
into one. You're small potatoes. Blake's the only one they're
after. Lovers' quarrel, words exchanged, he goes ballistic, offs her.
Simple . . . They don't care about you one way or the other. You
know what you get for murder, premeditated, if they certify you
and the jury convicts? Twenty-five years, minimum. Some guys I
know got triple life. Your lawyer don't believe you—bad sign. He's
not gonna do squat. We got to stick together," Orin added, wiping
milk off the Machete with his thumb. "Guys at the max study how
to hurt you without letting it show. They study it, they get good.
If they send you up for killing a fourteen-year-old—I know you
didn't do it—but guys in the can don't like little-girl killers."

Orin was tight with some of the guards and found out what was
happening on the women's wing where they were holding Blake.
"He's sitting over there like some prince on a throne," he reported,

"fucking everybody in sight, inmates, guards, you name it, he fucks it. And he gets special meals sent in, jail food's not good enough, all 'cause he's eleven months younger than you and he's got two hot-shit lawyers playing every angle."

Orin speared a macaroni. "You think they're cooking up ways to save your ass? They're gonna nail you, I've seen it a thousand times."

This was definitely a sore point, Blake's getting special this, special that, Tommy himself getting shit. And Blake had the whole Cook family helping him out. He had April. He'd had Ivory, too.

fifty-six

◇

Tommy's mom visited when she could. His little sister Romaine tagged along, too, big-eyed and scared to death. She'd gotten boobs and zits, he'd never noticed, going into seventh grade. She was the bright light bulb. He was proud of her, but he wished she'd stayed home; she looked too sad, like maybe he'd already died.

At the sight of his mother, her hair pulled back in a knot, her hands twisting with sorrow, he got a mouthful of lead. He'd just stuffed that kid's toy soldier in his mouth, he'd chewed it but couldn't spit it out, it caught in his throat. He choked so bad his eyes watered. Tears, it had gotten to tears. They slid down his mother's face and his little sister's. He'd clamp his down if he had to, but the lawyer'd left and Orin had a court appearance, it was just the women.

"It's bad," he said, shaking his head, looking down at his hands. They couldn't imagine, and he'd never tell, but the river of tears lapped against him, licked his stubbly face, he was bathed in sorry words, and nothing they could do: if we could change places, but they couldn't. "I'm okay, Mom. Go."

Life without parole. You'd never get out, never breathe real air or touch a woman except through wire screen. He woke at night, sweating: max cons sticking a screwdriver in his guts and fucking him so bad he'd never hold his head up again, maybe have to crawl because he couldn't walk. Oh, Sweet Jesus. His heart knocked in his throat, clattered in his head. His mouth so dry he couldn't swallow.

Mostly it was just marks he made on a piece of paper, stuff that didn't mean anything. He doodled, it calmed him down. AC/DC, he wrote and drew skull and crossbones, 666. Then he balled the thing up and threw it in an ashtray in the library. Later he swore he saw a guy checking trash, checking ashtrays, looking for scraps of paper.

"You're fuckin' paranoid," another guy told him.

"Tommy's just bein smart," Orin said, stroking the Machete, and the guy backed off. *You gotta pick who you trust.* Tommy trusted Orin, no question, and he surely wanted to please him, but he wasn't ready yet to lay shit on Blake the way Orin wanted him to. Some of the older guys looked at him with hungry eyes—not Orin, Orin was his friend. Guys screamed shit from their cages. Back and forth. At each other. At guards. Back and forth. Hours of shit. As far as he could tell, he was the youngest by a long shot, nobody else's mom visited, nobody else choked so bad they cried.

fifty-seven

Blake's court-appointed lawyer, Ray Monroe, was new to the business, his first murder defense, and he'd asked his favorite law school professor to help him out. Miriam Sonenfeld must be about forty-five, he figured. She stood almost a head taller than he did, long bones everywhere—legs, arms, hands, feet. Her eyes looked bigger than natural behind thick glasses with sparkly frames. In every other way except the sparkles, she was a down-to-earth type. Ray adored her. More than any of his fellow students, she'd been a kindred spirit.

One day while lecturing on defense strategies, Miriam had stopped, folded her arms on the lectern and spoken of something which had been *bugging her like a boil* for some months: *sophistry and cynicism, and that sardonic edge some of you seem so intent on cultivating.*

A stir, then silence. Miriam continued. *Right after college, I had a scholarship to visit Russia and Poland. I saw what happens when citizens' rights are taken away. I visited some extermination camps. I also spent a lot of time in East Germany. This was pre-tearing-down-the-Wall. We're the last chance, don't you see? Once criminal defense lawyers compromise, the system's shot to hell. Without us, Nazi storm troopers can beat down your door. Believe they can. And have. And will again, unless you do something*

*to prevent it. If this were Nazi Germany, I know some police officers who'd
be marching at the head of the line . . .*

That visit changed my life, she went on. *I decided defense law was worth
everything I've got—a lifetime,* she added, unfolding her arms and letting them hang at her sides.

Her words had struck him, but what Ray remembered most was
her eyes. How when she'd talked about a defense lawyer's task—
making it sound like a sacred mission—she'd lit up, her eyes blazed.
The relaxed, stick-figure woman vanished, and in her place burned
a flaming sword.

Now here she was in his office. He'd just moved in—up two
flights of steep winding stairs in an old brick apartment house, hardly
space for his desk and a couple of chairs, a file cabinet, some book-
shelves. Through an oak archway, his secretary's second-hand
teacher's desk with a single straight-backed chair for waiting clients.

Somehow Miriam had managed to stretch out, her long, sandaled
feet crossed at the ankle, covering most of his desk. She leaned back,
hands behind her head. She'd agreed to work on the certification
hearing and the trial, should it come to that. He felt nervous and so
excited he barely slept. Miriam was looking out the window, ignoring the city noises below on the street. Middle of August, a splen-
did summer, tour buses, seagulls, tourists buying ice cream and
lobster key chains, lobster shot glasses, T-shirts with lighthouses and
dancing clams.

"I looked at videotapes of Blake and Tommy's polygraph tests
this morning," he told her. "What a debacle. Inconclusive, to put it
mildly. Those state police clowns, what were they thinking? Just
scaring the boys into confessing, don't you suppose?"

Miriam nodded. "So our guys didn't do it, who did?" She was
still gazing beyond the dirty window into some middle zone.

"Anybody, the whole gang of them—den-o'-thieves, as my
grandfather used to say. They can't even prove it happened that
Sunday."

"She hitchhiked regularly—didn't you get friends to say that?

Anybody could have picked her up. I'd say this was not an example of random violence, though. Ivory lived a risky lifestyle. So Stan's cousin saw her go off with Blake and Tommy on a motor scooter. We've got kids lined up who saw her weeks after that."

"Buzz Carbon, how about him?" Ray said. "We need to follow up on his alibi. The cops didn't bother to interview the couple he and his wife supposedly rode around Maine with, getting loaded, the day Ivory disappeared. They just contacted them last week."

"Great." Miriam shifted her feet. "You remember where you were that weekend in July, two years ago, as opposed to the one before or the one after? Buzz doesn't strike me as the kind of fellow who saves his daily planner from one year to the next . . . His brother Ricky: another sterling citizen. What's with the *weird albino*?"

Ray laughed. "Every case should have one." When he grinned, he looked the same age as her kids, wild hair, chronic bed-head, crooked nose, trademark gaudy suspenders. But he was himself, clear about what deserved both probity and passion, easygoing about the rest of it, and so bright he could afford some foolishness.

"Meanwhile," Ray was saying, "Blake's life is going to hell in a hand basket. This gets smeared all over the papers during the certi-fication hearing, he'll never get a fair trial. Can we bar the media?" He looked at Miriam, who still stared out the window as if fascinated by the brick building across the street and a tiny morsel of sky.

She inflated her cheeks, then took a sip of lukewarm coffee. Her glasses glittered. "Highly unusual to close a felony hearing, even for juveniles. In fact, I can't think of a case—but we'll try it."

Last week they'd pored over Ivory's eighth-grade yearbook. Blake had it, he'd kept everything, every note Ivory wrote him. The book was full of messages from friends and acquaintances: *love ya*'s, i's dotted with open circles, lavish X's and O's. A whole parade of kids had trooped through his office, everybody who signed Ivory's year-book, yacky about inconsequentials, but tight-lipped when it came to anything close to murder. Although he and Detective Bergeron inhabited opposite sides of the moon, they agreed on this: teenagers knew how to shut adults out, and it drove them both crazy.

Miriam picked up the yearbook and flipped through pages. "Remember this one?" she said. *" 'U R 2 Young 2 Drink 4 Roses'*—I was always good at that kind of math." But beneath the attempt at a joke, it was sad enough that she dropped her head in her hands. She had a daughter entering eighth grade, a son in high school. Good kids, such peril. The more she learned about Ivory and Blake's world, the more she worried about her own kids. It was a new thing, this sort of dread: Their cocoon of safety looked much more fragile now than she'd ever let herself imagine.

"I wish there was a way to suppress Blake's juvenile record. Tommy's, too," she said.

"Down the road, after the certification hearing, I'd want to separate them. Blake's done a complete one-eighty, Tommy's on your basic downward spiral. If it comes to jurors, we don't want them thinking it's two turkeys for the price of one."

They worked long days, into the night, while all around them bars spilled beer and rock-and-roll and knots of twenty-five-year olds onto brick and cobblestone sidewalks. It was party time. They did take-out burritos. Ray felt super-charged. This was it, the high point. Miriam understood, the adrenaline rush before court.

"My kids are giving it to me," she told him. *" 'Is your guy a thug?'* *'Why Sammy'*—I bat my eyelashes, all innocence—*'would I ever represent what you so indelicately refer to as a "thug"?'* They're not impressed. Sonya's treating me like I'm the village idiot. I try to make the point that Blake's no angel, but that doesn't mean he's a murderer. They're such Puritans. Where did they pick up this Manichaean view?—must be their dad."

fifty-eight

Motion sickness, Ray called it. They wrote motions to suppress evidence and one to bar the media and the public from the certification hearing itself. Papers were strewn everywhere. One afternoon, only a few days before the hearing, the phone rang. Ray's secretary stuck her head around the archway separating their desks. "Some kid says she knows something about the case." He took the call.

It turned out to be Callie Viola—Callie Carbon—the sixteen-year-old who'd dropped out of school and married Ricky Carbon. Ray had read the transcript of Detective Bergeron's interview with Callie earlier that month held in a parking lot around the corner from the women's shelter where she'd been staying. Not a top-ten interview, nothing much, just things she'd heard, bad stuff Blake and Tommy had done, filtered through Ricky's grubby lens.

The next day she was sitting in his office. Miriam had taken her son to look at some colleges, so Ray was on his own. Callie perched on the edge of her chair, ready to run if need be. She must weigh all of eighty pounds, most of it pale blond hair that she first pushed off her face, then hid behind. There was a space between her two front teeth. She wore a blue striped tanktop and tight jeans. As she talked, she nibbled on her cuticles. Her nails were eaten down to the quick.

"I was scared to tell Detective Bergeron when he talked to me. He didn't want to hear about Ricky anyways, only Blake and Tommy, but it kept botherin' me, like I had to tell somebody. My girlfriend told me I oughta call you. Maybe it can help them."

She stopped, picked at her ring finger, then leaned forward. "Ricky told me he did it—he killed Ivory."

Ray felt caught between glee and horror, wanting to comfort Callie and cover his ears. His voice calm, though he was trembling, he backed the story up a little. "So, you were married right before Christmas, last year, right? When did troubles begin?"

"Before that. I didn't tell anybody, but he flipped out on me, got smashed last summer, he like yelled outside my house, ran in front of cars and kept crying about Ivory. Said he felt so bad, said he knew stuff, but didn't want to get his buddy in trouble. He tried breakin' into my house, my dad called the cops."

So how come you married the guy? Ray was dying to ask but didn't.

"Him and me moved to Lowell right after our wedding. We eloped. We both were looking for a job. I got one, bagging groceries at this market. I come back to our apartment, all excited. He's watching TV, he's been drinking, and he goes ballistic that I got a job before he did, he starts slapping me, starts choking me, calling me Ivory, Ivory, and then he says he wouldn't think twice about killing me the way he killed her. But he was drunk. You know how guys are, boasting about stuff."

Ray nodded.

"He was like trying to push me out the window. I got to the phone and called my gramps, then Ricky says he's gonna throw himself out, it's the third floor. My gramps finally gets me away and the cops take Ricky to the psycho ward. Then one time we're watching *Quincy* on TV—you know the coroner guy?"

"Yeah, I like Quincy. When was that?"

"Few months ago—and like Ricky's all calm and everything, but out of the blue he goes, *I like fuckin' dead girls, I fucked Ivory. I'm gonna kill you then fuck you like I did her.*

"I got away that time, too. He choked me so bad I couldn't breathe. I was scared 'cause I kept calling the cops to protect me, but they said he had to do something first—something you could see before they could do any protecting. He was gonna kill me, I know he was. My girlfriend said to call you. I can't sleep good, it's been on my mind, Blake and Tommy maybe going to prison . . . I'm hiding from Ricky. I just filed for divorce. He don't know yet."

She paused, curdled with fear, then brushed pale hair off her face and nibbled a thumb. "I'm telling you this, but I'm not going to court."

We'll see about that, Ray thought. He gave her a Pepsi and called a cab. When she left, he tipped back his chair, put his feet up on the desk, and gazed out the window, courting Miriam's resolve, her fiery sword. But all he saw were Callie's fingers, picked naked, and the empty space between her teeth. Still, she was the witness he'd dreamed of.

fifty-nine

The day before the certification hearing, Sid Moravian read through the latest motion out of Ray's office and sighed. He was an assistant attorney general, criminal division, in charge of prosecuting the Ivory Towle murder case. All morning flakes of ceiling paint had drifted about him and there was an early frost of plaster dust on file cabinets, the arms of chairs, his desk, his bald spot. Construction of a new addition to the courthouse would begin soon, that was the talk, but so much had already crumbled and flaked, a blizzard of decay, they ought to send over the snow plows and start from scratch.

He tapped the state police file. A cloud of plaster dust, fingerprints. He sighed again, wondering how Ray Monroe was fixing to twist this mountain of evidence against his client into something boggy and insubstantial. Let's see: *The cops screwed up.* That was good. Detectives like Charlie Bergeron had only a thimbleful of money and time to scour the crime scene. Then defense lawyers—all the time in the world—sent packs of private investigators back to the scene. You washed your hands with disinfectant, but get a powerful enough magnifying glass and scrutinize those hands again, they'd be filthy dirty.

How about: *Somebody else did it.* Yup, those rotten coppers fingered the wrong choir boys yet again. In part, he blamed that law professor, Sonenfeld, teaching perfectly good kids that evil didn't exist, that it was never anybody's fault. And they fell right into it, those defense types. Something unformed and adolescent about them, no matter what their age. It used to frighten him on their behalf; now he saw them for the menace they presented. Some of them weren't fooled, they knew full well their guy was guilty, they just took on the prosecution anyway, for fun, maybe the kid-glee of beating grown-ups. Some of them did believe in evil, he guessed, they'd just gotten it ass-backwards, seeing the government as the villain: crooked cops, crooked prosecutors, evidence tampering, conspiracy.

His hands ached, he popped a couple of aspirin with the last swallow of cold coffee. If he were defending those boys, he'd want to seal their juvenile records, too. Burglary, theft, arson, rape—it started at school, zero attention span, you stole candy, then a Budweiser suitcase, you lifted some tires, hey, why not the whole car, and let's get rid of the lady driving that hot GTO which by all rights ought to be yours. Tommy was a stupid con and always would be. Blake? Your average sociopath. Tommy'd never fool anybody, no matter how close they got his shave, but Blake was quite the accomplished actor, that clean-cut, turn-your-life around performance—Oscar-time.

And then there was the girl, shot once, shot again, and again, stabbed with some kind of ice pick or screwdriver, her breast bone so soft it probably hadn't even crunched. Or—Dr. Cooper's *periter-minal*—maybe they'd stuck her first, before they killed her, to see what she'd say, what she'd do, how she'd beg them to stop.

It was lunchtime, he felt hungry. Slowly he pushed off from the battered wooden arms of his chair. Arthritis, helped along by a swollen gut, was seizing up his joints. Doctors said, *Walk briskly. Walk briskly* to a guy who'd pitched one shut-out after another, magic-armed, who'd sunk every free throw he'd ever put up. Forty years ago.

He headed out of court and two blocks over to the only deli that still kept fat on beef and didn't assume you wanted sprouts. He got in line behind fellows with honest hammers hanging off their hips and a few diehards who liked sliced bread, not pockets.

"Mr. Moravian!" a voice called behind him. It took him a moment to make the connection, then he grasped a young woman's hand. She held his and squeezed hard, a satisfying shake.

"Sally Gregg, hello!" He beamed at the girl he used to know, grown into an officer of the law, blue uniform, badge, gun, shiny black shoes. "How long has it been since I've seen you—ten, twelve years?—since we moved to Concord—but just in the past couple of weeks I've read your name a dozen times, all those statements you took after Ivory Towle was murdered. I'm prosecuting that case."

Sally nodded. "I know, I'm glad."

"What'll it be?" the man behind the counter asked Sid, rubbing wide palms down his apron front.

"Roast beef on a bulkie, lots of mayo, large coffee, regular."

"I hope you nail them," Sally added, her voice over his shoulder vehement but soft.

He turned back to her, away from the counter. "That's my plan. I don't see any problem sending it to the grand jury. That young lawyer of Blake's is trying to bar the media, but I can't imagine the judge'll fall for it."

"Blake was so cold the times I talked to him after Ivory's body was found—but of course you've read that—he didn't even pretend he was sorry she died."

Sally was ferocious, Sid remembered that about her, the intensity she'd possessed even as a little girl, but tempered now. So different from Ray Monroe. She knew evil. He saw it in her face.

"What brings you to the city?" he asked.

"I'm a Big Sister. A group of us are taking our kids on a harbor cruise this afternoon, then I'm heading out to Mrs. Towle's—funny I should run into you. She called me yesterday. She's scared to death about testifying."

Sid noticed one of his colleagues at the door, he waved, seemed not to have heard what Sally said. "Your folks still live in the old neighborhood?"

"Same house."

When Sid and his wife Evelyn were first married and moved up the road from the Greggs, he'd imagined he'd father a girls' basketball team's worth of daughters, a string of Amazons. But instead they'd had one son, Mack, whose hands favored stringed instruments, not balls, and who somehow belonged more to Evelyn than to him. By some amazing fluke, Sally had turned out to be Mack's best pal growing up, a crackerjack athlete who smashed field hockey balls all the way to the States, who ran hurdles and distance and beat the boys at round-the-world. "Watch this, Mr. Moravian!" She'd dribble a three-sixty, a trick she'd picked up from her brother, just back from Swish Camp, and she'd flashed him a smile. His consolation, his yearning.

Sally's turn, she ordered turkey on white and a Coke.

"Any grandchildren yet?" she asked.

"Almost. Mack's wife's pregnant with their first. Big as a blood-filled tick last time I saw her."

Sally laughed at the picture.

"Don't repeat that. Evelyn'd have a fit hearing me talk like that. Mack's crazy about her and that's the sum of it. But she's the type who pays to have her fingernails and toenails painted, makeup, too. She's a singer—soprano—has her own career, kept her own name. The kid's going to be a hyphen. You have family?" he asked, then realized too late he'd stepped into catastrophe. He tried to remember—something Evelyn had told him—the death of a baby, divorce, he couldn't quite piece it together. He'd listened with half a mind—with his reptilian brain, Evelyn called it—the part that skimmed detail, that missed subtlety in favor of shadow and light. Now he stumbled over himself.

"I muck around with kids on the job, but otherwise I'm available." She understood, he thought, gazing at her face. Smile lines, sorrow lines, dark smudges under the eyes. Young still—Mack's age, thirty-two, he realized with a pang—but marked by wisdom's heavy hand, all those traces of living Mack's wife tried so hard to erase.

I love you like a daughter, he wanted to say, *I'd sooner drop into hell than cause you pain.* Instead: "You want my pickle? Doctor says it's got something I don't deserve—salt? cholesterol? taste?"

"Nice briny half-sour, sure. What's Mack up to?"

"Plays in a string quartet, teaches at the Boston Conservatory. He's making a living, if you can believe it."

They carried their paper bags outside, bright sun, to stand in the corner park where families in shorts fed popcorn to pigeons and snapped pictures of kids, backed up against a brick facade, painted to look like a carnival.

She took the pickle he offered.

"Tell Mrs. Towle not to worry. It's only a couple of questions— about the time of that phone call she got the Sunday Ivory disappeared."

She turned to go. "Congratulate Mack for me when the baby tick pops, Mr. Moravian."

"Boneman."

"Boneman?"

"Name I picked up in law school—I was skinny as a rail and so poor I lived on bait soup. Of course I want cons to think I got it for the pile of bones like theirs stacked outside the courthouse."

"Boneman," she repeated, laughing at the notion. The name moved her, why she couldn't fathom.

He held out his hand, that same firm grip. "You still play field hockey?" he asked, not ready to let her go.

She laughed again. "I haven't held a stick—a day stick—for about twelve years." She stood on tiptoe and kissed his cheek where the salt and pepper beard grew sparse.

She was short for a ball player, he'd forgotten that, still that wonderful athlete's body, and something else: the gift of kindness.

"Ivory played softball, her mom told me—back in grade school, beginning of junior high. She'd be sixteen now, maybe doing a fall sport—yesterday I saw kids out at the high school, preseason." Sally opened her arms wide to possibility, then let them drop. "Or maybe she'd be pregnant by now with a second child."

sixty

Geena hadn't planned to attend the certification hearing. It wasn't like anybody wanted her for a witness, fuck them, she thought. But a few days before it was scheduled to begin—somehow the date stuck in her head without her paying attention—through the stupor of heat and alcohol she'd sunk into, she woke with a shock. She and her mom had been doing some drinking, just the two of them. It felt good to be friends again, but the day she snapped to, it suddenly grossed her out, a mom sucking it down with her own daughter, passing out together, pretty picture, mid-afternoon and dark as midnight with the curtains closed.

She'd studied her mom, still asleep on the couch. Thirty-four years old, her face the color of a dirty pillowcase. She'd been snoring, head back and wobbly-throated, darkness where some teeth should have sparkled. *And you're the spitting image*, people said.

Risky behavior ages you. Mrs. Cadenza's words, not her own, Mrs. Cadenza in her goofball turbans, talking about ejaculations and sperms, saying how you had a choice. Caspar didn't believe in condoms, they hurt, he said, like he might explode, he couldn't get them big enough, so what could you do? Mrs. Cadenza made it sound like before you fucked, you sat your boyfriend down and had a meeting. Okay, let's have a report from the birth control com-

mittee—like you were in charge. Caspar was kind of a wimp, he
was fun to boss around, but when he got his dick out, there was no
stopping him.

For some reason, the day Geena had come to, it was Mrs. Cadenza—so nice it drove you crazy, like anybody could act that way
in real life—Mrs. Cadenza who floated around her brain, as if they'd
unscrewed a genie-bottle, not a fifth of Popov. So Geena had flown
into this cleaning thing. Cleaning herself up, her mom, the bathroom, she'd done five loads at the laundromat, mopped the kitchen
floor, washed windows, wiped dust off her horse calendar, tied the
burnt-orange curtains back until sunlight flooded her little corner of
treasures Dunc and his buddies had trashed looking for Ivory. Even
polished the ten silver rings she always wore and gave herself a perm,
which fizzed instead of curled, a headful of dark filament, gone hay-
wire. It pleased her anyway, who cared what people thought, it
matched the shock-blue of eyes that were hers alone, not her
mother's.

So there she was, the morning of the hearing, hitchhiking into the
city. The old guy who picked her up was okay but mouthy about
danger. If he only knew. Wanted to take her directly to the courthouse, but with some kind of badge-of-honor thing she didn't understand herself, she insisted he let her off before they got there.
Two miles or more from the courthouse, he warned, big city, girl
like you . . .

She hadn't walked this far since the day Detective Bergeron
picked her up at school in his state cop car and she'd showed him
the path from Ivory's house to Blake's, miles it had been, hours. It
was cool that day in the woods, leaves rustling underfoot. Now it
was so hot and humid the sidewalks jiggled, tight shoes, pantyhose,
what you wore to court. Her short dress stuck between her legs and
she felt out-there, naked and exposed.

It seemed harder doing this than running away from the two fist
holes in the plywood front door, from her mother, gonzo with
booze. Running away you turned your back, forgot, moved for-

ward. But this simple walk in broad daylight—through bus fumes, down grubby sidewalks, cement, brick, cobblestone, the noise of a city, past weird foreign people and retards and cool-looking, scary-looking kids her own age—her heart pounded. Now it was this way, she thought: You're walking backward, into the guts of what scared you to death, what gave you such pain you passed out and woke up in a clearing, blood on your hooves. Wishing for blood on your hooves. Instead, Ivory'd gotten murdered, her neck shot through, her back, her mane.

If she'd hit back, one blow to the head with her hoof—she did fight back, of course. It had taken three bullets to kill her. Probably she'd never believed it was Blake, even after she died, she couldn't believe it. Even when he'd shot her all those times and laughed. Happy Pastures, that's where they lived, Ivory seemed to think—so much in love, it felt so good. Geena couldn't imagine that kind of desire, begging for it, wanting it the way Ivory did. The facts: Ivory loved Blake and died of it.

Inside the courthouse she stopped to ask directions. Her heart banged, she tossed her head, beamed shock-blue eyes left and right, at secretaries, at sheriff-types, at empty chairs. She turned the last corner. It wasn't what she had expected: a wide door into a court-room, like TV, big enough so everybody could crowd in and watch. Instead, it was crazy, that hallway, narrow like the ones in her apartment house, lined with wooden benches on both sides. People standing, sitting, staring at her, not smiling, but whispering behind their hands. Everybody talking, except for pockets of quiet around Ivory's mom and dad.

Mrs. Towle's feet barely touched the floor. It had been over two years, since before Ivory died, the last time Geena saw her. But Mrs. Towle wasn't looking at anybody to recognize them, she was looking beyond the far wall, lost somewhere ashy and bare. Mr. Towle bit his lip, fidgeted, and rubbed his hands back and forth along his pant legs. He coughed into a bandanna.

She saw Detective Bergeron, who'd walked her through the woods, Blake's family, must be Tommy's mom and dad, everybody looking up in the air or down at their hands or quick back and forth, not to dwell on people they hated. It knocked her out: how somebody packed into this very hallway must be the mother of a murderer. Maybe two mothers, two murderers.

She was standing next to a girl she recognized from parties at the pit. "Can't we go in?" she asked.

"Not yet. Judge's doin' somethin, lawyers told us wait," the girl said. "I like your hair. I seen you at the pit, right?"

"Perm screwed up. Yeah, I'm Geena."

"Toni Sparrow. I gotta testify, I'm a nervous wreck."

Geena wondered what Toni had heard and what she'd seen. "Did you know Ivory?" she asked.

Toni shook her head. Her hair was black, pulled tight and smooth into a ponytail. "But I recognized her—she was so pretty, and one night at the pit she helped my friend Amber—she shot her own foot."

Geena nodded. She remembered the way Ivory had stepped into headlights and taken Amber's hand. "I wasn't there—the weekend she died—I would have been, usually, but I wasn't." She leaned against the beige wall and closed her eyes. She envied Toni, the chance at bravery in front of judges and lawyers, in front of murderers, a whole courtroom full, not just bravery in your head.

sixty-one

Florence opened her purse and rummaged. Blake's mother was nearby, she felt it. If she touches me, if she looks at me—Florence felt herself shrink. Duncan put an arm around her shoulders. His chest was big with trying to get enough oxygen, the rest of him grown so thin, his arm like wire pulled tight, though still a comfort. Don't fall to pieces. Don't fall to pieces. They took some water up last night, it'd been so hot and dry. Took some water up. Ivory's parched earth drank it down. Suddenly, the small door to the courtroom opened, and a lawyer wearing red suspenders came out, whispered, then beckoned to Blake's mom, to Tommy's parents, to that Detective Bergeron. Some talking, Bergeron looked like he'd ate something sour and hated to swallow, he'd rather spit. She turned away. Hard to hear, so many words, no sense, voices like glass, like dust.

But Duncan understood. He jumped up and made a fist. "We're the parents of the *victim*." His voice shook. "Our daughter got shot, *dead*."

Florence nodded. She opened her purse, she rummaged. She understood now: They were to wait outside.

sixty-two

Behind closed doors, the judge had met with Blake and Tommy's lawyers and with the prosecutor, Sid Moravian. The evidence, he ruled, was *so sensitive that making it public could substantially impair defendants' right to a fair, impartial jury-selection process.* Furthermore, these were juveniles and until they were certified as adults, the law required it be sealed. Therefore, he was barring spectators from the courtroom, including representatives of the media. He regretted doing this, he said, and didn't undertake it lightly.

Ray Monroe and Miriam Sonenfeld were jubilant. Bill Davis seemed pleased, too, though he didn't jump for joy. They'd won this one, a long shot, they agreed. Blake and Tommy dared to smile, weak, prisoner smiles, but still there was hope.

So sensitive, Sid mimicked—a girl, running away, shot three times in the head and back. But he masked his fury and went on to present the State's case. The evidence was clear, abundant, compelling, and damn sensitive because those two boys were guilty. He felt confident the judge would certify them to Superior Court to be tried as adults.

Outside the courtroom, in the hallway, on wooden benches: a small vigil kept by Geena and the Towles. No candles lit, no prayers, no placards, only silence and eyes that drilled unspoken questions whenever a witness entered the hearing room or left it.

Detective Bergeron was called first. When he came out again, he stopped and talked to Florence and Duncan. "I told the judge about the investigation, what we did, the place where Ivory's body was found, how we gathered evidence." He shook Duncan's hand then gazed at Florence, apologetic, as if to say, *I did what I could.*

You never called, Florence wanted to tell him, *after those first weeks, you just dropped us.* She didn't dare, and then she heard her own name spoken. She stood up, clutching her handbag.

She was small in the hearing room. It was quiet around her, the stillness of tragedy. "Tell me about the phone call you received that Sunday afternoon Ivory didn't come home," Sid asked her gently.

What time the phone call had come, how some lady needed Ivory to babysit while she rushed her husband to the hospital—Ivory'd be home late, she hadn't known who it was, hadn't recognized the voice.

How she'd laid awake that night.

How she'd called a friend the next day to drive her to Blake's and when she'd asked if he'd seen Ivory that weekend, he lied, but later changed his tune.

She didn't look at them, the other parents, she looked into Mr. Moravian's brown eyes. He was like somebody at Emergency, important-sounding but sorry to pry. Or she looked down at the worn clasp of the pocketbook she snapped open and shut, open and shut.

Then his lawyer, Blake's, had a few questions, if he might, just a kid in red suspenders, with a mop of messy hair. She didn't trust him. He'd do anything to get Blake off. How she hadn't asked to speak to Ivory, no, she hadn't. Small and painful, her voice gray with the torture of hindsight.

sixty-three

Ivory, digging with a spoon. That's what popped into Florence's mind toward the end of that first morning. She couldn't bear it, this narrow hall, Ivory in the yard, out behind the house, digging a castle underground that was nothing but a hole. Dunc tromped it, made fun of it. Later he helped her dig it out again, an act of kindness that dwarfed brother-sister cruelty.

Ivory's maybe three or four, out of diapers. She takes a spoon, a little one, the kind she eats her cereal with. In the dooryard she digs up earwigs, beetles, ants. *He's carrying a diamond on his back*, she says, *look, Mommy*. In her bony palm, it sparkles—a grain of sand, a bit of quartz, enough to raise a blister in your shoe.

He's got his arms up, look, he's holding queen-eggs. She has whistle teeth now, the two top ones missing. She sings, she's always singing. She must be six, she buries those fallen teeth and waters them with the hose. And Florence watches out the window over the kitchen sink. She wonders: what's Ivory thinking in her little head? She didn't wonder at the time. She marvels at that, and she wonders now. Ivory's digging with a spoon.

Somebody waiting on this same bench dug rough initials with a penknife: WT. Duncan ran his knuckles over the letters, back and

forth, rubbing skin raw. He understood why somebody would need
to gouge while they waited. He figured that was what it was. He
didn't picture a kid doing it, meaning disrespect—he saw a parent,
most likely, some dad kept out of the hearing room because it was
his daughter shot, his son knifed to death, and his wife who'd been
called as a witness.

For two years, he'd walked those paths in the woods, out back of
his house, back to where it happened, or at least to where they found
her body. Looking for something to clinch it, something the cops
missed because it was not their kid. At first they chased him away,
state police investigation mumbo–jumbo, but he stuck with it and
they gave up. Lately, though, he just didn't have the wind to walk
that far, and of course there were just too many ruts and stones for
his Falcon.

sixty-four

Sometime in the afternoon, it was Toni Sparrow's turn to testify. She'd been up and down, back and forth, bathroom, sodas. Over and over, tugging on her black ponytail, she'd told Geena how scared she felt, going before the judge.

When she returned from the hearing room she looked red-faced and pissed off. She waved to Geena. They'd become friends. Toni could just leave; instead she sat back down on the bench, and for that Geena felt grateful.

"I told the judge how Tommy come over and we went out and bought some coke, come back with this other kid, but then Tommy stayed and he forced me. He held me down, he's a big guy, stuck his dick in, and he kept callin me *Ivory, Ivory*. It still creeps me out. After that he asks if he can spend the night, he don't have nowhere to go, and he's so wasted, he can't drive anyways.

"That lawyer of Tommy's, he jumped all over me, he even laughed. *"Tommy raped you and you let him spend the night?"* Again, she yanked on her ponytail. "Made *me* sound slutty. I went out with Blake a little, then Tommy. I was all fucked up," she added.

Geena understood. She saw how Tommy's lawyer twisted things, how come, after a guy'd forced sex on you, you said okay, you can stay over, it's too late now, especially if you figured he was your friend. Drugs, they were beside the point. So you had a few snorts, like you wouldn't get it right that a guy *raped* you? Like somehow a few lines blotted that out, that you'd do it with anybody just for a hit, begging some asshole like Tommy to fuck you?

She worked her thumb over four of the rings on her left hand. "I bet you did good," she told Toni.

"Tommy raped that girl," Geena reported to the Towles, pointing at Toni's back as she walked away, "and he kept calling her *Ivory* the whole time."

"When was that?" Duncan asked.

"This past spring, she said."

Florence shuddered. It was cold in the hallway, too much air conditioning. Her feet and legs went numb. It was late afternoon when a blond-haired young man rounded the corner, shackled, hands and feet, but for all that acting like Elvis the King, like he owned the place and those sheriffs leading him had to be private bodyguards, he was so important.

"Who's that?" she asked Geena.

"Buzz Carbon."

"The one who gave the statement in Florida," Duncan said.

"I went out with his brother for a while, Ricky."

"Yeah, Ricky, I remember Ricky. He's been to our house, Ivory liked him, friend of hers," said Florence.

Geena zapped Buzz with her blue-shock eyes, but he just smirked. He was scary and cocky-good-looking, in spite of the handcuffs, up-yours, he zapped her back.

sixty-five

$\mathcal{B}$uzz was enjoying himself. The arraignment he'd just come from upstairs in Superior Court was no big deal: taking a hike from the joint, borrowing a few cars, details, details, who remembered what color they were and where they'd been parked? At least they'd stopped bugging him about Simon, the guy he skipped with, who shot himself on the first day of deer hunting season, sad fuck, and the cops tried to nail him for it, shit. Now he was the key witness, kingpin of the state's case.

Ape-Man, the prosecutor—fat gut, hairy face and hands—asked him questions, no sweat. He unwound his story, letting the line play out, not even bothering to make eye contact with Tommy and Blake. He could have, no problem, he was just telling the truth so help him God that he swore before the judge, but why bother, they were just a couple of chisely punks, years his juniors in experience and smarts. He'd got them by the balls, all of them.

"Me and my wife Lisa was over to my Grampa Stan's," he told the judge. "We had plans to ride around Maine with these friends of ours, neighbors over to Leighton Falls, so we got Lisa's niece to babysit—there was gonna be some drinkin'. The couple with the car, they went to church beforehand, so we didn't leave from Stan's till about noon or one o'clock."

193

He paused to check his audience, running a hand through his glinty blond hair. "When we got back, there's not enough room for all of us to ride home with my daughter and her stuff—I offer to stay the night. Then I hear Tommy's lookin' for me, waitin' in the backyard, out by the pool. So I go out, and he's there. He's wild, just wild—tells me the story, how Blake and Ivory'd gone walkin' out behind Stan's after me and Lisa left, then he took off on his bike until he got to this clearing. He says, *'I jumped out of the bushes when they come through. Ivory got scared and ran, Blake pulls a gun out and shoots her, and I take the gun and I shoot her.'* "

Buzz paused again to let the words explode, then, aiming at Ape-Man, he went bang in the air. In the witness box, no handcuffs or shackles, and he moved with the tawny joy of a cat. The hearing room couldn't contain his story now, it bulged, it split wide open, and he was the cougar, sniffing that clearing, his eyes gold in the fluorescent light.

"After I got out of jail, end of August," he continued, his voice coaxy soft, "Blake called me and asked if I'd meet him at the four corners near his house. I walk over—it's close," he added to edify the judge, "and he's standing in the middle of the road, firing shots in the air and sayin', *'I told you we was gonna do it!'* "

When Ape-Man pressed further, Buzz said the gun looked like a .22 Ruger. "I'm not positive, though, 'cause when I tried gettin' it off him, he wouldn't give it over. *'We shot her, we shot her,'* he kept sayin', geez, the guy was some wired."

Under Bill Davis's cross-examination, Buzz admitted that he had once implicated someone else in the murder, Small Runyon, a fellow allegedly camping in the woods at the time, and a weird albino kid that never talked, and he further admitted he'd once claimed Ricky, his own brother, offed Ivory Towle, but he'd only been teasing, you know, just fooling around.

Davis wasn't finished. "Isn't it true," he said, "that you once told state police detectives you returned from your excursion to

Maine at four p.m., but later testified it was almost dark? At the end of July, about what time would that be?"

"Isn't it true that it would be about fuckin' nine o'clock?" Buzz fired back. "I got my dates mixed up. That was like two years ago, Jesus Christ."

"Interesting, Mr. Carbon," Davis said. God, what a snide little bastard, big-bucks white shirt. "You've given several vivid accounts, in stunning detail, the most recent less than a month ago, but now suddenly, when I ask you specific questions, you can't recall . . ." He let his voice trail off. "You in the Nixon Administration at any time?" he added, that puff-face red as a boil.

Some fuckhead laughed—Blake's lawyer, Bozo the Clown. Ape-Man objected, the least he could do. Then Bozo started fooling around with questions himself.

"In one of your statements, Mr. Carbon, you claim you knew nothing about the murder weapon, but in another you went on at length, describing it. Isn't it true you were just looking for some kind of deal, telling the police detectives what they wanted to hear?"

"I never said nothin' like that."

"Let me refresh your memory." Bozo waved some papers. "Would you kindly read this section of the transcript of a statement you gave to Detective Bergeron?"

Buzz grabbed the pages and scanned them. "Ha, yeah, right. I said this," and he read: "*Tommy told me him and Blake threw their gun off the truffle*—'Truffle?' What the hell kind of thing is that? Some idiot type this thing up? Yeah, I said they threw it off a railroad truffle, that's just what I said . . ."

Buzz was riding high. It went on like this for the better part of another day, more stupid questions from Ape-Man, Bozo, and Davis, more incompetents who'd typed stuff up wrong he never said. Leaving the hearing room the second day, he walked by that dead girl Ivory's parents. The mom sat there, a red-eyed mouse, her legs not touching the floor, looking out, looking out. He turned away. Then there was that slut Geena who'd messed Ricky over so bad.

Beyond them, sitting against the far wall, was Lisa. Short skirt, legs crossed so you could see right up. God, she was hot, that tarty-apple smell and tight, dog-collar blouse she was wearing with the peep hole over her tits. The two dumb-fuck sheriff bodyguards walking him out, they got stiff just looking. They let him stop and kiss her mouth, God, she was hot.

sixty-six

Love you—that was what he'd longed to say, Lisa was thinking when they called her into the hearing room, though with the sheriffs there he used those soft, soft lips of his. She tugged at her skirt, feeling a little wobbly in the heels she'd just bought.

Yes, she'd talked to Ivory that morning when Blake and Tommy went off to buy dope, and Ivory was steamed 'cause she'd got her period and cramps wicked, she even thought she might throw up, and no protection to speak of. She had heard Ivory chewing the boys out when they got back, she remembered that, before her and Buzz had rode around that Sunday afternoon with their neighbors from Leighton Falls.

Yes, her niece had took care of the baby there at Stan's, and she was trying to remember exactly what time they'd got back, maybe headlights shining on the garage door, maybe not . . . But yes, she knew it was late, now, it was coming clear, because the baby'd been sleeping on the sofa in the den where her niece was watching TV, but his stuff was still upstairs in Buzz and Ricky's room, she remembered because she'd turned the light on, not realizing Ricky lay on the waterbed next to some girl she didn't know, so she'd grabbed the bag of baby clothes and switched the light off. Had to have been late.

Then later, right after Ivory's body'd been found in the woods, her and Tommy and one of her girlfriends were sitting on the king-size bed in that same bedroom, shooting the breeze and of course all they'd talked about was Ivory's murder, and she'd told how she got raped in Virginia, and how she'd yelled her head off, not that it did any good, and her and her friend got to wondering if Ivory had screamed for help while she was getting shot or maybe if somebody raped her first.

"Then Tommy blurts out, *No, she didn't yell or nothin'*, and we all go quiet. Afterwards, I went and told Buzz's grandma but she said it probably weren't anything much so I didn't mention it to the cops that first time they talked to me, but it kept eatin' at me, not feelin' right, so I told."

She dared to look at Tommy. He didn't dare look at her. The prosecutor guy, Mr. Moravian, he treated her good, not like Tommy's asshole lawyer, who said didn't you bartend at a strip club in Florida, and didn't your husband "on occasion" beat you up, scaring you so you'd second the story he cooked up.

No, she said, no. Later in the courthouse bathroom, she saw her face in the mirror. Two black zippers on her cheeks, runny eye makeup, he'd made her cry so bad.

sixty-seven

No matter how early the Slacks got to the courthouse, the Towles were already there, sitting on the bench outside the hearing room. *I'm sorry*, Doris whispered once to Florence, but there'd been no acknowledgment. Maybe Florence didn't hear. Sorry for what? That your baby was dead, that you couldn't go inside, but my son was fighting for his life today because of your daughter, and was that fair? He didn't do it, still he got locked up night and day in the company of criminals. He was just a boy. How fair was that? She knew it wasn't the same, she knew, and that sorrow, too, nested in her heart.

Certification hearings usually took an hour or so, but this one stretched on for four days, spread over a week, as fancy as a regular trial, they overheard Blake's lawyer telling his mom. The prosecutor presented all his witnesses—they listened to detectives; gun experts; the state medical examiner who did the autopsy; the man who said the three of them had gone off on Tommy's dirt bike together that Sunday and they'd had a fight.

But nothing had prepared her for Buzz Carbon's words—if she'd known, she'd have poked her ears out, not to hear—Buzz Carbon lying about her boy admitting he'd killed the Towle girl, lying with such a cool face, a smart-aleck face, so disrespectful she'd felt Harvey

coiling with rage beside her. It was horrible, and you not being able
to say a single thing to protect your boy. It was as much a blur inside
the hearing room as it must have been outside for the Towles, who
hadn't heard a word of testimony, a nightmare you woke up to every
morning, and dreamed about each night—some older man, who
said he'd been in jail with Tommy, said Tommy loved Satan things,
that he wrote devil worship numbers and letters on pieces of paper
then threw them in the trash so nobody'd catch him up, said maybe
him and Blake killed Ivory in some Satan church-thing.

He did it, Doris thought, Buzz Carbon did it, his gold eyes, gold
hair, unnatural handsome and cold as the grave. He was the Satan
that had dragged Tommy into getting caught for things he was too
weak to resist. He'd done it, Buzz Carbon, or his brother Ricky.
Terrible boys, sad boys, but why should hers pay for the Devil beat
into them long before they'd moved in with poor Stan and Nonie,
who'd gotten burned time after time.

It was better now, it was the other side, their side. But more
Blake's than Tommy's. Tommy was a simple boy who just followed
along, if you could fault him for anything that was it, slow to de-
velop, of course boys were that way, he was a follower, he'd go
along with things just to fit in. Now she hardly recognized him.
He'd lost weight, lost color, lost the boy-look, on the outside anyway, though he still had it, underneath that haunting mask of a man.

Where's Mr. Davis? she wondered. Too busy cracking jokes to
fill them in. He wouldn't return phone calls. Tommy said Mr. Davis
thought he was guilty, she'd always pooh-poohed that before, but
now she heard it for herself. He was silent. It was Blake's lawyers,
two of them, who called witness after witness on Blake's behalf: the
school social worker, the basketball coach, who said what a fine
young man Blake was, knew he'd *hit a rough patch in junior high* but
he'd turned it around, his little boy Skip idolized Blake, he'd trust
him with Skip's life, like once in the weight room, he'd let the boy
pretend to bench press a hundred pounds, Blake was spotting him
and of course Blake had done the lifting himself, but let Skip think

he was a regular He-Man, then let the bar down light and safe as a cloud.

And April Cook's dad, the man who'd hired Blake, who'd taken him under his wing, he let his daughter date Blake, for God's sake, and the parole officer, who had Blake on *informal adjustment*, one thing and another over the years, and Blake was the biggest success story he'd ever had.

Even Blake's mom got up there, said her boy misbehaved sometimes, he was just a kid still, but he liked nothing better than spending time with her and his little sister, and of course working on his car, you know how boys like to tinker with machines, and after he'd gone to that alcohol and drug unit at Youth Development, he'd dried himself out, no more trouble with *that*, he stopped going to AA meetings because he'd done so good, and how much he'd liked Camp Jeanette Winston he got sent to for two summers, up north where it was lakes and woods.

Listening, Doris wondered, How come my boy never got that— the kindly parole officer, Camp Jeanette Winston, a man like Mr. Cook giving him a break, a teacher at school who—well, if she'd known, she'd have found hundreds of people to testify on Tommy's behalf, she just didn't know, nobody'd told her, Mr. Davis hadn't told her, she thought he was doing his job, getting paid by the government, you'd think he'd do what was right.

If they'd let her, she'd stand before the judge, proud as all get-out, and talk about her boy, even show off the cutting board he'd made her himself in the shape of a strawberry, her favorite fruit, and the Mother's Day card: *You mean the world to me.* All the bad things they'd said, they just couldn't be thought inside a mother's brain.

sixty-eight

P lease state your name for the Court," they said, and she told them, "Callie Viola Carbon, but I'm back using Viola, I just filed for divorce," her voice so quiet the judge kept asking her to speak up.

She looked at him, just him, otherwise she couldn't speak at all. He wasn't that old, but he had pouches under his eyes and a wild head of hair—white cotton candy, like her gramps, who used to say, *Hurry and grow up so I can marry you,* and *Push those bangs off your face, you're too pretty to hide your light under a bushel basket,* and later swore at her for marrying Ricky, but saved her once when Ricky threatened with a knife.

Mr. Monroe, the guy she'd told her story to, he asked her to repeat what she'd said. She hated him for it, for making her talk in court. Telling it, she tried to put time and space between herself and the stories, talking as if it had happened to somebody else, but she couldn't, it had happened to her, and Ricky was going to find out, he'd track her down and that would be the end.

Her voice quaked, cataloguing the times Ricky had told her he'd killed Ivory or wrapped his hands around her throat and squeezed her windpipe shut. "He said"—her voice papery thin—"he said, '*I liked*—' She thought of the polite ways Mrs. Cadenza had talked

202

about sex in school—"He said, *'I like—doing intercourse with dead girls . . .'* "

The judge stepped into the quiet. "Under the circumstances, Mrs. Carbon, it's okay to use Mr. Carbon's exact words, though we appreciate the delicacy of the matter."

She nodded. "Okay." She gnawed at her thumb. "He said, *'I like fuckin' dead girls,'* that's what he said, *'and I'm gonna kill you like I done Ivory, then fuck my brains out.'* "

After she'd told it all, every time, the prosecutor guy, Mr. Moravian, said, "I gather it's an acrimonious separation you have from Mr. Carbon. And given that, you'd like to get the most you can for your trouble, which might account for your stepping forward now?"

She wasn't sure what he meant except the now part. "I didn't step forward," she said. "He—" she pointed at Ray Monroe—"he sent me papers saying I had to come. I didn't want to, I told you that before."

"Thank you, Mrs. Carbon."

The way he said it made her mad. "I'm back with Viola, I said that too."

"Legally, Ms. Viola, you're still Mrs. Carbon. Here we're speaking of the law, not raw emotions."

They let her go. When she stood up, she almost tripped. Her fingers stung, catching herself on the edge of the judge's desk.

sixty-nine

At the close of the hearing, Bill Davis wrote a letter to the judge, tearing the prosecution's case to pieces:

> *Did police detectives ever take fingerprints from the 1974 Cutlass abandoned about the time Ivory was reported missing and found not a quarter of a mile from where her body was discovered? NO. Did police detectives ever follow up on Buzz Carbon's alibi? NO! They failed to interview the couple he and his wife drove to Maine with until the week before the certification hearing.*
>
> *Isn't it possible that Buzz was flirting with Ivory around the pool before he went off with his wife, that he came back around 4:00, so he could flirt some more? And that he killed her when she rejected his advances? Buzz Carbon, a felon repeatedly convicted of crimes of moral turpitude, as both juvenile and adult, gave contradictory testimony about the murder on numerous occasions, always with the intent of making some kind of deal with the State.*
>
> *And what of Callie Carbon's testimony that her husband Ricky repeatedly confessed to the murder? It's as likely the Carbon brothers were involved in Ivory's death as the two juveniles*

accused. Has the State proved any kind of motive? NO! Blake was Ivory's boyfriend, and from all reports, there was great af- fection between the two. What about the telephone call Mrs. Towle testified to receiving late that Sunday afternoon? Could this call not have been made by Lisa Carbon, stalling for time to help out her husband? Had Detective Bergeron subpoenaed phone records, there would be a way to make a connection be- tween the Carbon household and the Towles. But those records are routinely destroyed after six months. The investigation so quickly narrowed to the two juveniles in question that no other possibilities were entertained. Is there any way now to track down that telephone call? NO!

seventy

In spite of the letter, the judge found prosecutive merit to the murder charge; he certified the boys as adults and transferred the case to superior court, where it would come before the grand jury. Ray Monroe wasn't surprised, he told reporters. "*Prosecutive merit* simply means a preponderance of evidence—fifty-one percent certainty—while conviction in a criminal trial requires proof beyond a reasonable doubt. In a way we're glad the case is rolling forward," he added. "We believe we'll beat this thing before a jury. We're just disappointed Blake's not being treated as a juvenile."

After the judge submitted written findings-of-fact to Superior Court, supporting his decisions to certify, he told the court clerks not to make them public until he'd learned if Sid Moravian, the prosecutor, or any of the defense lawyers might object to that release. Ray did. The whole point of closing down the hearing, he argued, was to keep inflammatory information from prejudicing potential jurors and, until Blake and Tommy left the juvenile jursidiction of District Court, and Superior Court accepted them, the proceedings should be sealed. Reluctantly the judge agreed.

By mid-September, Ray had appealed the judge's ruling, which bought Blake some time and separated his case from Tommy Slack's.

A transcript of the hearing wouldn't be ready for three months, Ray said, add another month for the appeal to be heard in Superior Court, no reason it shouldn't go all the way to the New Hampshire Supreme Court. Certification hearing were uncharted territory as far as the high court went.

In early October, the grand jury heard evidence concerning Tommy Slack and, during secret deliberations, indicted him for murder in the first degree.

part five

seventy-one

Tommy's sister, Romaine, counted ticks, school-clock ticks. You waited and waited, then the second hand leaped up-and-over, the way a cat pounced on a leaf it took for a mouse. It was the loudest silent noise she knew. There was a kind of rhythm to it, sometimes her thumbs tapped it out or her tongue clicked the roof of her mouth. But not in Mrs. Cadenza's class, you listened up. You never knew what words would pop out of her mouth: *intercourse, orgasm, masturbation.* It was thrilling, not to mention very weird.

Today, though, Mrs. C was wound up about choices you make. Romaine's mind blanked and returned to tick-counting. But ticks turned into heartbeats, lumps of blood slammed against heart windows and broke glass. Today, counting clock-ticks reminded her of Tommy, how the judge ruled he was a grown-up, one tick only between boy and man, one eye blink, one gunshot he didn't shoot. Figured a jury would convict him, would say, *Lock him up for what he didn't do.*

Mrs. Cadenza knew the story. She'd read the papers, and of course there was talk around school. Tommy had been sixteen at the time of the murder, he was eighteen now. Romaine herself couldn't be more than thirteen. According to the packaged Family Life curriculum, the time had come for seventh-graders to collide head-on with Personal Responsibility.

"How about you write down one time you did something that showed you taking good care of yourself, taking care of business, acting responsibly, and one time when maybe—"

Mrs. Cadenza heard her voice zig high—a tiny trumpet pinching spit, like the boys' voice-cracks, which made them curse and growl more than speak, afraid of going into vocal orbit. Hers was no crack in advance of deepening. Hers sounded high and flustery with loss of nerve. What to say to Romaine? What to say to the kids on Romaine's behalf?

Last night when she couldn't sleep, thinking about Period Two, she'd pulled Gertrude Stein off the shelf, the collected works. *You either serve God or you serve Mammon*, said Gertrude, in response to her question.

"I'd like you to write about one time when you took good care of yourself, the way you'd take good care of someone you love a lot."

"Like your boyfriend?" asked Michelle, straight up and innocent, not in her usual snit.

"Like your sister or your best friend," added Mrs. Cadenza. She couldn't help herself, she looked at Romaine, her face swollen with tears and leaked-out rage and heartbeats so loud and scared you could hear them from three rows back. *Like your brother*, she didn't say.

Romaine's eyes were big as holes in a tree trunk, the kind you dropped love letters into on your way to school, the kind Tommy supposedly hid the murder weapon inside of before he tarred it shut.

"Romaine's brother is in jail until he goes on trial. He's been indicted for murder, but he's innocent until a jury finds him guilty, or they set him free. For three or four or five months, maybe longer, he's going to be in jail. It's got nothing to do with Romaine, except that she loves him, he's her brother." Mrs. Cadenza ran this through her head, thought about saying it, did say it. Her voice shook, but it was an honest shake, the kids knew this and watched, spellbound, at the possibility of tears.

Romaine needs your kindness. She needs to be a regular girl who's waiting for something terrible to happen—or be over with. She didn't say that.

Bobby rubbed his palms back and forth along his pants' legs, asked to go to the lav, returned, and rubbed more. He had Tourette's syndrome and sometimes blurted things out—obscenities, girls' body parts in the crudest language. A small, beaky kid, sharp knees and elbows, Adam's apple. He liked Romaine. With the flat of his palm, he kept rubbing his jeans, he rocked, not to blurt, not to spoil.

Romaine was writing hard:

> *I don't have a self right now to take care of, I've got a leg that's my dad, an arm that's my mom, a rest of me that belongs to Tommy so he won't die, I've gotta breathe for him, eat for him, try in school the way he couldn't. I've gotta stay alive each time the clock ticks and kids turn away and stare at their feet when I walk by, or laugh and whisper, "Freddy, Freddy"*
> *"Halloween"*
> *"Friday the Thirteenth"*
> *"Murderer."*

She looked up at Mrs. Cadenza looking at her. Kids said Mrs. C still had cancer, her hair fell out so she wore turbans, but this year she'd moved to wide cloth headbands in a million different colors, sometimes a scarf with gold or silver threads. And there was the beginning of a hopeful pelt, pink it looked like, where her skull wasn't covered up.

"You want these?" Romaine asked, stabbing a finger at her paper.

"How much more time do we have?"

"Nine thirty-eight the bell rings."

Mrs. Cadenza smiled. "You've got it down to the second." She longed to pick Romaine up and carry her safely across the dark hole of waiting, the trial, the verdict . . . But you weren't to touch kids anymore, not to pat a shoulder, not to squeeze a hand. "I want them very much," she said.

seventy-two

Dunc climbed up spikes he and his dad drove into a white pine, maybe five years ago, until he reached good climbing branches, then the platform they'd built. It was November, and the season had opened. He wanted his deer. It was the first real stir of desire he'd felt since Ivory died.

A couple of months ago, one of his friends told him that Tommy was laughing about him, Dunc, wishing he could use him, Tommy, for fish bait. *"Shove bits of my hide on the end of his hook."* Tommy'd thought that was real funny, the friend said, "like he was taunting you." Before the indictment. Now Tommy was sweating, at least there was that. He'd get convicted, Blake and him, but how much time do you think they'd serve—few years, max, Dunc guessed. They'd wake up—mid-twenties, thirty at the most—with the door of that prison swinging wide open. Their whole long lives handed back. Go anywhere. Do what you want. Make mischief. Make hay.

He liked this deer stand, right over an animal path and high up enough for a clear view through hard woods, down to the understory—moosewood, hobblebush, some blueberry and witch hazel. In the winter, the deer slept here, nestled down, you could see the blue bowl of snow their warm hides made, their droppings thick as loam.

It was cold now and still. Most leaves had already come down, ripped off by the wind. The woods were thick with them, but a few Norway maples still hung on. Yellow leaves with spring-green veins. They pleased him, those veins.

One Halloween Ivory went as a tree. Two nights ago, when the doorbell rang, he'd stayed in his room, not to see kids trick-or-treating, knocking on the storm door he'd just put up, sticking their grubby hands in the candy bowl. His mom had bought eraser-sized Snickers, and she called him whenever a new group showed up, breathing candy steam through the open door.

Ivory couldn't dress up normal—a Glo-Worm or a skeleton or a sequinned Sleeping Beauty. No, she took a plastic garbage bag and duct-taped maple leaves all over it, some oak, some birch, waxy yellows and reds. She must have been six or seven, he thought, maybe eight, he didn't exactly remember. She worked hard. Everybody laughed, she laughed, too, and kept working, poked holes for her head and arms. He'd teased her, he remembered that, still it looked pretty good, that tree, he had to admit.

Two days later, Halloween afternoon just home from school, she stood in the kitchen, holding the garbage bag by one corner, some leaves like mummies, the size of cigarettes, some powdery as the end of a Count Chocula box. Only a few stems still stuck on, lots of duct tape. Big gloms of tears shot straight out of her eyes, straight out, not down. He punched her arm, a buck-up kind of punch, not hard, then he scrounged colored paper and helped her cut out hundreds of leaves and tape them back on that bag—then she glowed, lit up with joy instead of sunlight on that dark afternoon. Right there in the kitchen, she turned into a tree.

Or maybe I didn't help, he thought—the memory singed him— and he went off, playing Hobo Jungle, freckles made of shoe polish, a bandanna on a stick over his shoulder, screw-you to the little-sister-Halloween-thing, but of course wanting the candy, and he'd said, *Tie it around your neck*, he'd said, *You can go as trash*.

Below him, rustling in the leaves. He wanted an eight-point buck. He'd not lost his taste. The older guys did, he'd heard, they didn't even pretend to shoot. It was a mystery; he couldn't wait to shoot.

Ivory'd been excited about hunting, too young for the license, though. Still, it was one thing they liked together, the held breath, the electric current through their fingertips, that kind of waiting so sharp and sweet. Now she was dead and his dad was sucking up oxygen, emphysema he'd got, the doctors said, all those smokes, made sense all the smokes, all the bitter waiting they'd done that had nothing to do with blood-desire. The eight-point buck turned out to be a squirrel, grabbing acorns. He had to laugh, but he shot anyways. At night he heard his mom crying through the wall. Mostly after work he stayed in his room or he went out, just out.

seventy-three

Usually, Nicki attended Volunteer Fire-and-Rescue meetings Wednesdays after school and once a month Saturday afternoons. Her boyfriend Martin picked her up, and often they stopped for pizza afterward. Her mom trusted her, a long haul after that alcohol-sleeping-pill combo she and Roxanne pulled, which her mom never let her forget.

But this particular Saturday in mid-November, close to Ivory's sixteenth birthday, Nicki changed her plans. She told Martin she had cramps, she told her mom Martin's car needed new brakes, could she borrow the Pinto. Scary how well she still knew how to lie. No matter. She was about something else, Ivory's business. It came over her like a flood, a muddy torrent that just swept her along.

Instead of picking up Martin, she drove for an hour to Christmas Beach without even turning the radio on. She was new to her license, she loved to drive, and yet she didn't want to be doing this. But *want*, that famished mouth she couldn't ever satisfy, for once shut up. Right now she was on a mission, a test of valor that Ivory had set her to. *Don't make me feel this, don't make me, I can't help that they shot you dead . . .*

It was grouchiness, the smart-ass voice she used at school, but it didn't matter. Still, she braked hard—tire squeals, she jolted against

the wheel just to have that for herself—then, with dread and a chur-
chy feel to her steps, she walked out onto the sand.

A few red leaves, curled tight as her newborn niece's fists, had
tumbled to the water's edge. Ivory had been in the middle of a scare.
Nicki remembered that. Ivory thought she was pregnant and it was
so exciting to each day wonder yes or no in Mrs. Cadenza's class,
reason enough to stay alive, just to know for sure.

Then Ivory died, and all those hundreds of eggs she was born
with died, too, each and every one. Nicki looked at the zigzags her
sneakers made in wet sand. The night they'd stood here together—
just her and Ivory—and the sea squirmed with green plankton,
they'd got off planet earth, they'd got off on wind and the smell of
boys across the ocean in Portugal, boys they imagined might kiss the
insides of their elbows and lick salt off their bellies, boys with sperm
galore, seeds that just kept on coming—the thrill of such production,
the careless glut, not like those few precious eggs girls roost for life.

Daylight, November, it was a different place. The wind kicked
up sand and trash along the scallop of tide. When she stepped, something crunched. She looked down, knelt down: a hank of birch bark,
curled up. She'd broken it, a tangled thing, washed down some river
into the bay, jumbled and tumbled for weeks, maybe months.

Ivory ran from Tommy and Blake. Somebody said they shot her
in the back and she lost one shoe, running so fast to escape. She ran
toward the fence, toward open pasture, foamy with light from Mosey's barn. She might have gotten away, but stuff grabbed her ankles,
her shoelace snagged on a root, she tripped over a birch log fallen
across the path. New bark tore off, soft as skin. They shot her and
her few eggs broke on the ground.

Don't make me feel this, Ivory, don't make me.

Bark washed down the river in the swollen spring, it must have
tumbled for months, then garbled up on the full moon tide. Green-
plankton fed on eggs, even dead ones. She squeezed the birch bark.
No use keeping things. Ivory made her throw it back.

What is it that you want from me?
What is it that you want?

seventy-four

From day one, Manfred Grady, editor of the *Yankee Times Weekly*—circulation five thousand—had covered Ivory's murder and its aftermath. He'd interviewed her parents, reported on the funeral, explored how her sudden death had sucker-punched her friends. Periodically he'd checked with Detective Bergeron on the progress of the investigation and noted its first- and second-year anniversaries. He covered Buzz Carbon's car-chase escapades, his capture in Florida, the extradition. Pencil cocked, Man waited outside the jail for Blake and Tommy to show up handcuffed, freshly arrested for murder. And, long after the certification hearing began, he'd sat on the same wooden bench the Towles had, outside the courtroom, incredulous they weren't allowed in.

Right then, Man had smelled a good fight. Every First Amendment bone in his body was set rattling by the district court judge's secrecy ruling, then his impoundment of the hearing transcript and all other paperwork relating to the case. Quietly he'd petitioned the court for release of documents, hoping the *Yankee* might slide into an exclusive, but no luck. Things got noisier when he hired a lawyer and sued the court on his paper's behalf.

It felt beyond him how Ray Monroe could beguile the judge to begin with—some sob story about protecting poor Blake's life from irreparable harm. *Once the pirhana-public latched onto the underbelly of his juvenile record—psychological and criminal—it would suck him dry, then there'd be two shadow-bodies, all bone, no flesh, and another family laid waste . . .*

One fact Man left out of his bylines: the alleged weekend Ivory died, his hair had turned white, overnight. Of course at the time he knew nothing of Ivory's existence, let alone fate, until kids roaming the woods discovered her remains and police detectives did their backtracking. There he was, a strapping fellow on the husky side, thirty-seven years old, over six feet tall, who suddenly began traveling under a shock of ghost-white hair. His sister Loretta believed it was simply the physical flowering of a deep, psychic cord binding him to Ivory Towle. Loretta was a schoolteacher and she'd taught Ivory second grade. She knew these things, she said. Man himself laughed at the idea, still there was some odd personal connection he couldn't dispel.

Now, overnight, it was winter. A good nor'easter had dumped three inches of rain earlier in the week, and wind stripped the Norway maples. The trees stood bare. Except for splashes of bittersweet, the world looked gray or brown, and it got dark by four-thirty. It was still November, but cold, cold. Man didn't dwell on the weather, though. He wore a short-sleeved oxford shirt, no jacket. When his office-in-an-Escort skidded on some yellow leaves blowing across the road, he simply righted the fishtail and floored it. He was driving to the courthouse, toward the story of a lifetime.

After waiting for months, he was caught up in hurdy-gurdy motion. Judge Maietta of Superior Court had just ruled in his favor, releasing the certification transcripts. The district court judge made a mistake, Maietta noted in his decision. *Our judicial system is not served by secrets. The public has a right to know what transpires at juvenile certification hearings when serious crimes such as murder are involved. Citizens need to observe legal proceedings firsthand or at least through the eyes of conscientious media reporting. It is a backbone of our legal system and should outweigh a defendant's right to keep underage matters private.*

The danger of prejudicing a jury is slight, the judge added. *People read, people forget. Careful voir-dire of prospective jurors should weed out anyone unduly transfixed by newspaper coverage, by radio or TV.*

In a moment, Man would hold the documents in his hands.

The first person he saw outside the clerk's office was Ray Monroe. They lifted their chins in greeting, even smiled and waved. Amazing this civility when you'd like to whomp the guy, but it felt sporting somehow, they were sparring partners, not enemies. "See you up there!" called Ray. He took the wide marble stairs two at a time.

But when Man reached the viewing room and requested *State vs. Thomas R. Slack and Blake Parady,* Ray was nowhere about. A huge file, over a thousand pages, he guessed, and he had to read it all in this tiny, windowless room during regular court hours. He opened his notebook, opened the file. He'd plunged deep into Buzz Carbon's testimony when the woman who'd handed him the file suddenly demanded it back. Her high heels clicked as she carried it away, her pile of teased black hair wobbled and gleamed in blue fluorescent light.

seventy-five

When the judge released the documents, Ray had immediately appealed to the New Hampshire Supreme Court, first requesting a stay on Maietta's ruling until his own appeal could be heard. He still hoped Blake's case might end up back in district court where he could be treated as a juvenile. *The people's right*—Ray scoffed at that. The people's right to cut open a kid's guts, to perform an autopsy on a living boy, then report it, scalpel stroke by scalpel stroke, in the wonderful *Yankee Weekly*.

Blake's life was teetering over a cliff, Ray knew. Like a slow-motion movie, a white 1969 Chevy Monte Carlo, axle stuck on a rocky outcrop, chassis rocking back and forth. Dust rose, smoke, the smell of burning. The least wind, the least movement from the car's lone passenger, it would plummet, hit a granite boulder below the cliff, and explode into flames. Ray was wet with sweat. Inside, next to Blake, he felt the car moving. He was outside, too, pulling the car back from the precipice. Ridiculous, one small-size man, pulling tons of steel that slipped through his fingers as if made of wax. Still, he pulled that car, his hands on the bumper, he kept pulling.

And it worked. For a moment, it worked—until Justice Sommers, her first case on the high court, upheld the lower court ruling, which meant Man Grady got the file back. Ray watched the Monte Carlo teeter, free fall, accelerate. It built up speed, wasn't that what happened, sparks flew, the gas tank exploded, flames shot up, all of it obscured by thick black smoke.

"That's only one way to look at it," Miriam told Ray. They were eating bagels around the corner from the courthouse. She felt calm, seeing a rounded picture, not his youthful all-or-nothing. "We want Blake indicted," she said, cupping her long fingers over his and giving a maternal pat, "we want him to go to trial and get acquitted, end of jeopardy, end of story."

"Otherwise," she said, "it's always there, the whispered accusation. You can't fight the wind."

seventy-six

Man read and took notes until the court closed at five. Then, in darkness, he headed home. Callie Viola Carbon: *My husband Ricky said he did it, and he wanted to screw me, dead, the way he screwed Ivory. Buzz Carbon: I never said that, the stupid secretary can't type worth shit. Toni Sparrow: Yeah, I let Tommy spend the night after he raped me, too late by then, and he was wasted.* The kids Ivory cared about, hung out with. . . . Yellow leaves blown onto the road, causing skids, causing accidents or flattened under tires.

Loretta said Ivory was a quiet child in second grade, except every once in a while she'd get wild and laugh until she peed her pants. Big brown eyes, chapped lips, chewed hair. But of all the girls, she was chosen bathroom buddy for a classmate who was crippled. They'd lope down the hall together and end up racing, Ivory running backwards to make crutches fair. In the bathroom stall, Ivory unbuttoned her friend's pants, unzipped them, waited, then zipped the pants back up. Of course newspapers had no room for small remembrances like that, not even in obituaries.

He had goosebumps it was so cold, but the heater was on the fritz. He'd read too long. Seemed like every single oncoming car had turned on its brights, selfish bastards couldn't dim and his eyes smarted. He'd go to the office and bang out stories all night. *First*

Amendment Rights Triumph! The whole front page, minimum. He felt delighted; he'd won, the people had won. A light snow began to fall. Suddenly, the road was slick with ice, and glassy leaves blazed up yellow in his brights.

Tomorrow was Thanksgiving. Loretta had invited him over, he went every year. He'd never had kids, never had a wife, not even a pregnant girlfriend. Lucky thing.

We set a place for her, Thanksgiving, Christmas, Florence Towle said the first time he'd interviewed her. When he knocked, she'd invited him in. They sat at the Formica kitchen table, he in the chair closest to the door, looking out a small window at a bird feeder nailed onto the branch of a cherry. She showed him the special placemats, indicating his was the spot where Ivory's empty place would be. Mugs of instant coffee, a saucerful of Hydrox cookies. She smoked.

Thanksgiving, she said, *I always fix celery stuffed with cream cheese. She liked it so much she'd take 'em all and lick the cream cheese out if I didn't keep my eye cocked.*

No room for something small and plain and painful as that.

seventy-seven

As usual, Tommy sat next to his buddy Orin at breakfast. Tommy hardly ate—puke-eggs, flabby toast—he had no appetite. His trial was coming up in another week. Orin scooped everything off his own tray, then Tommy's, and shoveled it down. A good pair, him and Orin. Amazing, that guy, gut of steel. He swiped the Machete clean of crumbs, rubbed it with his napkin until every little hair shined. He was a finnicky fellow except for what he ate.

"Won't believe what Blake's got himself now," Orin was saying.

Tommy knew he needed to nod, at least, grunt, something, or else Orin wouldn't spill the beans—he was sensitive about not getting listened to. "So what's he got?"

"Computer. His own private hooked-up computer and this lady comes and tutors him. Paid for by your tax dollars." Orin played a drum riff with his forefingers on the edge of the table, then glanced at Tommy. "Bet that sits good."

Later, in his cell, Tommy had plenty of time to let the computer get under his skin. About five months of things like that under his skin. He was crawling with stuff, one big oozy sore. He'd not laid eyes on Blake since the certification hearing. Not once. Blake sat over in the women's section, screwing everybody, fancy brought-in food, now a computer, his own teacher.

Even not eating, Tommy was a beefy guy, but Orin had worked on him enough he knew just how small a potato he really was. Blake's lawyers were ready to sell his soul, to send him up for three lifetimes if it meant getting Blake off. *You gotta pick who you trust.*

He walked his cell until he made himself dizzy. Still, he walked, fist opening and closing in time to his steps. Smart enough not to smash the bars like some other guy had and broke his hand. Stupid, but not that stupid. His thoughts tumbled, angry waves that wouldn't break clear. He was stuck in a cage. Next week, a jury was gonna wolf down lies. They'd lock him up for the rest of his life, for three lifetimes, no chance of parole. But it was Blake, not him.

You gotta pick who you trust.

Orin said he could save himself, just telling the truth. Simple. Nobody selling nobody. You'd just gotta tell the truth of what you remembered, what you saw, what you heard. Davis, his so-called lawyer, had whispered to Blake's lawyers, they all laughed—that's what he'd seen. Blake getting all the goodies—that's what he'd heard. What he hadn't heard was anybody standing up at the hearing and saying, *That Tommy Slack, what a great guy.*

Instead, some teacher he hardly knew had told how the stuff they were doing in English was maybe sinking into his thick skull, maybe not, some other teacher called him a burnout. It all went for Blake— the parole officer, the basketball coach, Mr. Cook. His own mother so ashamed she'd hung her head, hadn't cared that her hairdo spilled all to hell, right there in front of strangers, that she'd sobbed too loud.

He paced, he paced, thoughts tumbling, memories of that steamy day, it all erupted through his skin and he screamed for a guard, he had something to say. He was screaming, but his voice sounded so quiet the guard asked him to talk up so he could record the statement. All about Blake taking his dirt bike while he slept in the tent, riding Ivory into the woods and shooting her dead, then waking him up to tell him the news. On the happy side of glee, Blake had been. That's how he remembered it now.

seventy-eight

When Bill Davis received the sheriff's call, he walked to the jail from his office through sleet that bounced off his overcoat and melted in his hair. In the elevator to the basement cells, feeling blistery hot with rage and sweat, he shucked his coat and his suit jacket, then yanked his red tie loose.

Tommy was waiting for him, heavy as a stone at the table in the interview room. The place stank of bad cafeteria food.

"Thanks for wasting my time," Bill said.

Tommy's thick neck and shoulders tightened, but otherwise he sat inert, stolid, his red hair matted and dull.

"Jesus Mary Mother of God, you gonna cook up a third story for the jury? You said, *Oh, yeah, Blake and I don't know anything, we're innocent, both of us, I swear it's the truth.* . . . I figured from the beginning you must be bullshitting me, but I—"

Suddenly, he just stopped, and the gale of words storming his head went quiet. Fury dropped to despair at the lump of life he saw before him, a kid probably so stoned or high or zoned or fucked-up at the time he had no recollection whatsoever of that Sunday afternoon. And he probably had shot that girl. Drunkard, doper, bullshit artist—why'd you even expect he'd remember, Bill asked himself. He sat down at the gray metal table opposite his client. He was exhausted. His face dried. His shirt, runny with sweat, felt cold as the shroud.

"That is what happened, Blake did it." For a big guy, Tommy's voice whined, mosquito-pitched in self-pity.

You're one sad fuck, Bill thought. "The minute the judge finds a new lawyer, I'm off your case," he said. He put his gray suitcoat back on, buttoned it, his navy blue overcoat, buttoned that, the cashmere scarf. In spite of the layers, he was still cold. Something in him wanted to slug Tommy, to make it clean; instead, he extended his hand and wished him luck. He felt burned, yet chilled to the bone.

Back in his cell, Tommy got the shakes. He hated Davis, but his trial started in a week, no lawyer. Three consecutive lifetimes. He wrapped his hands around the cell bars and squeezed them to steady himself. Once Orin told him about the guy who'd tried to rip apart this very cell, ended up bloody and knocked out, one steel bar with a little bitty dent. *He went berserk*, Orin said, *fear-of-being-locked-up, claustro-something, straightjacket, loony bin*. The other guys had sat around and laughed.

Don't forget to breathe, Orin said. Tommy breathed. Enough to stay alive until Orin got back from the library. Then, at dinner, letting Orin know what he'd done, his statement to the guard, the way he'd fired his lawyer, he felt what Orin told him he ought to feel: pride.

"They'll get you somebody better, somebody who'll stick Blake where he deserves to get stuck." And for the first time in four meals, Tommy ate.

seventy-nine

A few days later, two weeks from Christmas, Florence walked the aisles at True Value hardware, hoping something might jump off the shelf to please Duncan, who was still home in his recliner. In late November, he'd had to go into the hospital, steroids for his emphysema, and oxygen too. He wasn't death-pale anymore, but so shrunk and quiet it scared her. Ten days in the hospital, ten thousand dollars, and his work was nickel-and-diming them about insurance payments. When he talked at all, it was about that, and locking Tommy up forever—that was one good thing. Duncan couldn't go to the trial, he was too weak, but still. *Make those two boys pay.*

Hurry, she told herself, Dunc Jr.'s waiting out in the parking lot. He drove her to the mill, somebody there brought her home. A real imposition, especially with winter coming on. Hard without Duncan in the driver's seat.

There. A nifty window scraper with a chrome handle found its way into her hand. Duncan might like that. $4.99. She was heading toward the counter to pay when Sally Gregg came up a side aisle and put a hand on her shoulder. Her hair cut chin length, some nice style. Must be off-duty in a pretty checked wool coat.

"Hello, Florence," Sally said, "Did you hear the trial got postponed?"

Florence shook her head. Nobody had called.

"Tommy and his lawyer had some problem, he's off the case now. The judge assigned him a new lawyer, and she's asked to have the trial postponed so she's got time to prepare. More waiting. Somebody should have called you. I'm sorry."

"Nobody calls," Florence says. "What kind of lawyer is she?"

"Ingrid Salzman's her name. Just moved back here from New York. She was a prosecutor there after law school—I think a prosecutor. I've heard she's pretty good—it's her first murder defense, though, and she's no match for Sid Moravian."

"When?"

"Springtime probably. I'll call you." Sally hesitated, seeing the scraper in Florence's hand. "How's Duncan?"

"Gettin' over one of his bouts, but he's doing good."

"Your third Christmas and still no trial." Sally understood. Her dark eyes understood.

"Thank you," Florence said. "You have yourself a good holiday."

Dunc Jr. dropped her at home, then he went off. Duncan was asleep, see-through plastic tubing running up his nose, hands twitching on the arms of the recliner. He'd not opened the mail, which sat beside his water glass—a couple of bills, a Christmas card. Florence fixed herself a cup of instant coffee and opened the card. Pretty crèche scene, snowy boughs, some drifts, but with a cozy feel from the halo light. Inside, a school picture of some big grown boy. An acquaintance had sent it, not a friend exactly, somebody she used to sit near when she'd gone to the Baptist church years ago.

This lady, Corinne, had a baby four and a half months premature. They'd kept him in an incubator for almost a year and named him Willy Hope—Hope for a middle name since they figured he'd die. That's what the preacher had said and asked them to send prayers up like the wings of doves, straight into God's kindly embrace. Florence had prayed for Willy Hope. His foot tiny as the pad of a child's pinkie finger. She hadn't seen him at the hospital, not knowing the family to speak of, but she prayed.

God paid attention to those wings of doves—all that clatter, the feel of the wind as they'd flocked around Him—He listened. Now Willy Hope wore size 12 shoes. Corinne had written that on the back of his picture. A big boy, the usual growing pains. Looking at his face, goofy smile, crooked, friendly teeth, Florence wished she had one of Ivory's baby teeth or a lock of her hair. She hadn't thought to keep things then, not naturally of a saving mind.

Ivory was the family magpie. They said magpies steal bright things. Florence's mother had sworn she'd left a pair of rhinestone earrings on the kitchen counter, middle of summer, windows open, and a magpie'd flown in and carried those earrings off, one at a time, to decorate its nest. But their brains couldn't possibly be big enough, Florence thought, for them to love the way sun shined off glass. A magpie's brain was just plain too small—the size of Willy Hope's new-born foot.

Yes, Ivory kept everything. Duncan used to get after her about the mess—little feathers, bright stones, crushed flowers if that boy-friend's hand had happened to touch them.

Afterward, she and Duncan couldn't bear seeing Ivory's magpie things, so Dunc Jr. had cleared them out. It hadn't occurred to her to send them over to church after what happened. She believed in God and didn't blame Him, but she'd stopped sending up prayers.

I wish I had a lock of her hair, Florence said to herself, stirring her coffee into a whirlpool. She'd stopped thinking about Ivory every minute. She could work and eat and they'd taken drives, her and Duncan—before the latest trouble—and even when they visited the cemetery, she didn't always dwell on things. No use doing that. Third Christmas with Ivory gone.

But she wished she had a lock of hair, so she could remember the color, the sound of its staticky crackle when she'd brushed it hard, the smell. Ivory'd kept a cat tooth. Fuzzface went around for two days with his bottom fang-y tooth sticking out straight. Ivory used her babysitting money to take that stupid cat to the vet's. Bad teeth, the vet said. That's the poor thing's inheritance. Bad teeth. Ivory cried. But the vet said, *You'd be surprised what cats can eat without any teeth at all.*

Florence didn't have that cat tooth or Ivory's baby teeth or even a snip of hair. You forgot, if you could believe it. You forgot. The state medical fellow had known it was her from her teeth: perfect teeth, except one little filling. Florence had never imagined she'd die. If she'd had to worry from the beginning like Willy Hope's mom with one chance in ten, she'd have made Duncan name her Hope or Faith. Her hair was brown. Her eyes were brown. She was an average kid.

I wish, Florence thought, holding Willy Hope's picture, *I wish I remembered the sweaty feel of her head, heavy in my lap.* When she was born, her feet were big as tulips right before they open.

eighty

In early February, after a week of gray skies, the clouds blew off to the east. Bright sunshine at last. It actually felt warm when you stuck your face into it, which Manfred Grady stopped to do outside Hair Off the Square, around the corner from the *Yankee Times Weekly* office. *Since the winter solstice we've gained sixty-four minutes of daylight*, he'd heard on the radio that morning. Weather facts, pretty satisfying things this time of year. Hopeful or apocalyptic, there was nothing like records broken or tied. Man's just-trimmed white hair glowed as he lingered, chin lifted, eyes closed. Every inch of him glowed from the warmth of the sun. Then, regretfully, he opened the *Yankee Times'* door and forced himself inside.

Overhead, Miss Linda's Academy of Tap and the Balletic Arts—the *shoop, shoop* of too-young toe dancers, Mrs. Provencher's arhythmic piano rendition of "Slaughter on 10th Avenue" for over-the-hill Rockettes—sounds he'd typed in time to his whole career, from beloved Correcting Selectric II to his current PC. Come June, after the spring recital, Miss Linda would close up shop for good. Forty-three years. The flu had hit Miss Linda and her pupils hard. In fact, it had hit everybody hard, including the *Yankee Times'* self-styled "arts and entertainment correspondent," which was why the job of interviewing Miss Linda had fallen to Man himself.

Because of the sun, he felt spasms of unseasonal spring fever and he just couldn't sit down yet to wrestle a feature story from his notes. Still fidgety, he glanced at his mail. Promos, bills, one square white envelope, addressed in large, childish handwriting: Editor, % *Hearld Times World*, return address some apartment number in Danbury, Connecticut. Amazing it had been delivered. But since he was the only editor of the only paper in town, maybe not so amazing. Inside, printed in pencil on wide-lined composition paper, was a letter in the same labored hand as the envelope.

Dear Sir:

Two and one half years ago, July 19th, Gerald Homberg and me arrived at your State Prison. We were, (still are) federal prisoners.

This past September U.S. Marshals came to that Prison and brought us to USP Danbury, CT . . . In your State, I celled right next to Buzz Carbon! He was in cell #5. I was in cell #6!

Buzz Carbon told me several times at that prison that those two teenage boys didn't kill that fourteen (14) year old Toll girl!

Buzz told me by word of mouth, by notes we'd right each other, and in front of Gerald Homberg that his brother, (I believe Richard), Richard Carbon killed that girl! . . .

Buzz stated he grew up with them and that they had everything, and the Toll girl was in love with one of the teen age boys and that he hated them, (he was very jealous of them!!)

Buzz told Gerald and me his brother killed the girl while out walking in the woods and after Richard killed her he, (Richard) took off for Florida.

Gerald and me both done a lot of prison time, but we decided back in December to contact someone about this matter because we'd hate to know that two innocent teenagers could be found guilty for something they didn't do!

Buzz had escaped from the min faculty, got into more crime and is now trying to hang these two teenagers for murder so he can receive a lighter sentence!!

The other kid who escaped with Buzz supposedly killed himself with a shotgun, and Buzz can't be connected with that death—Buzz said he has to good of a alibi, (story to cover it).

Buzz didn't state he actually killed his escape partner, but he sure gave the impression he done it and covered it up real good.

But Buzz did state to me and Homberg that his brother did kill that girl!?

Your's truely,
Borden Casparius 87132-111

Man cackled. The newspaper editor part of him, who'd yearned for an exclusive, publishing the certification hearing transcripts first, out-and-out cackled and said, "Punch-and-Judy theater, print it" . . . But another self chimed in. The loosey-goosey cosmic one whose hair had turned white the weekend Ivory Towle disappeared and who felt some private, painful stake in her murder. That part told him, "Send it to Ray Monroe." Maybe it wasn't those two boys after all. It had to be, everything pointed that way, but maybe not. Buzz Carbon, sure, maybe he killed her, or that brother of his, Ricky, who'd tried to strangle his little wife Callie and nec-romance her the way he had Ivory.

Well, Man decided, he couldn't publish the letter anyway. He'd need to check authenticity, contact the Feds. Could be somebody's idea of a prank. He grabbed the phone and got hold of Ray. "Man Grady, *Yankee Times Weekly*," he said. "I'm sending you a letter. Something to do with the Ivory Towle murder. You're gonna love it."

When asked for specifics, Man smiled at the young lawyer on the other end of the line. More comrade than adversary, still there was friction. But Ray was someone who also burned to get whoever killed the girl, provided it wasn't his boy Blake. "Trust the U.S. postal system, my friend," he said.

Before sending Ray the letter from Borden Casparius, 87132-111, Man made a photocopy and wondered what Borden and his buddy were up for—drugs, rape, murder? When he finally did sit down with his morning's interview notes, every sentence he wrote ended with an exclamation point.

Long after the promising February sun set, Man kept working. The temperature plunged to single numbers before he was satisfied with the job he'd done on Miss Linda's life.

eighty-one

Man was right: Ray Monroe did love the letter, so did Blake when he heard about it, and Tommy. Soon after he ratted on his friend, Tommy recanted the statement he'd given, bullied and unnaturally influenced by that older weasel Orin, his new lawyer Ingrid said. Their futures would spring from the same root, Blake's and Tommy's, no matter how they diverged aboveground. Ray and Ingrid sought permission to take affidavits from Borden Casparius and his buddy Gerald at Danbury and planned to bring them up to testify at Tommy's trial. Fingering somebody else—namely one or both of the Carbon boys—figured large in his defense.

Tommy's trial was scheduled for mid-May. Blake's, who knew? Ray was still trying to release him on bail and move his trial back to District Court. It all took time. Which was good. But Blake was rotting in jail. He'd missed basketball season—he would have been j.v. captain—he'd missed making money working for Mr. Cook. He'd be driving heavy machinery by now. July was another lifetime.

Ivory Towle.

Sometimes Blake said her name out loud, just to remember, to make sense of why he was here, in the women's section of county jail. But mostly he tried not to think. He'd never been what you'd call an observer. Always he'd wanted to move—run fast, drive fast.

Now he couldn't, not big movements anyways, only pathetic, hamster-on-a-wheel stuff. Jumping rope, push-ups, he did those, things you repeated in place.

February, March. April visited him when her dad allowed it, every week or so, not on a weekday, Saturday afternoon. She brought news of high school, the greenhouse, the seasons. Inside, you didn't know time of day or night, let alone temperature, the feel of air, wind, rain. He missed weather. Once when she came, her hair was wet with sparkles and she smelled like snow. Without even closing his eyes, he imagined snow-blowing the long driveway for her dad— the powdery cloud kicked up, showers of white light, so different from the storm of dust when the sheriff's cruiser had picked him up.

Dot, one of the inmates, her husband over at the max, she said he sold knickknacks he made out of wood at the prison gift shop— jewelry boxes, lazy susans, blocks of cedar you gouged the word *mental* into and people used them for paper weights. Folks in jail were supposed to like crafts, that was what Dot said. *Takes your mind off. Rehabilitates you so you return to society all freshened up, you know, make a fortune huckstering mental blocks. It's your constitutional right to learn crafts in the can,* she said, *besides, you're just a kid, treat ya with kid gloves.*

She laughed, she had a wicked smoker's laugh. They'd made it together a couple of times. Dot was runty and practically middle-aged but she always managed to smell good, he thanked her for that.

The lady-cons liked to mother him and talk about their kids back home. He'd had all kinds of offers—extra desserts, hair combing, home-made tattoos. He'd considered *April* on his hand but Ray nixed that idea. His stutter was sexy, they told him, and they helped with homework when the tutor left. Once, Dot got hold of a tabloid newspaper and read some article about Cher out loud, that was where they got the expression *boy toy* they thought was so adorable.

One of the hookers cried on her son's birthday. *About your age,* she said. He let them fawn over him, tease and fool around, but he knew this: It was no big deal, it just felt good to forget where he was, how his life had gone up-in-smoke.

You couldn't hate them—a bunch of hard-lucks slinging *cute* around more than any other four-letter word. They came and went, the drunks, they cried the most, but there was one up for murder, her and her boyfriend killed the ex-husband, she said, *I done it and glad too*, but when it came to her five kids, she was mush. They got to see TV, one of those nature shows, female chimpanzees picking lice off each other's hairy heads. That was what they were like, the way Ivory used to be, always picking at him, but it didn't make him mad, it seemed more a comfort, since he couldn't by a long shot touch April.

April loved him. She said it every time she visited. It still felt like a miracle. No surprise the ladies got all wound up about April's birthday present. They were really into this romance. *Make her something, write her a song, girls love that, don't have to be good, just so you done it yourself.* They were full of sugar-sugar crapola on his behalf. *Geez, Blakey . . . Her pop must keep a close watch on her—I don't think I ever was that innocent-looking, even the day I was born . . .*

But underneath, some kind of wistfulness showed through. No one talked about Ivory, if he'd done it or not, who she was, what he knew. She was dead. It was only them now, but not real contenders, there was April and the chance at courtship.

His tutor Erica said, *Write a poem, I'll give you English credit. How about one using the letters of her name down the left-hand side of the page?* A clever trick he'd never heard before. *You know, like A is for A wonderful girl . . . P for so Pretty I can't hardly believe my eyes . . .* Erica found soft copper sheeting the color of April's hair and he tapped her name, letters like Michelin tire-babies, Dot said. In return for a tumble, one of the guards bought him tape and wrapping paper. His poem got copied on a homemade card.

April was bowled over by the gift. She got telling him about the junior prom, a month away.

"W-wanna g-go with me?" he asked, seat-of-his-pants.

"You'll still be here, won't you?"

"M-maybe R-Ray can g-get me out, j-just for th-that night."

Crazy, sure, but suddenly it was something he wanted more than anything he'd ever wanted before. Who gave a bloody fuck about a prom until the possibility got stolen right out of your hands? And holding April, feeling her up, her in a low-cut pink dress, smelling tropical and outdoors . . . He'd talk to Ray.

Some catcalls and rude remarks, but mostly the lady-cons melted. "The closest I got to *prom* is *romp*," said Dot, who'd turned dyslexia into an advantage she was that smart, Jumble Queen, they called her, crosswords, Crypto-Quip. Even did algebra in her head. She'd dropped out of eighth grade with her first kid, but her brains wouldn't shut up, she said, sounding almost regretful.

Prom. Another four-letter word the women latched on to. The idea—right out of some fairytale, like *castle* or *soufflé* . . .

If Dot was the second-smartest person Blake had ever met, that made Ray the smartest. *Hang on, keep your schoolwork up, keep your grades cool. You'll graduate with your class.* He'd be a good coach, he had the hubba-hubba down, not making it sound like b.s.

You'll graduate with your class, he kept saying, an impossible thing, Mr. Cook, too, and then this wacko idea about the junior prom. Here he was, in jail awaiting trial for murder, and he was supposed to rent a tux and get April carnations and figure out a ride—It wasn't his old crowd, it was her friends, college-track. The way he imagined it going down: He'd be like some celebrity with a contagious disease—you couldn't take your eyes off him, but you didn't want him breathing on your mucus membranes. He still wanted it, wanted her.

April Cook.

He longed to say her name and not stumble.

eighty-two

Ingrid Salzman, Tommy's new lawyer—he didn't think of her as a woman. She was taller than him—thick arms, a good corded neck, beefy shoulders—she looked like the Statue of Liberty, that solid and strong. She dressed in red, white, and blue—dark blue suit, white blouse with a collar that opened into layers of floppy stuff, foamy as the tide at Christmas Beach, but all up around her neck, not down by her boobs. "The Star-Spangled Banner" scratched at his skull.

No, you couldn't come on to Ingrid—he'd not dare hold that idea in a closed fist for more than a second. Tough even shaking her hand the first time. She'd squeezed hard but not mean, hard the way you did when you liked what you squeezed and you had faith.

Ingrid believed him. She knew he hadn't shot Ivory Towle that steamy July day. She didn't have to take notes, her mind was a tape recorder. She listened.

Not the kind of a woman he was used to—there was the frou-frou blouse, though, and that rose pin she wore on the lapel of her man's suit. A blooming rose, painted red. When they shook hands, he saw it was china, the kind his mom might wear, a pretty open-hearted china rose.

"Ivory was bullshit at Blake for leavin' her so long at Stan's," he told Ingrid. "And her with her monthly and all." It embarrassed him, talking about a girl's period in front of Ingrid, but it bounced right off her. "When Blake got her quieted down, we rode outta Stan's, takin' one of the trails toward her house. But after 'bout a mile she starts yellin' again and she leans so far I gotta pull over and stop. She said she'd rather hitch than feel Blake's dirty hands all over her. That's just what she said."

Ingrid nodded, and her eyes dug right into him.

"After a while she started crying and saying how she felt sick and we all got back on my bike and we rode a little more, then she yelled at me to stop again, so I did. And she just walked off, along one of the paths. So we left her."

"Was she heading toward her house?"

"I don't know. It's kinda messed up in my head. I was so stoned I fell asleep in the tent out back of Blake's and when I woke up, nobody was there. Later that night me and Blake hooked up again and he said he didn't know where she was. I never seen her after that day, I looked, too."

"What time was it—when you woke up in the tent?"

"About suppertime, I'd say. I was hungry, I remember that, and I rode my bike home."

Ingrid was a demon for details, that's what she called herself. She demanded every drop of his memory, which skidded and skipped over the very details she loved—names of roads, names of people, exact times and dates. He was missing whole hours, whole days, it seemed. It made her mad and she said so, but not accusing him the way Bill Davis had. She just let him know it wasn't good enough.

"How the fuck am I supposed to—"

"Clean it up, Tommy. You need to be so squeaky clean the jury could eat right off you."

She said stuff like that, socko-in-your-face like Melody'd never said. And things to his sister you wouldn't believe. Ingrid hired a private detective to follow his family, especially Romaine, it turned out.

"Forget the dope and cigarettes behind Gil's Variety after school," she said. "It's cheap and risky, and it could hurt your brother's case. Besides, it's beneath you. And lose those lowlifes you've been hanging out with."

Romaine's cheeks had blazed up like volcanoes and she'd looked about to cry, but she hadn't—the first time in all of her nine months of jail visits she hadn't. Later his dad said, "That lawyer is one tough lady"—but there was respect. Tommy was innocent: Ingrid believed that. She told him Orin was no real friend, stop telling yourself he cared one iota about your welfare. You're okay now, she said, tough, soft. A jury could like you, she made him think.

After Ingrid took his case, he was still locked up, everything the same. Guys with a hair across their ass at breakfast slugged each other over somebody passing ketchup. Once or twice a day, he still got panicky. He gulped, helpless before the terrors that flooded his cell. He still dreamed of sharp things, very sharp things that hurt, but then Ingrid would be waiting at the visitor's table, a gray suit this time. Her shoulders kept getting wider, but that china rose was still stuck on her jacket, the one womanly business she tolerated. And he thought maybe she wore it for him. A little tricky close-up thing between them—he didn't mean on-the-make—something that was both a promise and a pledge.

She wouldn't let him die in prison. The prosecutors, they wanted him up for a lifetime, maybe three lifetimes one after the other, not all at once. Ingrid wouldn't let Romaine smoke dope behind Gil's, either. It just wasn't allowed, by order of God. That's how Statue-of-Liberty-important Ingrid was. She'd make the jury understand it hadn't been him shot poor Ivory Towle.

He'd have *protected* Ivory if he'd known somebody wanted to kill her. In fact, he'd have wasted no-matter-who on her behalf . . . He remembered her hands that last time she rode behind him on his motorbike, how her fingers couldn't quite reach around to lace up his middle, just lightly pressed his sides. It meant something.

Ingrid understood that little bit of the story. The china rose on her chest was enough to let him know something was there, some man–woman thing, but he wouldn't dare breathe enough to ruffle those rose petals if they were real, for fear of spoiling whatever that hopeful thing might be.

eighty-three

It was raining, time to get up for school, but Pammy stayed plumped against the pillows on her single bed. Her mom promised a queen-size mattress if she kept up her grades. For now, though, Algebra was slipping through her fingers, the way letters of the alphabet did in computer keyboarding class. A single bed seemed fine. The spread definitely wasn't, a machine quilted thing that smelled like bad breath, and it was a gross peach color, no longer her heart's desire, though just what was she didn't know for sure anymore.

She still wrote poems, she loved that, needed to, and folded them up small inside the back cover of the yearbook dedicated to Ivory, behind Ivory's drawing of a Mustang, the car not the horse. She slipped the yearbook off the shelf; it opened naturally to the dedication page, to Ivory's picture with the perfect flippy-flip hair: *For Ivory Towle*, and Joey's poem about rainbows and angels that had inspired her so much she wrote something that sounded like Ivory talking to her from a rainbow's highest arch. Writing that and showing it to Mrs. Cadenza, Pammy had forgotten just how empty of talents she used to be.

She closed the cover. It sounded final, the way Ivory's death felt, over and over, but each new time hurtful and raw. In that photo, Ivory's hair was out of style—Ivory, who'd set so much store by her skinny bones and bangs that flipped up, against hair's very nature. Nobody wore their hair like that anymore. People who died couldn't ever be up on things again.

The last time she'd seen Ivory, she was walking along the road, gym bag swinging on her hip. She'd just washed and blow-dried her hair for the second time in two hours. Pammy herself was riding her bike fast in the opposite direction, toward home, water flying off her tires from the downpour earlier that night. She'd felt like whooping and maybe she had, but before the road angled off, she braked, skidded a bit, looked over her shoulder, and waved. Ivory waved back. Her bangs still curled up, dark and shiny in the single streetlight, in spite of raindrops hanging in the air, in spite of splashes from the pines along the road. Pammy's braids had thumped heavily against her back, more like ropes of kelp than hair.

The summer Ivory died, Pammy had barely even dreamed of boyfriends. She'd worn baggy sweatshirts and biked for pure joy. Now she had Anthony. But today it wasn't what she'd hoped. Anthony hated her prom dress, though he'd never even seen it. He'd forbid her wearing it or he'd stomp on her corsage and yell out loud in church that she was a harlot.

A fake black velvet number, long, to the ankles, with a slit practically up to her butt, tight and low-cut, and she knew her breasts looked great. Everybody in the store had said so without exactly saying so. *Pizzazz-plus* was what the saleslady had called it. She felt beautiful, and her mom had volunteered to pay half, then cried for rapture and the sorrow of a daughter grown, she said. Ivory would have loved the whole shebang—the black heels with lots of toe cleavage, the bead handbag her grandma bought her, the dress itself.

Last night, Anthony made her tell him just how much of her chest would show, and afterward he went crazy. She'd hoped a boyfriend would take her to pit parties, they'd drink and kiss and make out on the hood of somebody's car while they kept an eye out for shooting stars. Anthony said wanting that was trashy. He cared about her soul. *He* was waiting till marriage, but he wondered about *her*.

Ivory would understand heart's desire, body's desire. She'd never talked to Pammy about sex, but she let it be known without words that she and Blake made it, and for Ivory it hadn't been put on, it was real. So it wasn't wrong, Pammy felt that in the murky pond of her guts, and she wrote poems about love although that wasn't exactly it, either. Kids in Mrs. Cadenza's class laughed at the sexy-science words, but Pammy didn't know any others.

Ivory was at the store, and Pammy twirled in the black velvet prom dress.

"God, you look gorgeous. If I was a guy . . ." Ivory preened Pammy's hip as if smoothing feathers. And then she whispered, "Dump him."

But that morning, sitting on her single bed and late for school, Pammy didn't dare. She'd take the dress back. But maybe not. She could keep it and not go to the prom. She could take it out and spin in the mirror. In that low-cut dream she was beautiful and so full of talents she could just steam-roll Anthony-the-homo, she could buy herself a corsage of white roses and spin herself into joy on the Elks' Club dance floor. And early the next morning, instead of sleeping with her arm under Anthony's sweet blond curls, she could take Ivory the flowers.

eighty-four

It was early May, the weekend before jury selection began, and all over the state temperatures topped sixty-five, bright sun, warm soil, at least the top half-inch. Sid Moravian, who was still prosecuting *State vs. Thomas R. Slack*, in spite of defense changes and delays, felt he ought to be immersing himself one last time in the overwhelming facts of Tommy's guilt; instead, he'd been plunged into domestic catastrophe. He and Evelyn had agreed to take care of their eight-month-old granddaughter, Renata. Mack, his son, and Vanda the Soprano needed to get away. And Vanda was giving her first per-formance since Renata was born. Good excuse.

He admitted his relations with Vanda had gotten off on the wrong foot. But she was bleach on his burns the way she laid a fortune out for makeup and nails, wore rubber gloves to rinse out a glass, you name it. And *Moravian* wasn't good enough for her; she'd hung on to *Bell*, another sore point. She might be a fine singer, she just wasn't much of a wife from what he saw, which was exactly nothing, Evelyn reminded him.

But visiting on the maternity ward, he'd pushed that aside. Vanda had looked different, big pores, lines in her forehead from the effort, even to a guy who saw exactly nothing she looked different, like some grateful survivor—as if her plane had landed out of a blizzard into the Everglades, and she'd just slid down the emergency slide, that same look of trauma, but underneath, pleasure upon arrival. He'd lost his head, leaned down and kissed her forehead. Her lips quivered, had to be hormones, the smell of soap and iodine, the unexpected loamy heat of new animal life: Renata Bell-Moravian.

Later, the moment had flared out—Vanda didn't like nursing, Mack mothered too much—eight months later, Vanda had a recital and they dumped Renata off, a baby named for an opera singer . . . Still, it should have been okay. Evelyn couldn't wait. When it came to a grandchild, it was the Evelyn Show, she kept telling him. But two hours into it, she took sick. Terrible pains down below—some kind of female ill he wouldn't dare argue against.

On his watch, in the hours between supper and bedtime, Renata wrestled the cat over crunchy Friskies, then sat in the water dish. Later, she scooted away from a clean Pampers and peed on the beige rug before he caught her. A little diarrhea, another diaper, more pee, spaghetti sauce on her soft spot—but when the phone rang and he heard Mack's voice, calling new-dad nervous from the lobby of a Baltimore recital hall, he said, "Nope, no problem."

At that moment he had Renata wedged against him in the maroon recliner. She was sucking down a bottle like you wouldn't believe. "She's sucking down a bottle like you wouldn't believe," he told Mack. "She's just about ready to walk, it might happen tomorrow. No, your mother's fine. Don't worry. Listen," he added, high excitement, "Renata's one hell of a coordinated kid—eyes in the back of her head. I tested her peripheral vision today. She practically goes three-sixty. A climber, too. You should see her."

"I have, Dad."

Renata was a milky loaf at his hip, but already she was squirming, eager to shoot out of the chair. She laughed her rascal's belly laugh. Ready, Go.

"Eight months," he said to Mack, holding Renata back with one hand, feeling soft stomach and ribs. "Eight months, I can't believe it. You know, they've got basketball scholarships for girls." He wouldn't have dared say that in front of Evelyn, who would have hooted. But she was upstairs, asleep under a heating pad.

"Mmm," said Mack. Sid pictured him rolling his eyes at Vanda, who'd probably just bought Renata a baby-size violin, the way they did nowadays.

"Hope it's not too much for you and Mom. Don't you have some big trial coming up?"

"Just jury selection."

Crackling on the line, Mack disappeared. He and Renata were safe. She was his girl, the way Mack had never been his boy but Evelyn's. Later, she pooped again, they tangled, he won, she was snapped into her pj's more or less on the mark. She made significant eye contact and laughed, knowing it was him, Grampy, then fell asleep in the porta-crib, set up in his study.

He ought to pull out the Ivory Towle file, but he felt exhausted. For an hour or two he dozed next to Evelyn, then started awake, plagued by disturbing thoughts. "Ev-" he shook her shoulder, "—babies—are they supposed to sleep on their fronts or backs?" Crib death, he was thinking. "What was it that happened to Sally's baby?"

Evelyn groaned.

"Sally Gregg, the baby that died. Was it sleeping on its back or front?"

"Mack slept on his tummy and he survived."

Sid stood above the crib, carrying a flashlight pointed at Renata's diaper bag, not to wake her. He watched. Soon his hips and knees and hands ached. His law school nickname Boneman seemed prophetic. Strange how arthritis turned you to bone. He drew the chair over from his desk and sat beside her. She lay on her back, head toward him. Breathing beautifully—a natural athlete, economy of motion. But he beamed the light at her chest, just to make sure. You don't see, Evelyn told him. Sometimes he saw. Now he saw. Renata's eyelashes cast shadows on her cheek, which glistened with streaks like dried snail trails where he'd swiped her nose. Through the open window, the smell of soil.

Reluctantly he got the state police file off his desk, sat down again, rigging the flashlight so it lit the page, not anywhere near Renata's face. He scanned statements from Tommy Slack, from Ivory Towle's friends, witnesses who'd seen her that last afternoon, the crime scene, where Sally had kept vigil until daybreak.

The body is badly decomposed and appears to be that of a young girl, he read.

He lay the file down, open, on the floor. Softly, thumb moistened with spit, he rubbed the shiny trails on Renata's cheek.

eight-five

*T*ommy *waits for the motorbike in the clearing. Late July, early evening, and sunlight splashes the crown of birches. These woods have been logged before and before that. The stumps of oak trees are home to ants who've carved dark paths underground—full of mystery and damp smells, like the paths above ground over decayed roots and leaves.*

So Tommy is waiting. His lips roll an unlit cigarette from one side of his mouth to another. He's edgy. Flashes of sunlight hurt his eyes.

He hears it, the motor of his dirt bike, coming down the path from Stan's Redemption toward his rolling cigarette. His heart is beating everywhere but in his chest—his wrists, his neck, the knot where his stomach ought to be. He smells the bike before he sees it. The wind's blowing clouds of greasy smoke that burn his eyes.

Blake's on the seat, Ivory behind him. Tommy's heart thumps in his knees, his forehead. Blake stops the bike, gets off, Ivory gets off, stands close. She belongs to Blake, Tommy sees, though he pretends sometimes she belongs to him.

"Tommy," she says his name, just that.

Blake reaches into his jeans jacket. The gun he pulls has a brown handle. Over their heads the birch leaves rustle. Tommy can't see very well, his eyes are smarting.

It happens so quickly and yet with no motion at all. The wind stops, the

*leaves still, his cigarette falls from his mouth and doesn't move it drifts so
slowly to the floor of the clearing. Sunlight tangles in the top branches of the
trees. Night's falling, but slowly, without movement.*

*A shot is fired. Tommy's eyes glisten. Blake did it, he really did it. Just
what they planned back at Stan's house after she got mouthy one too many
times.*

*But Ivory doesn't fall, she runs. Suddenly the motionless world tumbles
with sunlight daggers and the smell of blood when Blake shoots again. Birch
leaves clatter, ants, carrying sawdust, knock loudly against the walls of their
tunnels.*

*Her eyes are open, her mouth is open, Tommy sees when Blake turns
her on her back for a moment before he flips her over again. The gun's in
his own hand now and he shoots, just to do it, like Blake. They hop on the
bike and head for Stan's. She's wearing some perfume—the heat of the
bullets through her skin makes the smell rise up and sting his eyes. His heart
that broke into splinters and traveled to his wrists, his stomach, now rides
high in his throat. The sun's down, the sky is a sweet rose color he turns his
eyes from. He bends to pick up his cigarette and lights it.*

That way, it lasted only a moment. But it might have taken
longer, Geena thought. Tommy was waiting in the clearing, yes, but
Ivory'd been the one who jumped off the dirt bike and started yelling
at him and Blake again. She acted like Blake had cheated on her
when all he'd done was take two hours on a dope deal and leave her
behind. But he quieted her down soon enough, he always did.

"C-come on, Ivory," Blake said. All of a sudden he'd got a blank
and hungry look. "C-come on, come here, b-baby."

He motioned Tommy over. "W-w-we want some, b-both of us."
He held the gun, pointed toward a stump.

"You both want some," Ivory said, hands jammed into the hip
pockets of her jeans. She burned Tommy's eyes with her look. *I'd
rather die than screw you*, it said.

Suddenly she was jumping, one foot to another, the slowness of
an hour ago replaced by speed. Her hair wild, falling across her
cheeks. She was snarly and full of sneers, her teeth shiny.

She stood, legs apart, and seemed to grow taller, high as the tops of birches, her face in the light. "Do each other, assholes. That's what you really want, isn't it?"

And she laughed, a whole-body laugh, and they shot her, they both did, for making fun of them, for daring to laugh. Then one of them pulled an ice pick out of his back pocket, something he'd thought to carry in hopes of stabbing live flesh, and he stuck it in, thrilled at knowing the catch and the give.

This was how Geena imagined it, a scene she'd run her mind away from except the after-part—revenge—when Ivory turned into a horse and stomped the killers dead. Inside the courtroom this time, listening to the voices of witnesses she'd only watched walk into the certification hearing, Geena saw it straight on, the picture Mr. Moravian wanted her to see: the truth, she believed.

She avoided looking at Tommy and his lady-lawyer with the creamy blouses and classy suits. She avoided everybody but her certification hearing friend, Toni Sparrow. Toni had cut her black ponytail off, her hair was short and tight along the line of her jaw, but otherwise the same: back to tell about Tommy raping her. Tommy's lawyer made Toni sound like a slut, the way his first lawyer had. But no matter how they slimed Toni herself, the words held up: Tommy forced sex and called her by another girl's name, Ivory Towle's.

You did have to give her credit, Miss Ingrid Salzman, blond hair knuckled into a twist. Even if you knew Blake and Tommy were guilty, she still slipped the Carbons into the picture. Ricky waving that butcher knife, sick-yellow from the porch light, it felt as close to slicing Geena's throat now as three years ago, the weekend before Ivory died. Maybe Ricky had stuck an ice pick or a screw driver into Ivory's chest, maybe Buzz coached Blake and Tommy through the whole thing and helped them move the body from behind Stan's to a mile away, everything just so. Then, easy as you please inside his own story, Buzz managed to forget that part. Of course he was there, all over the trial, Mr. Star In-Your-Face Witness, hour after hour, hair and eyes glinty as a tawny fuck-you tiger cat.

Buzz had eyes like her boyfriend's, no relation, thank God. Ralph

was an older guy, couple of kids she babysat, brats, and he was clue-
less, but after a fight, he bought roses. And with Ralph, you could
line yourself up for certain favors, like borrowing his black Trans
Am. At the moment he was pissed—*Did I ever say four days, did I?*
But sitting in the courtroom, sitting there for Ivory's sake, it didn't
feel like a choice. Not one single other friend of Ivory's had showed
up, not one single one.

Ivory's remains—Geena couldn't push them away. According to
Detective Bergeron, Ivory's skull sat next to her hip, and the stuff
in her purse lay every-which-way. Whatever the details though, she
was gone. Somebody or two killed her. Other kids knew and didn't
tell because dead, Ivory didn't matter anymore. But before the ice
pick, before the bullets, Ivory opened one small window, a chance,
a hope—she got reckless, and the gift of courage opened her throat.
She yelled at the boys, she taunted, she laughed.

To stay alive herself, Geena needed this one small thing, desperate
as words in a bottle: Ivory had been more than a girl left for coyotes
to tear apart and maggots to breed on, more than a girl whose skull
ended up by her pocket. For the quick moment of a window's rushing open, she ruled.

eighty-six

Second floor, Superior Court, Judge Maietta's courtroom: "All rise," said the bailiff after lunch recess; all did rise to await the judge himself. Ingrid liked the morality-play decorum built into court procedures. Just that little fanfare to make heartbeats quicken, the pounding of a baton, the anticipated rustle of black robes, the fox hunt–chess match allure. Oak wainscoting, oak window frames, oak judge's bench, witness stand, jury box. An old room in an old building, slated for renovation. On the backs of some of the spectators' benches, she'd seen nicks and gouges, a few initials carved, but at least the bare wood had been shellacked over. Crowding the benches were media types, including the red-faced newspaper reporter from the sticks with his bright-white head of hair; poor kids from those same sticks, by the look of them, friends of the deceased or of Tommy Slack; his family; a few gawkers, neither family nor friend; a knot of lawyers, here for the show.

For that moment of waiting, Ingrid was aware of how tired she felt. Unusual, even this flash of vulnerability, but it was there. She held the rail. Nails perfect, clear polish, no rings to distract. She'd worked ten days straight, eighteen hours over the weekend, so immersed in preparation that it had startled her when her secretary pointed out the open window: *Ingrid, look, the dogwood's in bloom.*

One quick break on Saturday morning for ballet class and buying a new blouse, the weather heady enough for a brief fling with disorientation. Otherwise, focus. A boy's future. A botched police investigation. Witnesses ripe for impeachment, to put it mildly. The day the jury was selected and sworn in, she'd labored fifteen and a half hours. Fourteen hour days the rest of the week. Now it was Thursday.

But really, she didn't feel tired, it was a body reflex, something to observe, then clamp down on. Like ballet. You couldn't possibly do those things, stretch that far, lift bone and muscle that high, leap, pirouette, cantilever a thirty-seven year old's frame, and then, oh God, Smile. It was a new interest, ballet, a since-law-school interest. Discipline in service to beauty, to the redtail hawk soaring on an updraft. She loved that combination, what happened in court. Hundreds of hours, meticulous groundwork, argument, counterargument so that during the trial itself, she was free to let the force of her personality carry the courtroom aloft.

The jury was buying it. She liked this group, half men, half women: a fifty-ish supermarket executive, male; an accountant, whose part shone white as a drinking straw; an environmental engineer; a toll collector; a stockbroker; a part-time security guard; a fish-processing-plant worker, barely twenty-one, so skittish about responsibility that at significant moments he gulped; a housewife; a retired grandmother dressed in homemade neon crochet; one schoolteacher; one telemarketer with henna hair; one single-mother college student, who sneezed throughout the forensic entomologist's testimony; a graphic designer; and the night desk clerk at the Wishing Well Hotel.

She liked Gram best. Gram was a hot ticket, don't let the loopy crochet fool you. She listened, squinting her eyes like she'd been around that barn before, but more than once those same eyes had drifted to Tommy's mom, herself gazing at her boy for the quick chance this nightmare might evaporate. A serious bunch, as they ought to be, not easily hoodwinked by the State.

In Ingrid's hands, demon for detail that she was, they'd see things the right way. Details like the sparkle of a cut-glass necklace at Lisa Carbon's throat, which had begun its life at Ivory's. Details like a .22 caliber gun Small Runyon and his buddy the autistic albino had stolen before Ivory's murder. When cops hauled the guys in for questioning after the body had turned up, nobody bothered to test if the bullets matched the spent casings found at the murder site. Details like the 1974 blue Cutlass, abandoned in the woods less than a quarter of a mile from that same murder scene, no fingerprints dusted, no connection made. Details like phone records for that Sunday afternoon, a young woman's voice saying Ivory was baby-sitting late, some emergency, records nobody had bothered to sub-poena and which, after six months, the phone company had destroyed. Detail upon detail: Buzz Carbon's most febrile of alibis, shot through in an hour by the private investigator she'd hired, how about that?

What defied belief was the prosecution's case. Sid Moravian's arrogance or stupidity. No eye-witness, no weapon, no motive. The testimony of liars, drug addicts, and convicted felons. So the cops were under heat from the AG's office. Two years and no indict-ments, let alone convictions. Come up with somebody, anybody, was the gist, one warm body, maybe two. Who seemed likely? The boyfriend. They'd had an exchange of words—witnesses attested to that, the only witnesses to anything, by the way. They'd said Ivory was steamed and there was yelling back and forth. At an impromptu gathering, by the way, at which dope and alcohol had been freely dispensed. So nail the boyfriend and his burnout buddy, a poor sad kid who dropped out of ninth grade, Special Ed written all over him. You know, rustic violence . . .

So they'd delivered up to Moravian, plump and rotating on a spit, two kids from the wrong side of the tracks, fingered from day one. It made her boil, this adopting of scapegoats instead of solid, pains-taking work. The whole scenario made her boil. Where were that girl's parents? How come adults let these kids go unsupervised, nobody even followed up on a questionable story, these were teenagers, what did you expect? And how come so many adults gave them whatever substances they wanted? Kids ran wild. Break-ins, arson, assault, not to mention promiscuity.

If she were queen for a day, she'd get some effective parenting going, first off. Parents who could say no and stand behind it, who smelled a lie and chased it down, who had the moral strength to lead by example. Her dad, a single father, military doctor, into her business all through high school. It had driven her crazy, but she appreciated it now. She wouldn't have dared lie to him, and not for fear he'd do her, either. Schools: she'd search lockers. Take control and take responsibility.

Send the case back. Do it right next time. That was what she wanted the jury to think about, not that Tommy might get off, just that the State hadn't even begun to do its job right, why should two kids forfeit their futures for one shoddy piece of work?

Well, she'd gotten them going. Detective Bergeron—she did like the guy—but she couldn't let his testimony slide. He told the jury that during the certification proceedings he'd heard something when the boys were brought in—Blake mouthing to Tommy, *Did you say anything?* and Tommy whispering back, *No, did you?* During cross-examination, she and her assistant had stood far apart, the distance Bergeron must have sat from the boys, and reenacted the incident, her mouth like a ventriloquist's. Of course the jury almost snickered, which made Bergeron mad. Lip-read? Yeah, right.

Dr. Cooper, the State Medical Examiner, he hadn't seemed to mind her style. An early prosecution witness, he'd corroborated the State's estimated time of death as consistent with that late-July Sunday. *In fact, Dr. Cooper*, she'd said during cross, *that date is not scientifically precise, is it, it just matches the scenario given to you by the prosecution.*

He'd had to agree, but his mouth twisted slightly, a coroner's smile, off-kilter and sweet. A hard-working, genial man, nothing personal. Something even told her he was partial to the way she'd handled cross and re-cross. She held the sarcastic edge in check. In

New Hampshire, it was civil inside the courtroom. No *ad hominem*. In retrospect, the Bergeron-business was risky. Close quarters, this community of cops, prosecutors, defense lawyers, judges. You kept running into each other, if not this year, then next. It behooved you to show respect. She'd just wanted to do one thing: corrupt the idea of an absolute time Ivory died, make room for plausible alternatives, days, even weeks, and, just maybe, begin to unravel the State's emperor's-new-clothes self-styled colossus.

She could still taste the sharp pleasure of Buzz Carbon on the stand. Ha, she'd riled him.

Mr. Carbon, she'd said, *during your residence at the correctional facility, did you ever tell Maury Winchester that you were worried the cops were too close to solving Ivory Towle's murder and that you might have to shut some people up who knew too much, like your wife? And that's one reason, in fact, why you escaped?*

No way! yelled Buzz. *You know where Maury Winchester spent most of his time up there? PC—protective custody—'cause everybody hates his guts.*

Did you ever tell Maury Winchester that your wife had moved in with a man named Stevie Cameron and that you wanted to kill them both?

No, I did not! By then Buzz had crouched low, weaving back and forth, fingers locked on the witness stand. *I never said nothing like that!*

You don't want to kill him?

Moravian had objected—hostile badgering—she backed off, as if innocently amazed at all the hubbub her questions had caused. Point made, anyway. She'd riled him, the glinty gold eyes, the rage. One little step of the jury's imagination: a quick slide to the murder of Ivory Towle.

She folded her arms across her chest. *Mr. Carbon, did you have a vehicle waiting for you when you escaped from the correctional facility?*

Buzz sulked, glanced at the judge, ran a hand through his cougar hair. *I'm taking the Fifth on that one.*

Guffaws might have been in order from Judge Maietta. Instead, he'd simply said, *In this situation, Mr. Carbon, you have no Fifth Amendment rights.*

Why not?

Just take my word for it. The judge's bald head ridged into sharp pleats: amused, exasperated, Ingrid hadn't been sure. But that scalp had a wrinkly, expressive life of its own, more than the judge's precise features or eyebrows that twirled into question marks two inches from his face.

eighty-seven

◇

Late afternoon, and Lisa Carbon had spun her own lame tale into Sid Moravian's hefty hand. Now it was Ingrid's turn. Lisa really got her—the blond-bimbo-weepy-wife, pregnant with Buzz Carbon's second child. Come on . . . She was as all-over-the-place about the hour she and Buzz had supposedly returned from their booze-cruise that Sunday as Buzz had been himself. But she absolutely positively swore to this: She hadn't called Mrs. Towle, pretending she needed Ivory to babysit. Ingrid could hear Lisa's mind noisily laboring: *What answers will help Buzz the most? How to cover for him and Ricky?*

"Did there come a time, Mrs. Carbon, soon after Ivory Towle's disappearance, when Mr. Carbon gave you a necklace?"

"He gives me lots of stuff, he's my husband." Lisa looked at Ingrid's finger, no wedding ring, as if to say, *One up on you.* "Buzz gives me stuff all the time," she repeated, "but never some necklace belonging to Ivory. No way, I don't know nothing about that."

Ingrid paused. She fingered the ceramic rose on her lapel. "So, let me get this straight. Witnesses who say they saw that same necklace in the back of your pick-up truck—even remember your wearing it—those witnesses are all lying?"

"That's right."

Ingrid glanced at Gram, her bellwether. Gram was picking at her crochet vest but she was leaning forward, listening hard. Lisa-abuse-victim, scared for her life. Lisa-plucky-young-mother, hitched to a scumbag she still loved. For the purposes of reasonable doubt, either picture would fly.

Before Judge Maietta adjourned for the day, Ingrid tapped Tommy's thick hand, inert on the table in front of them. "It's okay. Things are going just the way I planned," she said. "Better." He couldn't smile, he was in shock, but he believed her, she could tell that. *Spine up here, fella, don't let me down*, her look said. She knew he wouldn't dare.

Just then, a folded note was slipped onto her stack of documents. It was from Ray Monroe, who'd been coiled tight for days, excited about the cons from Danbury arriving. Since the letter had come to him first, he'd acted as local liaison. Anything the guys said about Buzz worked not only for Tommy, but for Blake. So, the two sheriff's cruisers must have showed up—ninety-mile-an-hour ride from Connecticut.

"Call me," the note said.

Nice, she thought. Nice.

eighty-eight

They'd been late leaving Danbury USP, it turned out. The sheriff in charge had gotten squeamish about Gerald Homberg. *Extremely dangerous* wasn't a label you messed with, and a federal con up for a hundred eighteen years—assault, armed bank robbery, two prison escapes—*he's got enough 'a nothin to lose, he's capable of troubles you can't imagine.*

That had been how the delay was explained to Ray Monroe over the phone. Even separated from his buddy Casparius, handcuffed and shackled in the backseat of his own private sheriff's cruiser, Homberg needed an extra deputy for company on the return trip to New Hampshire, and rustling one up had taken time.

Your fellas won't be arrivin till ten, ten thirty tonight, said Dube, the phone deputy.

If the two had been prosecution witnesses, Ray figured things might have run a little faster, a little smoother. Sure, they'd gotten Judge Maietta's writ of habeas corpus, still it felt like conflict of interest, cops transporting convicts to testify on behalf of a kid the Attorney General's office had already certified a murderer.

"Why not bring them up tomorrow? Save a few bucks. We won't need them till Monday the way things are going," Ingrid told Ray. They'd met for a beer at the Bilge Water, a bar with the gritty feel he favored but so much polished brass your face shone gold as a cherub's, whichever direction you looked. And Ingrid said she liked that.

She drained her draft, then scooped a palmful of nuts. "Moravian's taking his time, one peachy witness after another. Toni Sparrow— well, she said the same stuff at the certification, but hearing it's different than reading it. *Tommy told me he killed Ivory 'cause she was a bitch and wouldn't sleep with him,*" Ingrid mimicked. "Not a problem for Toni herself," she noted dryly. "*I invited him for the weekend but we didn't have sex Friday night*—like how could she even remember they were so hammered? No, they're just friends, so, bingo, Saturday night he yanks down her jeans and forces himself on her and she's crying rape—but only to him. Like she was just friends with Lisa Carbon's brother, a one-time fiancé, like she was Ricky's *just friend.* Incredible, isn't it, after a two-year investigation, two prime witnesses materialize within a couple of weeks?"

Ray nodded. "Incredible."

"And how about her take on motive, huh? *Tommy told me he offered her because she was gonna rat on him about stealing some guns*—A robbery which, of course, happened after Ivory died . . ."

"You're preaching to the converted, Cupcake." Ray couldn't help himself, so far was Ingrid from cupcake paradigm.

She took off her suit jacket and loosened the bow on her pink silk blouse. In this light, it turned burnt orange, more October than May. "You remind me of my little brothers," she said.

"How many are there?"

"Five."

"You're the only girl, let me guess."

"And the oldest. For lunch I'd open a loaf of Wonder Bread, slap half the slices down on the counter, then order Benny through with a jar of peanut butter, Timmy with Fluff. The baby did tops."

"Your own Cub Scout pack."

"Den."

"Yeah, den."

"How's Blake holding up?"

"All psyched about the prom tomorrow night."

"My God, Ray, you're breaking new legal ground. A month ago—indicted for murder, tomorrow—dancing the cha-cha."

"With his girlfriend and two sheriffs."

"More of a conga line. You rented him a tux?"

"Of course. His mom's getting the corsage." Ray tightened his suspenders, another glint of brass. "The kid's a junior in high school and the cops fucked him over. The least they can do is pay for chaperones."

"Tough going back to jail after-the-ball. What's his curfew?"

She was a funny one. Not that much older than he was, maybe six or seven years, but very ship-of-state. Still, it felt good to joke around. And he meant it about Blake's life getting fucked up; after nine months in jail, what's cooking next fall? Instead of a senior year, a murder trial.

eighty-nine

It must have happened while he and Ingrid were at the Bilge Water, shooting the shit, Ray realized later. His own prime witnesses . . . Casparius—pockmarked, ham-cheeked, flabby as your wino uncle, and his buddy, Homberg—tall and blue-tinged, a great blue heron with that same cocky crest of hair.

He'd interviewed them twice at Danbury, and he had their affidavits. They both swore Buzz Carbon told them he'd been present when Ivory Towle was murdered, that his brother Ricky shot and killed her and that he'd helped his brother hide her body in the woods, that he'd done it to get back at Tommy and Blake for having stuff he didn't have, and at Ivory for *acting stuck up* and for rejecting Ricky's advances on the day of the murder. Buzz told them he'd implicated the boys because he was jealous of them, to protect his brother, to lighten his own sentence. He had also boasted about lying under oath and called it *perjury.*

Ray figured it had happened somewhere on 495, hooking around Boston. The cruiser carrying Casparius right behind Homberg's— left lane, blue light the whole way. But the deputy guarding Casparius must have noticed something first: how the closer they'd gotten to New Hampshire, the more riled his guy looked, agitated, as law-enforcement types liked to say. Pale lake-eyes gone cloudy with congestion at the effort it took to pinch off his heart. Probably couldn't clamp down such feelings any longer. They were speeding north, Crystal Gayle on the radio: "Don't It Make My Brown Eyes Blue," maybe the crackle of the CB. And then Casparius blew.

Homberg's the one got me entangled. He's broke outta two places before. I didn't want nothin' to do with it, 'cept to please him.

Something along those lines, maybe squeezed out over a couple of mile markers, or rapid-fire while they caught highway lights and darkness in the rear view mirror. The guy was a goner, his hammy cheeks scorched by hurt. Maybe that was when it had come out, in the back of the cruiser, how they were lovers, but Homberg'd been acting high and mighty 'cause it was *his* plot that was gonna lay the golden egg, and Casparius couldn't stand it another second, Homberg fuckin' some other guy.

It was after midnight when Ray got the call. Since leaving the Bilge Water at eight, he'd been at his office, waiting. "The Sheriff says, Bring along that box of evidence the Danbury cons sent you. Seems like we got ourselves a hoax," said Dube. "The whole story's made up," he added.

Ray was close enough to walk to county jail, adjacent to the courthouse. He ran. The smell of seaweed and fish bait clattered, the way his footsteps did on empty bricks. As he ran, the cardboard box pressed his belt.

"Yup," said Dube, "Pure fabrication. Like I told you, those fellas got less than nothin' to lose." Another deputy lifted the box off the Formica counter, then disappeared.

"That fella Casparius—refused to shut his yap once he got going." Dube lighted a cigarette, drew slow and deep. "Told me everything, soup to nuts—after he'd already spilled the beans to Hennessey on the drive up. How him and his boyfriend Homberg—'course he made it sound like, himself, he was one reluctant dame-at-the-dance—how when it was Homberg's turn to testify Monday, his brother'd already be sittin' in the gallery, playing with a machine gun. And he'd take you hostage, Mr. Monroe, if need be, so him

and the other fella could escape. Ho!" Dube frisked Ray with a quick
up-and-down, one fatherly grin, one slap on the back. "Then a
sister'd be waitin outside in some get-away vehicle," he continued.
"New Hampshire with no death penalty, 'course, worst thing they'd
get's more years on top of life-plus . . ." He chuckled. "Ya gotta
think these things through ahead of time."

Ray attempted a smile. Better to play along, he figured. The
world's little brother, very funny.

"What they got in that box, anyways?" Dube asked.

"Documents."

"They writin' a book?"

"Street clothes, too, for when they testify." Who was this guy—
Columbo?

The sheriff appeared around Dube's desk. Buzzed hair, mud slide
of a gut. He was holding up a zip gun, the way you'd hold a headless
mouse your cat just mauled. "False bottom," he said. "I had this
intuition. Handy prison-made job, 'course it can kill you, provided
they got it rigged right."

"Jesus," said Ray.

Dube whistled. "Looks like Peabody here saved your life."

Past C & A Florists, past Cookie Boutique, past In-Town Cinema,
closed for the night. Ray's legs walked while his mind exploded with
consequence and contingency. What if? What then? Empty bricks
talked back. It felt like a movie. The con, free of shackles on the
witness stand, rummages in his cardboard box full of evidence. Under bogus handwritten letters, his fingers first touch balsa wood, then
steel. And he pulls out a gun. Before anybody realizes what's happened, he's standing up, his face blue-cast and terrible. Heron-eyes
greedy with excitement. The gun works, he believes it will work.
He's got nothing to lose.

It was one thirty when Ray called Ingrid and woke her up. "You
might want to rethink your defense," he said. "Starting now."

ninety

Friday morning the judge was a little slow getting things going. Etta noticed. She flipped up the watch-pin Leo had given her and checked the time, which was right-side up to her, upside-down to the rest of the world. Her and Leo's joke. All week she'd worn the orange open-weave crochet vest he'd bought her three birthdays ago. So it clashed with her blue dress, no matter. Like the watch-pin, it was something real, something tangible from the history of her own life. Etta noticed details, scanned the room, and kept track of time, the least she could do.

From the moment she clipped on her JUROR badge and entered the courthouse at eight thirty each morning, she was aware of secrets. Knots of lawyers talking on the wide marble staircase—they stepped back, lowered their voices, a nod of thanks for this important work you were doing, citizen. But she couldn't help wondering what was withheld.

For a few dollars a day, plus parking and mileage, she and her fellow jurors were coddled and instructed, admonished, beseeched— a parade of witnesses for their exclusive benefit, and yet Etta learned only what others had decided she should learn—all of it carefully crafted ahead of time. Forensic specialists, crime-scene photographs, the ins and outs of spent shells, bullet entry and exit points, alibis,

whereabouts, but it was pieces of a story only—pinpricks of illu-
mination, not windows opened to wide landscape. And she herself
wasn't allowed to ask a single question. She couldn't just turn to the
defendant and say, *Son, tell me what happened.*

Once she and Leo had watched a TV program about some important fellow who'd years ago traveled in Russia, she believed it
was, and along his route he'd seen peasants waving with sheer high
spirits and villages painted the colors of chicory and sunflowers.
Come to find out the peasants were convicts in front of plywood
false-fronted buildings. But at the time the government official had
been fooled. She meant no disrespect. She admired the judge. Such
courtly manners, such knowledge of law. He'd told them more than
once that this jury they were part of, it was one of humankind's
greatest inventions, and they'd rise to the occasion, each one of them,
in ways they weren't able yet to imagine.

All true, and she was thrilled. Leo would have loved it, her being
picked for a murder trial jury, her name in the paper: Etta T. Sweeney, Retired Retail Sales. Their both being conscientious types,
humbled at the notion of civic duty, of course he wouldn't have
asked a single question or breathed a word, though it would have
killed him. He'd have clipped articles and made her a scrapbook for
after the verdict and taken a day off from the bakery to sit in the
audience, not waving or anything, just to know what she'd been
living through and live it with her, so when they'd gone to bed and
he held her against him, his arms and chest would have heard the
same painful words she'd heard, maybe even found things out she
wasn't allowed to. He'd have told everybody at the Spanos-Luttrell
Senior Center that Etta was serving Blind Justice. He'd have laughed
and just acted so tickled. But without her needing to explain, he'd
also have felt what she'd felt in the jury box, the surprising burden
of bitterness she'd been asked to carry.

Keep your mind open. Don't jump to conclusions. Listen to each
witness and weigh their credibility, what they have to lose or gain,
how their testimony supports or refutes the defense's case or the
prosecution's. Don't imagine: think. But separating thinking from

what your nose took in, the metal taste of anger on your tongue
when you sensed somebody was lying, what your heart felt in empathy, it was a weighty task.

Mrs. Towle—she'd never forget that sorrowful soul. No makeup,
no color at all. Three small questions, answers like scraps of flesh
torn away. If it were one of her own kids murdered—well, she
wouldn't travel down that path, except to suppose she'd be front
and center every day. But Mrs. Towle had testified, then she was
gone. And what of the father? And Tommy's family—that mother,
still in shock, whose baby had turned into a killer, or at least a boy
so tangled in trouble he'd found his way here. And the sister, it must
be, though no one had said, a kid who'd become nothing but puffy
blue eyes. Snappy Ingrid, the prettiest clothes, like a young school
principal, a take-charge type not unlike herself in younger days. Mr.
Moravian, she liked him too, rumpled in a stumbly way, annoyed
when Ingrid got snide, not that Etta blamed him, though you'd got
to enjoy Ingrid's flair. Who to trust? What to believe?

After lunch, it was single-file out of the jury room, back to the
prosecution's case. They'd just settled into their chairs, her hands
cupping the ends of armrests, when Mr. Moravian called a young
girl, big as a minute, who provided an alibi for one of the Carbon
brothers. Then suddenly the judge read a message the bailiff slipped
him and said, "I apologize for the interruption, but we need to call
a defense witness out of turn."

Mr. Moravian nodded, like he wasn't surprised, and returned to
his table. The girl was let off but told to stick around. Then they
marched back to the jury room, and so little time had transpired that
smells assaulted them—her BLT, the foreman Mr. Hokinen's tuna
salad and vinegar chips, somebody's meatball sub. They had to laugh.
Such a small room, fourteen wooden armchairs, like the ones in
court, a long table, a chalkboard. No windows, no ventilation. Etta
felt a touch of claustrophobia, knowing it was so beautiful outside,
one clear fine day after another.

She'd just asked if anybody knew about delphiniums because
Leo's prize Blue Niles were bleaching out, the stalks and leaves. As

the world greened around them—pulses of green, throbs of green—
the poor things got whiter each day. What pest or peril could be
sucking their life blood out? she wondered—such an odd and scary
thing, this failure to thrive. But before anyone ventured an opinion,
the bailiff escorted them single-file back to the courtroom, like so
many aphids and him the ant.

From the jury room to the courtroom, from lunch smells to lilacs.
Even at the courthouse, elixir of lilac tumbled through open windows behind the jury box. Just an instant it distracted them, contrary
to nature it seemed, this time of year, to sit indoors and pay rapt
attention.

"The defense witness will not be testifying," Judge Maietta told
them. His face without expression, like Tommy Slack's. "But you
are not to speculate about this turn of events one way or the other."
His black-robed wings lifted up. "Let's resume with your witness,
Mr. Moravian."

And by the end of the afternoon, the State rested. "It's time for
you to rest, too," the judge said, thanking them for their week of
hard work. He smiled, their kindly shepherd. "Take advantage of
the fine weekend. Relax. Tend your gardens. But please don't talk
about the trial with anyone, don't read newspaper accounts, don't
listen to reports on radio or TV. See you Monday morning at nine
o'clock."

Back in the jury room, Etta gathered up her string bag. Mr. Hokinen said, "About your delphiniums. Any evidence of mites?"

"No, none."

"Must be some kind of insect attacking the roots."

The youngest juror, almost a boy, shook his head. "Virus," he
said. "Gets in the soil and they're doomed. Disease just hangs around
year after year. Might as well start over, new seedlings in a fresh
bed."

Etta thanked them both. There was some friendly chitchat: Red
Sox, parking validations, mowing the grass. They walked out. She
waited a moment, then left by herself. Her head was pounding. Leo
walked with her, the absence of Leo. She felt exhausted. In the

bathroom downstairs, Tommy's mother was just drying her hands. They pretended not to recognize one another. There was awkwardness.

Etta pushed open one of the heavy courthouse double-doors and she was washed in lilacs. One day next week, then, they'd begin deliberations. Once, she and Leo had seen a movie about Queen Elizabeth, the first one, how all that power made her proud, but it gnawed at her like a canker of loneliness. It had been her joy and her sorrow, both things, how she couldn't, in the end, take anyone's advice but her own.

Mrs. Towle. Mrs. Slack. One family, two families, maybe three, five, twenty. It had sucked the life blood out, their green vitality. Failure to thrive . . . It wasn't something caused by micro-bugs or disease-germs too small to pick off with your thumb, it was the sorry afterbirth of three bullets and a sharp hurtful tool. No matter the verdict, there was no help for it.

ninety-one

Two hours before the prom, it was a crowd-scene down at the jail—like Blake was King Louis-the-Something of France, Dot said, some big cheese that needed help pulling up his fancy pants. She'd made a mental list of everything he'd need—socks, shoes, cummerbund, shirt, cufflinks, tux—and she'd told Ray to order white. She kept babbling about Blake's being an angel from-on-low who'd return to them at midnight with news of the happy outside world.

You're our sugar-baby sweetie-pie doll-baby, the lady-cons kept saying. Though he'd gotten fed up with the company of women, they were kind and all-over-him, so it could be a lot worse, Ray reminded him. For jail time, it wasn't hell.

Dot tweaked his white bowtie, they all did, for good luck. And, she said, for the chance that a cell or two of their own skin might hop aboard and sneak into the prom, a pack of microscopic stowaways. His cummerbund was pale pink, a match for April's dress. She'd smuggled a scrap of material into jail so Ray would get the cummerbund right. He did, and the lady-cons oooooed and aaaaahed. Some of them wiped away tears, then laughed. They reached for April's long skirt, frothing it up like egg whites.

"Honey," April called Blake, out loud, in front of the women, and he said it back. Ray snapped pictures. Blake-April. April-Blake.

Then Dot-Blake, and a tumble of lady-cons, eager to slip their arms around his waist and take credit for this one fine night. Until he got back, they'd stay awake, he figured—so many moms, locked up, hungry for details and him home safe. Except there'd be no wee-hours-of-the-morning confidences over a cup of hot cocoa. Lockdown at eight thirty, they were incarcerated, they'd wait alone—hearing the scuff of shoes if they stayed awake that late, the thud of heavy doors.

Before they left, April opened a white paperboard box. Under the cellophane lid was his boutonniere, a pink rose with a couple of leaves and some dotty things around it. She held it up for him to smell. "My mom bought it. She wanted to be the one that pinned it on you, but she's home throwing up—bad potato salad, she thinks. She told me to tell you, *Be-have*." Which seemed to Blake like the finest thing a mother could have said right then, a soft kind of poking fun.

April paused, unsure of herself. In that moment Dot muscled forward to do the pinning, then she pinched Blake's cheeks to draw color the way a girl would. And it was Dot who helped April with her white rose corsage. Blake knew one thing: April wouldn't ever find out what had passed between him and Dot. It wasn't important, just a kind of comfort, the underbelly of a kind of comfort he hoped she'd never need the way Ivory had.

Ivory.

She was there. Spoiling things. Ivory herself a memory too smudged to recognize. But he knew her still for all the misery she'd caused. Ivory. He pushed her away.

And then he was out into open air. Quick rush into an unmarked cop-car. April beside him, two sheriffs up front, all duded up themselves. Beneath the shock of lilacs, he smelled salt and diesel fuel from the waterfront. He'd gotten used to the smells of jail—the women's bodies, the guards' bodies, food cooked so long a vegetable became a meat, and immediately they served it up, it bled so much water the tray was awash.

But Ray had taken care of that too. He'd arranged for healthy stuff to be sent in. Blake was a kid, still, Ray had reminded the judge. On the other hand, watch him act like a man.

But acting like a man sucked, Blake figured, if it meant another year or two in jail. Ray knew he couldn't take it much longer. In July, then, they'd go to trial, no more appeals, no more waiting.

His hands were unfettered. He couldn't believe it. April's dress spread out onto his lap, scooped low and it had little dark pink blops, like flowers somebody'd painted or jellyfishes. They almost stung his fingers, touching them, so pretty did they look. That color really got him. Some splashy mollusk. A fine color with the memory of nakedness attached, a little tank top she'd worn nine months ago. Holding that color in his mind—it had kept him alive, him handcuffed, riding to county jail, under arrest for murder.

Around them on the dance floor, as he'd imagined, stood a ring of disturbance. He was being watched, she was being watched. By everyone. Kids still thought he killed Ivory. Teachers, too. They shrank back, leaving some distance. In that short pocket of emptiness, horror bubbled up, and a kind of glamour. Talk swirled under the DJ's slow dances, but it didn't reach them. Nobody mentioned Tommy's trial—shit, he was right in the middle of it—or Ivory or his painful months in jail. It felt like he'd just switched schools for a while or got quick-froze, and now he'd unthawed. April's college-track friends said hello, talked ruffles, hairdos, song dedications.

Prom dresses and tuxedos—they blotted out normal habits of mind. Amnesia night . . . It was okay. April's coppery hair done up in curls—no touching or it would fall apart, and underneath her dress she wore something hard, a corset or whatever. That was okay, too. When she went to fix her makeup, he waited alone, then spotted some guys from the basketball team, packed into folding metal chairs along the wall. They made room. He sat with them. It felt strange. He would have been captain. He'd wanted autobody at the voc-tech, a two-year deal, though too late for him, no matter what happened. New basketball uniforms, new bleachers in the school gym, how crappy the speakers sounded, the line of dogs by the refreshment table, except for the two hot ones in red strapless dresses.

It didn't matter. All just preamble to putting his arms around April, nesting his head, letting his two free hands slide down her satin butt. He drifted. Long ago, so long it was the ghost of a memory lived by some other kid, he'd spent every Saturday night at the pit, zoned out on a truck hood with Ivory's sharp bones digging in. Now he drifted again—April's skin, April's smell—how you must party on some sweet planet.

ninety-two

Ivory's prom. From the moment Pammy stepped out of Anthony's mom's Dodge Dart into the gravel parking lot behind the Elks' Club until her black spike heels crunched their last crunch before he shut her door, it was Ivory's prom. But for once, what Pammy felt wasn't empty missing. They'd figured a way to talk. She wrote *Dear Ivory* letters—in her head or in her diary—like girls wrote to "Ask Lois" in the newspaper. She answered the letters herself, but in fact it was Ivory's advice.

Ivory had told her to surprise-model her prom dress for Anthony. And when she had, he'd right away apologized for calling her a harlot. Just like that. Ivory'd already convinced Pammy he was just an accessory, neither more nor less important than the off-white orchid he bought her, than the heels with toe cleavage, than the dress. Actually, he was less important than the dress, way less, and he knew it. So she was only a sophomore, it wasn't even her prom, who cared. If need be, she was willing to wait till next year, it mattered that much. And he just caved in. All his Sodom and Gomorrah stuff—poof.

It's Blake she hadn't expected. He'd come with bitch-queen April and her preppie friends. Even on this starry night, there was separation: preps with preps, jocks with jocks, burnouts with burnouts, except only a few of them had showed up. Pammy didn't belong to any group, neither did Anthony. He went around with some religious kids who wore neckties and played chess. Ivory would have helped with that, knowing some of everybody. Tonight, though, Pammy was the centerpiece of her own table, and Anthony stared, google-eyed.

It was Anthony who'd sized up the situation with Blake. The two men near him all the time—pretending to be regular chaperones—they must be cops. They had lots of time to watch since Anthony wouldn't dance. He wasn't allowed to, he claimed, God wasn't big on that.

"He is too," Pammy said.

"Cite me a verse."

"You cite, Anthony. God likes joyful noises, that's what my mom says. Come on." She steered him by the elbow, and he was simply swept away. Whitney Houston: "The Greatest Love of All." She knew all the words. He counted until she told him stop. Then it felt dreamy—silver crepe paper trickling from acoustical tile, silver balloons, a disco ball.

"You're beautiful," Anthony whispered.

Ivory nodded.

They stopped by Mrs. Cadenza, who stood beside the food table, laughing with a bearded, mustached man, her husband she introduced as Guy, not Mr. Cadenza. She wore a loose silver-blue dress. It swung and sparkled, and her head was bare, no scarf, no headband, just ear-length gray hair: amazing she wasn't cancer-dead. It felt awkward making conversation with Guy there.

"What are you up to this summer?" Mrs. Cadenza asked. Guy went for punch.

"I applied at Twin-Mart. I'm hoping. Plus I got my poems."

"How's that coming?"

Anthony acted bored, staring at her toe cleavage. But she said, "Good, they're going good. I got some to show if you want."

"I'd like that. You're a Renaissance Girl, Pammy," she added, "a writer and the Belle of the Ball."

Later, Pammy was about to pop from too much punch, but her Algebra teacher who'd given her a D was sitting right outside the bathroom, so she stayed away. Finally he went out for a cigarette. She was standing alone, waiting in the hall, when Blake came up and smiled. All in white. Her heart flipped, not with desire, but with hate and dread. He killed Ivory. She looked through him. He turned away.

In her high, high heels she clacked over to the DJ and requested a song. She had blisters and her feet killed, but during "Only the Good Die Young," she led Anthony onto the dance floor. He jerked all over the place, it was a fast one, no steps went; still, it felt life-and-death to dance. This was Ivory's prom.

ninety-three

At the trial, there was the prosecution's side and Tommy Slack's side, but nobody took Ivory's part. The way they had at the certification hearing, they made Florence talk about the mystery lady's terrible babysitting phone call which would plague her to the end of her days: *You didn't ask the woman's name? You didn't ask to speak to Ivory?* And that was it.

No chance to say, *For my birthday, she gave me a back scratcher and she fixed a moist box cake. She loved her kitty-cats. She ran like the wind and drew things lifelike. Thanksgiving, she licked cream cheese out of celery sticks. Smurfs and pink roller-skate pompoms, she liked those too, and the count to a hundred while I brushed her hair.*

Three years ago, when Ivory disappeared, Florence had shut down. She didn't smell or taste, hear, see or touch, except the shoot of itches up her spine. But now, since the start of the trial, she was a chaos of too loud, too sharp, too hot. After she testified, she wanted to stay in the courtroom in spite of the painful things they said about Ivory—how at fourteen she'd invited murder, behaving like some awful monster of need, and they'd killed her for it. In spite of that, she would have stayed to watch Tommy Slack, to take the jury's measure.

But the day before the trial began, Duncan woke up coughing so bad they ended up at Emergency. Though it turned out to be the asthma not the emphysema, still he was forbid from attending the trial, doctor's orders. Nothing but skin and bones. There'd been pressure at the dealership, push him out, that's what the talk was, so many years and just push him out. Up against Duncan's health and no paycheck and the mill's rules about days you missed, hers seemed a small want.

Back at work the next day, the lunchroom buzzed. "You're a celebrity," one of the girls said, hearing Florence's name on TV. Another shushed. Just curiosity, this talking behind their hands, they meant no harm. And then Friday, the girls marveled at the hoax those two prisoners from Connecticut almost pulled off: zip gun, lawyer-hostage, get-away van. Of course none of it had happened, including that story about Buzz Carbon confessing to them his brother killed Ivory. There was satisfaction in that. But imagine, snipers on the courthouse roof, cop cars circling the whole downtown. Just like New York City, they said, all agog.

Now it was Monday noon. Florence bit into a stale cupcake one of the girls had brought, leftovers from a three-year-old's birthday party on Saturday. Chocolate cake, cream frosting stuck with rainbow sprinkles and some little person's finger holes. Lots of the girls had kids now. Toddlers. Kindergarten. The mother of the birthday boy switched on the news, a lunch habit ever since the new supervisor had let somebody bring in their old black-and-white TV.

Outside the lunchroom, a sudden rain squall blew up. A spate of drops against the glass and scraps of green, soft as skin, torn off a leafing ash. On TV, an ad for Duncan's dealership, the whole family of the owner—three blond kids and a pretty wife—waving from the bucket of a yellow front-end loader. Then the reporter live at the courthouse:

> *This morning, in a surprise move, the defense in the Ivory Towle murder trial rested its case without calling a single witness. In his closing argument, Assistant Attorney General Sid Moravian*

urged the jury to convict Tommy Slack of the murder of fourteen-year-old Ivory Towle. The evidence is clear and compelling, he said. He asked the seven men and seven women to question why the defendant had changed his story midstream if in fact he weren't trying to cover up his own guilt. Consider also, he said, the number of State's witnesses who offered testimony damaging to the defendant. Although these included prison inmates and a former substance abuser, none had anything to gain by lying.

In her own closing argument, Tommy Slack's lawyer, Ingrid Salzman, attacked the police investigation which, she alleges, immediately focused on the defendant and Ivory Towle's boyfriend, Blake Parady, ignoring other important leads. In spite of police bungling, her client cooperated as best he could. The State's two key witnesses failed to offer any credible evidence. Tommy Slack has been jailed for nine months in the company of hardened criminals. "It's a travesty," Ms. Salzman told jurors. "He did not kill Ivory Towle. We don't know who did, but that murderer is still out there somewhere among us."

She urged jurors to find her client not guilty.

"Oughta string him up by his balls," said the birthday mother, a big girl with a healthy appetite, big hands and feet, big laugh. The walls were sweating. Florence stood, pulled damp jeans off the backs of her legs, kept standing. So the jury was out. Just once, as she entered the witness box, she'd dared look at them, one by one, and they seemed like decent people who might try to understand a corner of what it was like. But they'd spent all those days in the company of Tommy and his mother, not with her and her empty hands.

Ivory's face filled the screen, the eighth-grade picture with black-ringed eyes and pale, pale skin. Pretending to look sad. Maybe in fact feeling sad. The picture they always used, newspaper, TV. Florence turned away. Everything hurt. Green blankets to fold, zipper cuts, she fell behind, the unbearable heat. And Ivory's face. It couldn't be today. It couldn't be.

"Josie, I got to get home," she told the supervisor, who simply nodded and said, "You do what you need to, dear," and for once didn't listen at the pay phone.

But it wasn't home Florence needed when Dunc Jr. picked her up, rush-rush snatched away from his job at the stove foundry. He understood. The jury was out. Click, click, his jaw worked, under the skin, she felt it helping the jury. Click, click.

"Stop here," she said, outside Floral Magic. He parked, opened her door, then held her arm, like they'd survived some terrible car wreck together, though he was still afraid she'd hemorrhaged. He'd got Ivory's long skinny face, but he'd grown past childhood, and it was killing him. She was the mother of one dead girl and this tormented man.

Inside, she bought a basket of cloth flowers with plastic ferns for support. Not like any one flower from real life, they looked too big and bunchy, the sharp purple color Ivory loved, the color she painted her fingernails and once her lips, for a joke, the color of her shaggy rug. They wouldn't shrivel and die, these flowers, not like the corsage Pammy'd brought down yesterday. It wasn't meant to disturb, Florence knew that. It was meant to comfort. Pammy swinging through the screen door, still shiny from the prom, saying, *Ivory told me, Dump Anthony, but we changed our minds. He bought me this.* Into Florence's hand she placed Anthony's gift: silver-threaded elastic, green stuff, a see-through orchid, spotted brown from a finger's eager touch.

I wanted you to have it, she said.

That dying, mummy thing with its sad, sad smell of gone and good-bye. Because you wouldn't ever wake to a daughter's corsage on your kitchen table.

On their way to Hilltop, the sun came out though the wind still flashed the backs of leaves. Dunc Jr. drove down Ivory's lane. Almost Memorial Day, and flags adorned the graves of soldiers and sailors, a few Merchant Marine. They parked by the chainlink fence. Apple trees were blooming across the way. Mary was there with kindly, outstretched arms. Florence knelt by the Halliday Funeral Chapel tag and set down her basket. It was a bright thing, Ivory would like it, but she wouldn't say so the way she did to Pammy. Grass grew in fierce tufts, hard to keep mowed this time of year. Dirt between the tufts, turned muddy by the squall.

"Your jury's out," she said.

Dunc stood and toed his boot into little hills of soil the ants were piling up after the rain. "Want me to repaint the cross?"

Apple blossoms had stuck to the gold arms, the red heart, riddling them with what looked to Florence like bullet holes. Or it was winter still, and those were petals made of snow.

"Wait," she said. "We just wait."

ninety-four

It was time. Judge Maietta had instructed them, they'd finished their sixth sandwich lunch together, oily wrappings balled up and stuck in brown bags, they'd drunk their sodas, and suddenly the bright boy-juror who'd diagnosed the trouble with Leo's delphiniums had to leave. After all that terrible listening and fascination, all that conversation in the jury room about everything in the world but why they'd been assembled, he turned out to be one of the alternates, along with Mrs. Frye. How could he stand it, Etta wondered. Herself, she'd just feel so cheated, so bollixed up.

"I took your advice, Leo's Blue Niles," she told the boy as he pushed back his chair. He sat at the other end of the table, she'd not had a chance to talk to him yet, and now he had to leave. "My son-in-law dug up the flowerbed yesterday, he's got a new Kabota, he scooped two feet down, then it all went to the dump, I couldn't bear to watch but I knew it was for the best. Tomorrow he's bringing a yard of new loam and we'll start over. I'm thinking not flowers, maybe shrubs or a tree, something with red berries for the cardinals this winter—"

At the door, the boy waved. "Flowering crab," he said. He looked relieved. During testimony, he had chewed his bottom lip nonstop—teeth pressing down the way the court stenographer's fingers did, translating sorry words into some sort of encryption. And wouldn't it be tough, too—he was a smoker—not to smoke while you deliberated.

So be it. Etta wiped her fingers and folded her paper napkin, wishing she could wash her hands before they began—something formal to call wisdom down while they decided. But it was too late. The door closed on the alternates. A chair scraped. Mr. Hokinen, the foreman, cleared his throat. The moment so big it filled the space around them and emptied their lungs of air. Etta's heart thumped. A living boy, a dead girl's family. *You'll rise to the occasion*, the judge had told them. It was time to rise. She flipped her watch-pin: ten after one.

One weekend in late July examined from so many angles—*he said, she said*, eyewitnesses from that last gathering when Ivory's period had started beside the pool—then the discovery of the body—and still just a small scrap of time. She wished she'd been allowed to hear Tommy speak. Not the words so much, the sound of his voice.

It was the Why that troubled her. Why had he killed Ivory Towle? Or maybe one of the Carbon brothers had done it or Ivory's boyfriend they kept talking about, maybe the weird albino, maybe somebody else who'd happened to pick up a hitchhiking girl, maybe some mix-and-match.

At the Spanos-Luttrell Senior Center, Mrs. Persky had them act out a murder mystery—one of those kits you sent away for. The directions said, *Think Means, Opportunity, Motive.* Here, with ample opportunity and means enough—guns, knives, ice picks, if you believed a word, though no weapon had ever materialized—it was motive that stuck in her craw. Mr. Moravian had proved there'd been arguing that morning and something about maybe Ivory turning Tommy and Blake in for a burglary—but Ingrid Salzman squashed that. No matter who killed Ivory, there was no sense to it. Somebody got angry, got high on drugs, got bored, let's see what would happen. Motive—there was none. All that sorrow and no point. It broke her heart.

But of course you're not to feel, you're to think. *You are to weigh testimony*, the judge said, *and measure guilt. Don't trouble yourselves with the implications of this verdict*—upon a son, upon two mothers and one girl-child, gone. All very purposeful, as if your mind was a poodle under voice control. But whenever Mr. Moravian objected and Judge Maietta said, *Disregard the witness's last statement*, wasn't it already too late? The information had entered your brain and left a mark, yet you were supposed to erase it before those words forever stuck. Of course life taught you to rein in worries, to stop imaginings right in their tracks or you'd never let kids leave home, you'd never let a husband die who needed to.

Here, twelve jurors, a body of evidence, they began to talk, but no casual swapping of opinions, no quick thumbs up or down on guilt. It felt important to follow a protocol, they agreed, something as clearly defined as the part down Mr. Hokinen's head. There was formality, a discipline of mind that felt almost holy.

"Did the State prove beyond a reasonable doubt that Tommy Slack murdered Ivory Towle? That's the question," Mr. Hokinen reminded them, "not: Did he in fact kill her?" A difficult point but crucial.

"So," said Mrs. D'Amico at Etta's left side, "it's possible for us to believe he had a hand in it but not convict for lack of evidence—hypothetically, of course."

"Exactly, yes." Mr. Hokinen nodded, his forehead glossy with sweat. The room was hot, close. Etta pulled off her orange crochet vest and draped it on the back of her chair. To refresh their memories, they took each witness in turn—what the medical examiner had said, the insect expert, ballistics, the state police detective in charge, Ivory's mother, some grownup relative at Stan's Redemption who'd seen Ivory drive away on a motorbike, wedged between Tommy and Blake. It went quickly. They all seemed believable, no reason to lie. So Ivory died, most likely, that Sunday afternoon or evening. Common sense said a teenage girl, obsessed with her looks, if in death she'd worn the same outfit she disappeared in, then she died that same day. Unless, after the fact, somebody clever had changed her clothes, which here just didn't ring true.

You did have to wonder about the other witnesses, and now, together, they could wonder out loud. The drug-rehab girl, Toni Sparrow, who'd taken cocaine with Tommy, then claimed he raped her but she let him spend the night. She said he boasted about killing Ivory. But you couldn't convict on that story's flimsy thread.

And Buzz Carbon. *Leo,* she'd have said after the trial ended and she felt free to talk, *Leo,* she'd repeat, squeezing spots in his hand, *When Buzz testified, I couldn't help but think I was staring into the eyes of evil.* Poor Lisa, Buzz's wife, all youthful blond, breaking down on the stand the way she did, defending him—scared to death he'd harm her, Etta was sure. It shocked her, that fear, a world she was innocent of. Not that Leo had been an angel, still, in thirty-seven years never once had he given her cause to be afraid. For Lisa Carbon, though, love and fear wore the same cocked hat.

The *booze cruise* Buzz and Lisa had supposedly gone on that Sunday afternoon three summers ago with some churchgoing friends— according to Ingrid Salzman, police hadn't interviewed that other couple until a few months ago. This nagged. Three summers ago— when Leo took his nose-dive. The hospital disinfectant, the color of his IV drip, his toenails turned to wood—all the details of decline still close, but the exact date it began—no, that had slipped away. And the kids involved with Ivory back then, they seemed to float somewhere off to the side of time, calendars, responsibilities. Maybe they'd had jobs, but nobody mentioned them. Who then could distinguish one weekend from another, one month, one day? Same for Buzz's brother Ricky, sleeping in somebody's van overnight with girls her granddaughter Tisha's age . . .

Toni Sparrow, Buzz and Lisa Carbon—nobody at the table seemed to believe them, at least not one hundred percent. So, they went around:

"He knows something, I'll bet on that—"

"Any one of those fellows could have done it—"

"They didn't prove a thing by me—"

So far, everybody had spoken up except the Silent Four on the other side of the table. Then one of them raised his index finger, a nice loud voice he'd not used before: "I'm convinced it's him," he said. "That defense? It's just mirrors and smoke."

"*Mirrors and smoke?*" Sarah Brown repeated, a sturdy girl, a first-grade teacher close to thirty, with patches of eczema inside her elbows.

The smoke-and-mirrors person—Etta couldn't remember his name, something Mayflower-y, though—Davenport, Bradbury. "It's a classic defense," he continued. "If you're stuck with a client as obviously guilty as Tommy Slack, your only option is to attack the prosecution. You hope to impeach witnesses and make the whole investigation look shoddy. Didn't it strike you as ludicrous when Ingrid Salzman tried to make even the *medical examiner* look disreputable, as if somehow he were in cahoots with the State? She's very good, very slick. Reasonable doubt's her only avenue. Notice she didn't present a single defense witness, and she sure as hell wouldn't have called Tommy himself to the stand."

Etta listened carefully, he had a well-spoken point.

But Sarah Brown was not impressed. "The judge said we weren't to draw conclusions about Tommy's not testifying," she told Mr. Mayflower. "Strikes me it's not she didn't have any witnesses to call, but if it ain't broke, don't fix it." She took a deep breath and scratched. "The prosecution didn't have a case. Nothing. I'm amazed this even came to trial."

Somebody down by the blank chalkboard groaned. Mr. Mayflower's lips pulled tight as slingshot rubber bands. Etta reached for the pitcher, poured water in a Dixie Cup and offered it around. No takers.

"We're not to speculate, that's clear," said Mr. Hokinen. Etta wasn't sure who the speculator-in-question was supposed to be—Mr. Mayflower or Sarah Brown. "We're trying," she said.

Yes, one of the Silent Four agreed.

Now Jerry spoke up, the bulky roll of a genial fellow three seats down. "Maybe there's something for us in Tommy's own statements," he said. "Remember how that detective talked about each statement? As I recall it, the first time Tommy was interviewed—

right after the body was found—he said he slept through the whole afternoon in some kind of pup tent over to Blake's—didn't know anything about where Blake or Ivory got to, and his motorbike was on the fritz, I think he said."

"No, he never said that, somebody else did," Mrs. D'Amico corrected him. Hands folded on the table, prematurely gray hair piled high, she looked calm as Lady Justice, but with a curtain rod for a spine. "He said he woke up and Blake had borrowed his bike to drive Ivory home."

Quarter past three, Etta saw. "We need to hear it again," she said. "You know, get the stenographer in here—the judge said we could do that if we had a question—and she'll read us everything Tommy told the police—three or four different times, wasn't it?"

ninety-five

The court stenographer sat in the boy-juror's empty chair. All heads turned toward her noncommittal voice, deciphering the secret code she'd typed. Etta wanted to concentrate, but she was enthralled by the back of Mrs. D'Amico's head. In the jury room, they'd hardly talked. Mrs. D'Amico was the self-contained sort who'd never chit-chat at the movies or spill over the border into somebody else's seat. Face-to, Mrs. D'Amico felt like a stranger, but with her shoulders, her nape, her mount of gray hair, Etta was on friendly terms. Because of where they'd sat in the jury box, Etta in the row behind Mrs. D'Amico and a little to the right, every piece of testimony contained with it a morsel of Mrs. D's neck. They'd kept secrets from her—the defense, the prosecution—but this secret she'd seen for herself. From behind, Mrs. D'Amico leaked emotion. She raged, she grieved. Without ever once guessing it, she'd been a small, fleshy buffer between Etta and the terrible information she'd had to sift for truth.

Now, Mrs. D'Amico's hand cupped the back of her neck and tried, blind, to tuck in a strand of hair. It escaped her fingers. If she knew—such intimacy Etta held her breath.

According to Tommy's first statement, taken the day after the body was found, he didn't know anything about Ivory's disappearance and murder. Later there'd been something lame about a broken-down bike so it couldn't have been him and Blake—*Ha, I'm right*, she imagined Jerry Staghorn thinking—and then two statements from jail. The first time, Tommy said Blake confessed to the killing. A chaos, that statement, talked in a tumble, in spite of the stenographer's spooky-flat tone. A few weeks after that, he changed his mind, claiming that under the influence of an older inmate, he'd lied. Mr. Hokinen thanked the stenographer and she left. They were alone again, twelve citizens.

"He was scared, he lied up and down, protecting himself—"

"Not once did he come close to confessing—"

"I believe he served Blake up to get the cops off his back—"

"If he didn't do it, why change his story?"

Now everyone had an opinion. But finally they felt talked out, even the prickly couples. Sarah Brown and Mr. Mayflower agreed the statements weren't conclusive, one way or the other. When by mistake Jerry Staghorn knocked over a Dixie Cup, Mrs. D'Amico offered her handkerchief and he accepted. The sky tipped. Somewhere, the sound of a blower but no air moved. Etta's vest fell off the back of her chair. She picked it up and cradled it on her lap, where it helped her think.

Over the weekend, she noticed, Mr. Hokinen's part had sunburned. He was pressing it gently, the way you'd test the doneness of a cake. Sarah Brown scratched. Jerry Staghorn twisted his wedding ring. Instead of delphiniums, flowering crab. She flipped up her watch. "Four thirty on the dot," she said. It was time now. *Hush, Etta. Hush your chattery brain.* She felt herself rising.

part Six

ninety-six

The court clerk asked the foreman of the jury to rise, while Ingrid Salzman lifted Tommy's elbow so that he stood up beside her, and Moravian, the prosecutor, also rose to his feet, a yellow jacket bulleted through the spectators' gallery, slowed and circled Man Grady's head. A moment later, it lighted on the back of his hand. It took a few steps, tickling his skin. Spellbound, he waited, eyes fixed on its hectic stripes. Shock traveled up his arm, up his throat to the roots of his white hair. He was allergic to bees. The thing navigated the trough between his middle and index fingers, then shuddered before stepping onto his thumb.

It made no sense, his connection to Ivory Towle. The weekend she died, the weekend his hair turned suddenly white, he'd never even heard her name, let alone met her. He hadn't known her people. Back then he hadn't cared. And now? He felt on heightened alert.

"Has the jury reached a verdict?" the clerk asked the foreman.

"Yes, we have," Mr. Hokinen answered, his voice strong and clear.

"Does the jury find the defendant guilty or not guilty?"

Mr. Hokinen's part bisected his head with surgical precision.

"Your Honor," he said, looking at Judge Maietta, "we find the defendant not guilty," and he sat down.

After nine months in jail, Tommy was free. Man saw him turn. His face cracked, the fracture of stone. Ingrid Salzman hugged him. He looked flushed. In the next row, his mother exploded into tears, she laughed, wiped, blew her nose, hugged the sister, then wrapped one arm around Tommy's neck. Awkwardly he patted her back, as if his arm had just come out of a cast. The dad nodded and shook his son's hand.

At the State's table, quiet consternation. Sid Moravian loosened his tie, then loosened his collar, not to rupture an artery, it looked like. Forgetting the yellow jacket, which groused a bit before flying toward a window, Man rushed forward and nabbed Moravian first.

"Unbelievable," Sid said. Otherwise, he'd leashed his angry tongue. "I'm not sure what this verdict means, but we're moving ahead on the Blake Parady prosecution."

Not a politic fellow, Moravian. Even without elaboration, it seemed obvious what he thought. His case so strong and straight-forward—how could it happen, this catastrophe he'd not seen coming and still couldn't believe: The jury let a murderer go.

In the hall outside the courtroom, Ingrid basked. Her first murder defense, first win. Ray Monroe, Blake's lawyer, flashed his red suspenders under a sober suit. Ingrid was busy so Man talked to Ray. "This is what we hoped for," Ray said, eager funny-nosed kid. "You gotta love the jury process. The State's got less of a case against Blake than it did for Tommy—he'll be out soon. This time next year, he'll be marching at his own graduation, you can be confident of that."

Ingrid joined them, her hand on Ray's shoulder. "When they called for the read-back," she told Man, "I knew we were home free. I figured the jury had rejected testimony from the State's witnesses and they were looking to find out if Tommy had incriminated himself in his own statements. Of course they couldn't find a thing."

She turned and whispered in Tommy's ear. *I told you they'd like you*, Man thought he heard her say, but not sure enough to quote.

Tommy was all over himself, needing to please. Not what Man had expected, this adoration. Ingrid wore lots of gold today, thick necklace, clattery bracelets, big confident teeth. She'd hooked Tommy's elbow and held him there to talk.

"She told me I'd be home for supper," he said. Slow speech, slow and deliberate, again the gratitude.

"So who killed Ivory?" Man asked him.

Tommy frowned. His ginger eyebrows ran together. Then he grinned a cocky grin and shook his head. "I—have—no—i—dea." In spite of a new haircut, he was one shaggy beefalo of a guy. He looked at his mom. "I'm out-of-here," he said.

"You're out of here," she repeated, as if those were the first words he'd ever spoken.

"Excuse me, sir," she told Man, "but we got a welcome home party at home to get to. She's been wonderful," she added, daring to touch Ingrid Salzman's pretty silk sleeve. "Just wonderful. To all of us."

The dad agreed. "Friggin' nine months it took 'em to believe my son," he said, a small man, prone to injury. Tommy bore him little resemblance.

ninety-seven

Man felt stunned, light-headed. In shorthand, legible only to himself, he wrote, *TS: I have no idea.* The courtroom had emptied out, but he found a girl, one lone girl, in the hallway, hunched on a wooden bench. She had bug-zapper eyes, all the bluer for her crying. "I'm Geena Winter," she told him when he asked her name. "Ivory was my best friend."

A poor kid, dolled up in short polyester, sprinkled with rusty flowers. "She fooled the jury, that lawyer of his," Geena said, "but Ivory knows he did it."

She refused to say more, and he left her, vaguely chilled and ashamed of himself for intruding. At the end of the hall, he caught a corner of orange crochet. The oldest juror, Mrs. Sweeney, rushing from his questions and yellow pad. Abruptly he walked back and sat beside Geena.

In that way teenagers had, she ignored him—he was invisible, of no consequence—but he'd felt that same wall on January nights in the aura of burning clapboard apartment houses, victims wrapped in blankets and outsize firefighters' jackets; he'd felt it at Willow Run Quarry when the grappling hook snagged a child's hand.

"The weekend she was murdered," he said to Geena, setting

down his pad and pencil, "my hair turned white. Overnight it happened, and there was nothing to account for it, no sickness or
trauma."

He felt better telling someone, one of Ivory's friends, if not her
own people. He thought of another murder he'd covered, a high-
school quarterback, beloved jock with important parents. Shock
waves through that community—*It's like it happened to my own kid,*
everyone agreed. But no shock waves for Ivory. Rumor-shocks, that
was all, no widespread ripples of grief. Only her family, a few Geena
Winters. It should still feel big, raw—

The verdict would be big. He'd sell lots of papers, banner head-
line: JURY ACQUITS. But it felt like pitiful news, distant news. Three
years ago a poor kid came early to no good—And Ray Monroe was
probably right: If they couldn't convict Tommy, they couldn't get
Blake.

Suddenly, Geena spoke, her voice like sleet on a windshield. "A
person could kill him themselves."

He was far away and didn't understand. She grew impatient, he
saw. "A person could kill him, Tommy, on their own, fuck the
jury."

"I imagine her family'd like to do that, but maybe he really is
innocent." In his own mind, the Carbon brothers rose up. After
reading the certification hearing transcript, you had to wonder about
Ricky, the psycho threats, the jealousy, and his alibi sounded flimsy
at best.

Geena gestured up, toward God, toward Ivory, toward the pale
courthouse ceiling and its flaking chips of paint. "Ivory gave you
white hair so you'd remember—and you—oh, please—"

For the second time in her presence, Man felt ashamed.

She relented, as if forgiving his age and his stupidity. "Dunc'd
love to kill him, and her dad, I imagine. But what good would it
do?" She paused. She wore lipstick paler than her lips, no color at
all compared to the jolt-blue eyes. "The summer we thought she
was missing—before they found her—one hot night a friend of

Dunc's called him up, he'd been out walking, mistook me for Ivory, sitting on my mom's windowsill. Dunc busted into the apartment, him and his friends, tore everything to hell. He thought Ivory'd run away and we were keeping her hid."

Everyone had left. The corridor was empty. "You need a ride?" Man asked.

"You won't put that in your paper," she said—statement, not question.

"No. No, I won't."

"Thanks, but I got my boyfriend's car. I babysit his kids."

They waited a moment longer, not speaking.

Over the weekend, he'd babysat his twin seven-year-old nieces so Loretta could catch a movie. He'd gotten stuck reading *Bootsy Barker Bites* a dozen times. They begged, they pinched, they fought over who owned his lap. According to Loretta, Ivory was a quiet kid—not like those twins. Only sometimes, something funny would get her going. The little crippled girl she helped in the bathroom— Loretta couldn't just leave it at that, she had to burden him with the particulars—the unzipping and the zipping back up. *Then those munchkins'd have a race back up the hall to my classroom,* she said, *Ivory stumbling backwards beside flying aluminum crutches. And they'd both be hooting so loud the librarian'd fill her doorway, one giant frowning finger across her lips.*

Because of his own strange hair, Loretta kept telling him Ivory-stories. He had a responsibility and a need, she let him know. But Ivory had been dead three years. Even back then she weighed next to nothing. Now she was fainter than the sneaky lick marks her tongue left on cream cheese.

"Did you know her in grammar school?"

"Third grade on."

He wouldn't ask what she'd been like, Geena wouldn't volunteer. Already he'd heard more small rememberings than he could bear. They struck him like forks of electric current, light as a drop of venom strolling his thumb, and that dangerous.

ninety-eight

The headlights of Uncle Gary and Aunt Edie's pickup had already angled out the drive and onto the road, and red crepe-paper streamers Romaine taped up had sagged hours ago, it was so humid. Before they'd cut the cake, Doris had asked Tommy to climb on a chair and tack up a streamer that was about to droop into the cake's frosting letters: *WELCOME HOME.*

Miss Salzman had told her it was important to give Tommy responsibilities so he felt part of the family again. On the chair, he'd teetered a bit, acting the clown, and Doris had reached out and grabbed his ankle so he wouldn't fall, but he pushed her hand away. Nine months locked up, his instinct now to push away.

Later, when he'd jumped down safe and she was pouring ginger ale on a block of orange sherbet, she felt fingers over her eyes, then a man's arm around her shoulders. The surprise of it, he was hard as stone, he'd had to make himself hard. He showed her his palm, the stark white pads of his fingers stained from crepe paper dye. He was sweating—the scalded freckly spots on his cheeks—he'd kept those from his boyhood-self, he was the same boy inside this grown-up fellow with red fingerprints.

Harvey had fallen asleep in his chair. She turned the TV off, he needed it to sleep, but he didn't pay attention. And the kids had gone to bed. Wonderful to think she had them both under the space of her breath, safe inside tonight.

We find your boy innocent was the sum of it. She'd believed that all along. She'd bought sliced ham and cheese, onion rolls, enough for a crowd, Aunt Edie had asked to bake her caramel cake. You needed faith to make a celebration when the jury might have locked him up a lifetime, two lifetimes if you believed newspaper stories. He didn't talk about it. Not what happened to him, not what others did to him or what he did back.

Once when she'd visited, he'd asked for a map.

A map of where?

Anywhere, he'd said. *I like roads.*

When they let you go, we can take a car trip.

A world map, he'd said.

The expanse of his new thinking amazed her. At the daycare, she'd told one of the moms that when your kids grew up they spread wonders before you from places you'd never showed them, from places you'd never dreamed of. *My Tommy asked me for a world map,* she'd said, smoothing the idea down with careful pats.

Harvey found a map of New Hampshire in the glove compartment, but it ruptured at the folds, cutting across Lake Winnipesaukee like some huge tidal wave.

My son wants a world map. When he's free again, we'll take a trip, maybe in an airplane to someplace he picks.

A harmless wish. In shop class, before he'd dropped out of school, he made her a cutting board, the shape of a strawberry, her favorite fruit. Nine months she hadn't been able to touch him. He'd changed. To keep him safe, she'd oiled the cutting board. The foolish things you did when your child went away and you couldn't check him in the night, couldn't pour him a glass of Kool-Aid or wash his scraped knees. Your hands had to do something to show they cherished. They needed it like sleep, like water.

He'd forgotten about the map. The next week when she'd brought it, he said, *Great, Ma, you pick me some spot I'll never get to and I'll try picturin' it while guys are screamin' their guts out.*

She hadn't recognized this boy. He was asleep now, and he had his freedom. He acted uneasy around the house the way Miss Salz-man said he might. But he'd remembered where his dad kept rum—no secret, in the cupboard beside the fridge. Rum-and-Coke, his favorite. He'd almost fallen off the chair, his fingers red from crepe-paper streamers. His knees gave—she held him up at the ankles.

He's celebrating, she'd told Harvey.

He's drunk, he said.

He'd earned the right, she thought, this one night out of all his wide life to come. When he recovered from nine months away—tomorrow it might be, maybe not till fall—she'd spread out the map on the kitchen table, she'd smooth down the folds, and they'd laugh at the strange names they couldn't pronounce. They'd make it a game—her picking a spot and him with his grown man's finger going down some lucky foreign road.

ninety-nine

The truth was: Florence felt glad. When Sally Gregg had called from the courthouse, breathless with running to the pay phone, she'd said, *They let him off!* like she couldn't believe it, like the bottom of the world had a sudden hole and she was tumbling end over end, the way nightmares tumbled you down an empty well without water or a place to land. But Florence just didn't much care. Of course she howled and snarled and one self inside her scratched her own eyes out at how a murderer could go scot-free. But the other self just shrugged.

It'll give you closure, the girls at work said. The kindergarten mom who'd brought leftover cupcakes for break and said, *I hope he fries* when the jury'd gone out, she'd taken a fresh bandanna with red triangles and hearts, wiped oily sweat off Florence's forehead and soft as a lullaby whispered, *Either way, she's gone.*

She'd been kneeling in the dooryard, digging holes for the marigolds they bought, twelve sturdy seedlings in peat pots, you planted the whole thing, not to disturb the roots, and the peat decomposed into soil. Some fancy thing, she'd marveled at True Value, and Duncan bought the flat because he saw it pleased her, that one small thing.

Blue-gold sky, a handful of pudgy clouds—it was the finest day since time began. If you only had one thread of a reason for staying alive, this day fed it and helped it grow. The feel of sunshine on your forehead—which didn't remind you of anything now that your child was gone and wouldn't ever feel it with you—it was sweet heat anyways.

And then the phone had rung. She dropped the marigolds. They bounced, she righted them before running into the kitchen, ahead of the banging screen door.

The jury voted to let Tommy Slack go. Three years—since he was sixteen—she'd hated him. He must be nineteen now. She'd talked to three ministers, one for each year. About—whatever happened—forgiveness. About—whatever happened—small pleasures in the here and now. *Cradle your memories, rock yourself in the bosom of Abraham, help some soul worse-off than you.*

But you did what you could do. They lied about prayer. It always led back to where you were just a dry sheaf, a barren field. God didn't fill you up. He let you take care of yourself and watched from the other side of the road like the newspaper reporters at Ivory's funeral had, snapping pictures like progress reports. God saw everything you did.

Now she and Duncan were playing cards. He opened the card table. He was brittle as a wishbone. Veins, tendons, heartbeats showed through his skin, and he'd gave up cigarettes he coughed so bad. It was Duncan who'd turned out to be the sickly one. Even a nice easy breath wasn't something he took for granted anymore. Herself, she was husky, she'd live forever, one self inside another, one self saying, *Go Fish*, and laughing at the foolishness of just them two, set at a game for three or four.

"Do you have an ace?"

"No! You just asked me."

"Maybe you drew one."

"Then I'd have put them down—"

Ivory's eighth-grade picture watched them. Under its sheet of glass the paper watched them. Brown hair, black eyeliner she just would wear, the long Towle chin. Beside that frame on the mantel

another paper, more glass—the picture from seventh grade in the
sweater Gram Towle knit. Pink-purple, purple-pink. But just paper
and glass, no daughter smiling down from Heaven.

Where is she? Florence still wondered.

At peace, all of the Reverends told her.

But peace wasn't a place you could picture when the last real
picture you imagined showed a leafy clearing in the woods, heat,
stillness, bits of skin, a tender hank of hair, scraps of memory leached
from bone.

When he'd heard the verdict, Dunc Jr.'s jaw had clicked, he'd
bowed his head. Now he was out, punching a sand bag, stopping at
Turcotte's Wayside Tavern . . . something to forget, she guessed, but
they didn't know for sure. He never talked about what he did at
night. Maybe someday a steady girl, back to school, kids. For now,
they couldn't live without him, day-to-day.

Duncan so lost at the news it was like an acid IV drip.

"Do you have a ten?"

"Yes. You looked," she said, mock-accusing him before handing
it over.

The fabric of the couch scratched her calf. She was ahead of Duncan. She might win. One self kept asking for cards, picking them
up, passing them across the table to his waiting hand. The other self
sat in the clearing. It wasn't waiting for a picture to turn into a girl.
She knew it wouldn't. That self shrugged at Tommy's not-guilty
verdict.

When the worst thing that could happen had already happened,
though you still managed to shuffle cards and pour water on coffee
crystals, to get pleasure from marigolds in the empty patch where
Ivory had planted baby-teeth, and you could sigh at the happy taste
of sunshine and thank a girl who wiped sweat off your forehead, you
knew you'd keep falling, end over end. A boy dying in prison or at
home, squeezing his wife's hand while grandchildren fooled with his
boot laces, either way it didn't much matter. If you said it did, you
spoke a lie.

acknowledgments

I'd like to thank long-time friends and trusty readers: Cathy Wright, Joan Memering, Agnes Bushell, Joan Kidman, Geraldine Kennedy, Mary Cushman, and Lynne Mansur. Thanks also to Nicole d'Entremont and to the writers at Sudden Fiction for fresh inspiration every week.

I'm grateful to my agent, Jennifer Carlson, and editor, Laura Hruska, who saw this project into the light of day.

To those who shared their stories, thank you for your candor, bravery, and kindness.

And thank you to Peter Fauver, Paula Hatem, Ken Rice and Kate Debevoise for help with verisimilitude of various sorts.

Special blessings and thanks to Eleanor Morse and to my wonderful family—the Kennedys: Nancy, John, Marianna, and Jim; and the Greenes: my husband Nate, Annie, Nathan, and Rachel. You've made this world a welcome and hopeful place.